THOROUGHLY SEDUCED

Book 4 of the Aldbey Park series

Chantry Dawes

ARE YOU SIGNED UP FOR DRAGONBLADE'S BLOG?

You'll get the latest news and information on exclusive giveaways, exclusive excerpts, coming releases, sales, free books, cover reveals and more.

Check out our complete list of authors, too!

No spam, no junk. That's a promise!

Sign Up Here

www.dragonbladepublishing.com

Dearest Reader;

Thank you for your support of a small press. At Dragonblade Publishing, we strive to bring you the highest quality Historical Romance from some of the best authors in the business. Without your support, there is no 'us', so we sincerely hope you adore these stories and find some new favorite authors along the way.

Happy Reading!

CEO, Dragonblade Publishing

PROLOGUE

Outside of London
December, 1813

M ISS BIRDIE DARLEY urged her horse on as she stared at the other riders galloping away on their horses in front of her. They galloped on through the cold mists over the colorless heath.

She spit the cold mud out of her mouth and held the reins in one hand while she wiped the mud from her eyes.

She bent lower over her horse's shoulders, rising off its back as its massive hooves raced over the churned-up earth.

All she could see were the back hooves and the haunches of the horses racing away with the lead.

"Thunder an' turf!" she called out. *"Run, Mo, run!* We'll not let this bunch of boasting, bamboozling boys beat us!"

She was surrounded tightly by the other racers. They penned her in, not letting her surge ahead like they knew she could.

Suddenly, one of them slashed their crop at her thigh encased in boy's breeches.

A stinging pain raced from her knee to her hip. She hissed out a breath. It became a white cloud in the chilly air.

She looked over at the rider with narrowed eyes.

"Swallow your spleen! That was a slum skiver scunner of a thing to do!" she called out. When she was angry, she liked to use her beloved Great-Aunt Eggy's old Scottish words.

She dug her booted heels into Mo's sides and surged past the rider who had struck her, almost into the haunches of the horse in front of her.

More mud flew at her, spattering the arms of her woolen coat, her breeches and boots, and the cap covering all her hair. It was on her face, even on her lashes, and dripping from her eyebrows, making it hard to see.

Two more riders galloped up beside her and flanked her.

Too close!

They were crushing her legs against Mo's sides.

"*Run*, Mo!" she begged her horse.

She felt her big horse's hind end push even harder as Mo surged past those two racers as well.

The chaos of the race was deafening as the riders called out to their horses and to one another.

The sound of the many hooves pounding on the ground filled Birdie's ears and made her heart rush with excitement.

She listened for Mo's breaths through the chaos, and watched as his ears flicked back to her, listening for her voice. The big horse was eager. Birdie knew that they just needed an opening to get to the front, and then Mo would race ahead of all of them and they would win!

There were more horses ahead of her, though. She just needed to get out of the crush of riders!

She looked left and right, looking for a hole to guide Mo through.

The man riding to her left urged his horse dangerously closer. He knew what she wanted to do and used his whip to try to strike at Mo's head.

Birdie screamed at him. "Don't you dare hit my horse! Lud, you are cruel, callous, and cold-blooded!" She slashed at him with her own crop, knocking his longer crop out of his hand.

He yelped in pain and clutched at his hand.

"Run, Mo!" she called out as the man and his horse fell back.

Birdie guided Mo to the left and through the now open space.

They hurtled forward as even more mud pelted them. She lowered her shoulders and her head. She was trying to miss the worst of it as the thunder of hooves and the harsh breathing of the horses surrounded her.

She gritted her teeth and narrowed her eyes, trying to see through her horse's ears. The flying mud coming off the hooves in front of Mo did not seem to faze him. Mo liked to win as much as Birdie did. Birdie knew that Mo would do anything for her, just as she would for him. He ran on, his giant hooves eating up the ground.

A horse in front of her suddenly lifted his head. His rider, a young boy, called out and screamed as his horse went down. The horse slid sideways on a patch of wet mud onto his haunches as his rider flew off and rolled over and over on the ground. The boy rose and knelt there a moment, stunned.

Birdie whirled around as she raced past. "Are you hurt?" she called out.

She watched with relief as both the horse and rider rose from the ground. The boy waved her on. "Beat 'em all, Birdie!" he shouted.

Birdie dug her heels in and called out encouraging words to Mo.

The horse lowered its head as its shoulders stretched forward and its hind end pushed. Birdie moved effortlessly with him. The two had been a pair since Mo was a young colt.

Looking ahead of her, she saw the first of the hedge row jumps come into view.

Birdie gritted her teeth. The conditions were not the best for jumping. They had had some thawing this past week. The ground was perilous. It was muddy and slippery in some places, frozen and hard in others.

Only the best would make it now.

Mo sailed effortlessly over the first row of hedges. Birdie lifted, looking ahead to the ground below.

Her breath hissed out of her. The mud was beginning to freeze and she noticed that there were small patches of snow here and there. From the gray sky, fat snowflakes began to fall.

As Mo landed, she held the reins tighter, bringing his head up to help him rebalance, and off they raced.

There were only a few horses left in front of her now.

On they raced as she passed them. Mo jumped anything she aimed him at with ease and eagerness until, finally, there was only one rider in front of her as the snow began to fall.

The boys never wanted her to win the coins that they all had to toss into a hat to enter a race. The men were more ruthless. The rider ahead of her was the worst of them.

The winner took all, and Birdie liked to win.

She did not care that the men did not like that she wore breeches or a boy's cap, or that she rode astride. Or that she was a better rider with a better horse than them. And won.

She caught up to the last rider.

The two horses galloped over the ground side by side. The other rider looked over at her, his face grim. He gave her a chilling, threatening smile as he lifted his crop and struck at her face. *"Girl!"* he spat out viciously as his whip hit her.

Birdie covered her face just as he was about to swing again, but instead, the rider reached down and yanked upwards on the leather strap of her girth, unbuckling it from Mo's back.

Birdie felt the saddle sliding sideways. She quickly kicked out of her stirrups and leaned forward onto Mo's neck as the saddle slid off and fell to the ground behind them.

The rider sneered back at her as he pressed his horse on faster.

Birdie sat back down, holding Mo's sides with her legs as she continued to race on, bareback.

The two horses took the next jump side by side, but Mo's thrust was stronger and he passed the other horse in the air, landing well ahead of him.

Birdie cheered and pushed him on, faster, and then faster as

Mo's huge strides ate up the ground. Within moments, she had crossed the finish line to win.

Later, after Birdie had put a wool rug on Mo's back, the snow began falling in earnest. She was leading Mo through the crowd of racers when she passed the boy who had fallen.

"Are you able to get home? Tare an' hounds but that was quite the fall you and your horse took!"

The boy blushed. "I am fine, as is my horse, Miss Birdie. I thank you, and congratulations on your win," he said, doffing his cap to her. "Hold tight to your horse, now. Some have gone missing!"

"What do you mean *some have gone missing?*" she asked before he could walk away.

He pointed to a group of men and young boys. They were racers that had dropped out and left their horses with a groom so they could go back and watch the finish of the race. They were all shouting and agitated.

"Their horses are gone," the boy said. "*Stolen!*"

Birdie stared at the angry crowd. There on the outskirts was the man she had beaten, the one who had unbuckled her girth.

She was lucky to be alive, no thanks to him.

He was also watching the crowd. His horse stood beside him, heaving with exhaustion, its flanks covered in whip marks.

Her mother's words came to her. *"'Tis the truth that a man that is neither kind nor gentle to an animal is not a man you should desire for a husband, or even an acquaintance for that matter."*

"*Lud*, that man is a mockit, mingin, manky, mauchit *scunner*," she said to the boy.

"That is Davis, and *I* think he is a cheat," the boy replied. "I think he gets away with it because his father is rumored to be some great general that fights Napoleon." He shrugged as if that did not matter to him. "I'm glad that you beat him and won the money."

"I am going to go have a word with that bowfin, boggin, bampot man."

The boy looked at her quizzically. "I don't know what all those odd words mean that you keep saying, but I would not bother with him." He shrugged and looked over at the man. "He may be a fine man, like his father. I cannot say, and my ma would say that I should not have spoken ill of him."

"'Tis foolish to give merit to a man that does not place others over himself. To me, that includes animals. *All* animals. *Pish*, just look at his poor horse!"

The boy shrugged. "As I said, I wouldn't tangle with that one." He looked up at the darkening sky. "I must get myself and my horse home, for the snow is coming down harder. Besides, I don't want my horse to get stolen like those others! Some say they are being smuggled to Napoleon." He shook his head at that, and then grinned at her, looking her over. "You are covered with mud and snowflakes, Miss Birdie. No one would take you for a girl now!"

The boy doffed his cap and walked away with a wave.

Birdie bit her bottom lip and narrowed her eyes as she stared through the falling snow at the man the boy had said was named Davis. She had raced him many times and beaten him always. Each time, however, he had tried something, and each time it had been worse. He was indeed a cheat.

She started leading Mo toward Davis. She knew that he was not that much older than herself, and he certainly did not look intimidating. Much less, she could not get over that his poor horse looked done in and he was not tending to him. She noticed he was speaking to a much older man whose back was to her.

Snippets of the older man's words came to her.

"—the shallow inlet of the channel. 'Tis perfect for the ramp."

Birdie frowned and paused in her steps as she tried to hear more, but the man abruptly stopped speaking. She began walking toward them again, determined to have a quick sharp word with Davis and then go see about those horses that were stolen. She needed to get Mo home before the snowstorm got worse.

The man named Davis turned toward her. She could see that

he recognized her, for his face turned ominous. He smiled threateningly and took a step toward her. The older man he had been speaking to grabbed his arm and mumbled something, but Davis shook his hand off his arm and kept coming toward her.

Birdie did not falter in her steps, but continued determinedly toward him when suddenly, a massive dark horse cut her off. She peered up through the falling snow to see the outline of a rider in a great cloak whose collar was turned up high on his face. He also wore a top hat pulled down low. She could barely see him through the curtain of white falling snow.

"Move along, boy. You have no business here." He waved her off.

Birdie frowned and shivered. She looked back to see that snow had begun to accumulate on Mo's wool rug.

"Get your horse home, boy. There is nothing here to interest you. *Go!*"

Birdie took a step back at the warning in his voice. With a glance back at the big horse and the man, she turned towards home.

CHAPTER ONE

Along the Thames
February, 1814

T HE ANCIENT DRAFT horse's spine was digging into her bottom where she rode on his old, bowed back.

"Thunder an' turf, *please* run," Miss Birdie Darley begged the wagon horse in an urgent whisper. "I am *rescuing* you! Well, 'tis the truth that I am stealing you back from those men who took you, actually! But you must go *faster*, please! I know it is very cold, but can you not at the very least trot? Or better yet, canter or gallop?"

Birdie peered behind her into the dark to see if the smugglers had returned and noticed the missing horses. She saw nothing but a few falling snowflakes in the night.

The boy had been correct. The horses were being stolen to sell to France. It had taken her over a month to find just the right shallow inlet along the channel, and sure enough, she had also found smugglers. She just needed to live long enough to give her report!

She turned back to stare ahead of her, through the horse's ears.

"I cannot help you escape if you mean to walk the whole way!" she whispered in exasperation to the horse. "We must get to Mo!"

Once again, she kicked her booted heels into the horse's sides, but the old horse stubbornly continued in a lazy walk just as it apparently did pulling a wagon for its master.

She clutched the ancient draft horse's mane with one hand. She held the lead ropes of two other horses and one rather wide, shaggy, black pony with her other hand. They had all been huddled together, standing in the snow, tied to a post in the cold night by the smugglers.

Birdie shivered and pulled the collar of her jacket up to her chin and her cap down further over her long black hair, which she had tucked tightly up into it. The brim of the cap served to help conceal her bright blue eyes. She wore snug but warm breeches on the cold February night to keep her legs warm. She had borrowed the cap and jacket from one of the stable lads back home at her family's estate of Aldbey Park. It was the same outfit that she raced in, and she felt that it concealed her quite well. She knew her mother and Aunt Eggy would be horrified if they knew what she was doing. *But we Darley girls are known to be willful creatures,* she thought.

Birdie looked back toward the channel. She could barely make out the water and the eerily odd, bulky, almost invisible shape of the ship anchored just offshore. It was painted completely black with black sails. She knew it was a smuggler's ship, painted to blend into the darkness to hide the nefarious deeds of the men aboard unloading the illegal goods it carried. It was a menacing, shadowy hulk sitting in the blackness of the water in the dark of night.

Birdie also knew that this ship sailed clandestinely each night, back and forth across the channel from France to England. The goods it carried were in high demand, as any imports from France were illegal during the war.

Tonight, the ship carried barrels of French brandy. She had secretly watched as the sailors rolled the brandy barrels down the specially made lower berth port ramp. They had rolled the barrels silently into the water of the channel. The smugglers then pulled the barrels from the water into their much smaller fishing boat.

Birdie knew that the return trip to France would also have cargo. She had overheard their plans as she watched from behind the bushes earlier before sneaking out to take the horses. That lower berth ramp was there for a reason, and it was not necessarily *only* to roll barrels down into the water. It was to load and unload livestock when docking was not possible.

Just then, Birdie heard the two men talking as the boat they were rowing reached the shore with its load of barrels. She turned her head just enough to watch the men as she urged the horse down the dark path away from the channel.

"The tide will be coming up in an hour or so and it'll be too deep and the water too cold to swim them. We'll not be able to get those horses out to the ship and up the ramp into the horse port if we don't hurry up with these barrels. They'll not want to winch this lot up onto the ship if those horses can't reach the ramp," one of the two men spoke in a warning voice to the other.

A short laugh came from the second man. "We'll be done in time. I can't believe *La Grande Armee* will want those horses if they have to winch the bony nags aboard. The winch will snap their ribs!" He laughed wickedly. "Those two coach horses look like they've been run from London to Yorkshire without a break, the third is a pony, and the last is an old, decrepit wagon horse. They are the worst lot we have stolen so far."

"What do we care?" the first man said. "Napoleon's army is desperate for horses after their defeat in Leipzig. With his remount campaign conscripting trained, rideable horses over six years old, I'll take their money! The coach horses should be rideable. That old horse will be pulling an artillery wagon, I wager, and 'tis the heavy drays that they are paying the most money for. He'll be killed on the first day, but what do we care with our pockets jingling with coin? That's if we can even get them out to the ship before the tide comes in and they drown."

The two men laughed until another man wearing a short,

light-colored top hat and fitted coat with elaborate puffed shoulders strode up to them. He was taller in height compared to the two others and walked with an air of authority. He looked around and then gestured angrily. "Where are they?" he barked as he looked all around in the dark. His eyes landed on the shadowy figure of Birdie at the top of the steep bank that ran along the channel, riding the draft horse away from the water. "You there! Boy!" he hollered angrily.

Birdie bit her lip as her heart raced within her chest. She twisted back around, clutching the lead rope tighter to the three other horses.

"Please run! *You must!*" she pleaded in a desperate whisper to the horse as tears began to run down her face. No amount of kicking her heels or pushing with her seat would incite the horse to break into a canter. "Do you want to be hitched to a French cannon on a battlefield? *No*, tare an' hounds, you *do not!* T'would be nothing but destruction, doom, disaster, your downfall, *your certain death,*" she cried through her tears. "I know I have a propensity for drama and my great-aunt Eggy says that I do go on, but what I profess in this instance is true!" She sniffed her tears back in frustration. "Please, please, *run!* 'Tis only a short distance to Mo and then you shall no longer have to carry me! But you must run! *Please!*"

Suddenly from the side of her vision, a man ran out from the darkness of the bushes at the side of the path. He ran close behind her. She felt him smack the old wagon horse on his haunches.

"Get them out of here, boy! Now!" he growled in a low voice to her.

The sharp hand to the horse's flanks was all it took. He bounced into a jarring trot and then rolled into a canter with the other horses immediately following.

Birdie glanced back just before she rounded the bend, which would take her out of sight of the channel.

She watched as the man hurtled straight down the bank to the other three men. They immediately lunged at him, but he hurled his fist into the man nearest him. In an instant, he was reeling around to strike the second man. The third man with the short top hat made to rush up the bank after Birdie and the horses, but the man in black tripped him. The man in the short top hat rose from the ground, looked at the man in black handily fighting the other two men, and quickly ran away in the opposite direction.

Birdie twisted back around on the cantering horse's back.

"We've been given the benevolent assistance of a most heroic stranger," she said to the big wagon horse. "Let us make an earnest effort to escape! I vow I shall get you all back where you belong before the night is over. You shall not be forced by those *mockit, manky, mingin, mauchit* men to swim in the freezing channel to a dark ship that will take you to your inevitable, deplorable destination of doom and death! Now, *run*, old boy!" she said as her hips moved with the horse's canter.

She looked back at the other three horses behind her and felt relief rush through her.

Birdie peered ahead toward the turn in the dark path they were on. She managed to purse her cold lips together and whistle for Mo as she squeezed her heels into the horse's sides. This time, he reacted instantly, lunging into a lumbering but massive gallop with the other horses doing the same.

A grin bloomed on Birdie's face as the cold wind and snow-flakes flying past bit at her cheeks and blew her tears away. "Thunder an' turf! I knew you could run!"

CHAPTER TWO

London
A few days later
A ball at Carlton House, the Prince Regent's residence in London

T HERE IT WAS *again!*
Something inside the tall, dark-haired gentleman's fine navy tailcoat had moved. Miss Birdie Darley watched as he placed his hand protectively over the upper part of his chest. No sooner had Birdie witnessed this curious happening when suddenly, a group of guests blocked her vision.

She sighed and looked away, thinking she must have imagined it out of boredom.

Birdie took a deep breath as she stood there, tapping one white satin-slippered toe and swinging her white ostrich fan in time to the orchestra as she looked all around the opulent, oval ballroom.

She felt rather out of place here. No one had asked her to dance. Of course, she had beaten most of these men in races on their expensive Thoroughbreds, and those that had not raced her had heard of her exploits on horseback and avoided her most thoroughly.

She had to admit, however, that dancing and going to balls no longer held her interest as they had before. Their only purpose was to garner a good marriage, and had she not already selected her husband? A family friend that she had known forever. Yet, strangely, he had not paid her a bit of attention this season.

She frowned. *"'Tis foolish to give merit to a man that does not place others first over himself."*

He had not asked her to dance, though he had not missed a single set this evening, not with such a bevy of very young ladies in white gowns with fluttering lashes and pouting lips begging for a dance with him.

She sighed with a sudden longing to flee. Her favorite place was on horseback, sometimes just galloping away from everyone and everything to explore whatever was on the horizon.

She continued looking around indifferently at the richness of the room and the guests in their finest gowns and tailcoats.

The crowd parted just then and Birdie could suddenly see the gentleman in the navy tailcoat once more.

There it was again! She had not been imagining it! Something inside the chest of the gentleman's tailcoat moved.

And then moved again. In fact, something very tiny reached up and tugged at the ends of his cravat.

Birdie watched as the gentleman once more placed his hand gently over that spot on his chest as he continued talking to the large group of women around him.

The music in the elegant, golden ballroom did not hold Birdie's interest. Nor did the young ladies wearing the older fashioned, enormously wide hoop-skirted gowns of white with narrow trains required to be worn when presented to the queen in their first season out.

Birdie moved from her position near the dance floor for a better look, giving only a cursory glance to the other ladies in gowns of every color of jewel imaginable in lovely satins and gossamer nets. Each had one or several plumes of ostrich feathers in their hair, vying for who had the most or the tallest, it seemed.

She passed by the tea board, noting its offerings of cups of coffee or tea, syrupy sweet orange orgeat, weak lemonade, cups of ratafia cordial flavored with almonds, sweet Madeira wine, or watered-down Negus wine. Her eyes were caught by the other tea board, heavily laden with dried meats, biscuits, jellies, pastries, dry cakes, cheeses, and delectable tarts.

She walked over to her tiny great-aunt who was also staring at the gentleman. She glanced at the top of Aunt Eggy's pink and balding head to her tiny little bun of dyed green hair that had tilted over the side. It had come to rest on the top of her ear. Without thinking, Birdie pushed the bun back to the center. She also righted the ostrich plumes that had listed sideways along with it.

Aunt Eggy patted her head and mumbled, "Thank ye, dearling," without taking her eyes off the gentleman in the navy tailcoat. They stood there, intently watching him, the man who had brought some sort of small creature hidden within his finely made coat to the Regent's ball of all places.

The creature was moving and had already made use of the ends of his cravat as something to be played with.

As Birdie watched, a very tiny paw darted out and grabbed at the cloth again, missed, and then attempted it once again. The gentleman calmly pushed the creature back down into his tailcoat.

Great-Aunt Eggy grabbed her arm. "Och, there 'twas again! My auld eyes dinnae deceive me," she whispered excitedly.

Birdie nodded as her bright blue eyes sparkled beneath the five grand chandeliers of the ballroom. "I saw it too, Aunt Eggy! What could it be? 'Tis surely a small creature of some sort." She tried to get a better look, but the ostrich feather-plumed headdresses of the ladies around him obscured her view. "Perhaps 'tis a mouse or a rat and he plans some sort of mischief? I shudder to think what all those ladies around him would do if 'tis a rodent and it was set loose in the ballroom."

Aunt Eggy grinned at Birdie. "Dinnae get started on one of yer dramatic descriptions too, dearling! And I dinnae think ye would shudder in fright at anything."

"Well, I must confess, Aunt Eggy, that indeed, you are correct. I would not shudder a' tall. Thunder an' turf, but I would find it most amusing! A rat running amuck at the Regent's ball! How scandalous. Imagine the screams of the ladies of the *ton* and their debutante daughters as they leap up upon the chairs! *Lud!* And then there would be the men, scurrying around, with some even crawling on their hands and knees, I should think, vying to see who would be the hero who caught the rat. Indeed, it would be quite an entertaining read in the Morning Post, of a certainty!"

A voice arriving at her side had the answer. "'Tis a baby cat."

Birdie's head whipped around. "Tare an' hounds! *Princess Charlotte!*" Birdie covered her mouth at her outburst, but recovered hastily. "I bid you good evening, Your Royal Highness." She grasped her skirts and dropped into a deep curtsy to the Prince Regent's beloved daughter and only child.

"Please, dear Miss Darley, no need for that," Princess Charlotte murmured. "I am so very pleased to see you this evening. You are the only lady that does not stare at me and watch my every move and remark on every piece of my attire."

Birdie smiled at the princess. They had become friends of sorts, seeing each other at several balls. This evening, the princess's gown was indeed particularly beautiful.

"Then you must forgive me, Princess Charlotte. *Lud!* But your gown deserves to be stared at, and indeed, I find that even I cannot help myself." Birdie grinned and stared at Princess Charlotte's royal gown with unabashed enthusiasm.

The gown was an exquisite dress of white lace with wide, stiff skirts over a hoop in the old style of the aristocracy. It was richly embroidered in lama silver with a fine over layer of silver tissue. The sleeves were of silver patent net with elegantly embroidered diamond points. She wore beautiful armlets to match the gown. Her headdress was made up of several white ostrich plumes. It was, of course, larger, grander, and far taller than the other ladies' headdresses in the circular ballroom. It was supported by a stunning diadem matching her necklace of rubies and diamonds.

Her train was narrow but long and showed off the embroidered lama silver to perfection.

"Thank you, Miss Darley. It is beautiful, is it not? For once, I must admit I do like this gown, but I would be the last person to confess this to my grandmother. The queen would forever be choosing every gown I wear, as she did this one." The princess grinned secretly to Birdie. "'Tis beautiful indeed, though I must confess 'tis quite heavy and the train is an annoyance."

Birdie smiled and shook her head. "I feel positively plain next to you!" Once again, she realized her outspokenness. "Though, of course, that is how it should be. How silly of me." Birdie shrugged and looked down at her simple lavender gown. She reached up to feel the two small, white, single ostrich plumes, one of which was curving over the top of her hair. The plumes were supported by a white velvet band that wove through the waves of her midnight hair piled atop her head.

The princess smiled kindly at her. "You always make me smile with your honesty, Miss Darley. May I say that I think you look lovely? You do not need anything a' tall to make you look more lovely than you are."

Birdie shook her head. "'Tis just a simple gown and two plumes—"

"'Tis the simplicity that lets your beauty shine. I would wish to have the freedom to choose to dress as you do, but my grandmother expressly wishes we follow the royal tradition of wearing these hooped, elaborate dresses. I did try to tell her that Marie Antoinette was executed in part due to these overly grand dresses she so loved to flaunt." She made a little moue with her lips. "I do not have your beauty, Miss Darley, so my clothing makes up for what I lack, or so says my grandmother." Princess Charlotte opened her bejeweled fan of silver ostrich feathers and waved it slowly back and forth in front of her face. She looked around. "The queen is here somewhere. I am sure she will remark on my choosing this gown and then find something or other to critique."

Birdie stared knowingly at the pretty, blonde, blue-eyed young princess. "'Tis very vexing that, for I believe you are lovely. But one cannot disagree with the queen, can one?"

They shared a smile before the princess looked beyond Birdie.

Her eyes were drawn to the gentleman and the small, moving bump barely visible under his tailcoat. "I cannot imagine that the poor creature is comfortable in his waistcoat."

"Indeed," Birdie murmured absentmindedly as she looked around for her great-aunt, who was suddenly no longer near her. She saw that she had taken a few steps away from her side to better stare at the gentleman, or rather, the object in his coat.

Birdie hastily pulled her back to her side. She smiled at the princess. "May I introduce my great-aunt Egidia Ross to you, Princess Charlotte?"

"Och! 'Tis the princess," Aunt Eggy crowed. She dropped into a stiff, very deep curtsy with a rustling of her stiff, black, bombazine skirts and cracking of her knees.

"Lady Ross, 'tis a pleasure to meet you," Princess Charlotte murmured with genuine friendliness.

Birdie heard her great-aunt groan. She leaned down close to her. "Aunt Eggy?" she whispered as she reached out to grasp one of her great-aunt's bony elbows. "Whatever is amiss?"

Aunt Eggy tried to look up at her, but could not raise her head all the way, much less see past the ostrich plumes drooping down from her head in front of her eyes. "I am quite as I should be, dearling," she said wryly. She blew at the feathers in front of her eyes blocking her sight.

"Do not jest, Aunt Eggy!" Birdie said in an urgent, low voice.

"Vera well, I fear I am quite stuck, as it were," Aunt Eggy said with a soft groan.

"Let me help you up," Birdie whispered quickly.

"'Twill take more than ye tae dae so, dearling." She glanced stiffly to the side and then said with relief, "Here comes Bibi Hibi." She tried to look back at Birdie. "Did the princess say 'twas a baby in his tailcoat? Or did she say a cat in his tailcoat? Or was it his waistcoat?"

Birdie groaned inwardly and whispered, "*Sards!*" as her great-aunt's friend trundled over.

"No need tae swear, dearling," Aunt Eggy said as she stared stiffly at the floor.

The small, round empress said loudly in her high-pitched, staccato voice, "In Persia, we do not dress our cats in coats. You are most strange in this country, my very best, good friend Egg Lady."

Birdie lowered her head and bowed to the tiny and very round Persian empress. "Good evening, Supreme Imperial Majesty Bibi Habibeh Qajar." She gave a furtive glance at the empress's thick, kohl-blackened brows, or rather her thick, single brow.

Bibi's brows went from one eye, across her lower forehead between her brows, and over to the other eye. This single brow was made even thicker and darker with the addition of kohl. This was considered beautiful in Bibi's country. Bibi wore an overly full-skirted gown of layer after layer of white lace, with every kind of flounce and ruffle that could be added. She wore a long strand of gold beads that hung from her neck to her knees. The overall effect was a peaked, round, and overly decorated sugar-coated cake.

The empress also reeked of hashish, which made Birdie wonder if Empress Bibi had brought her argila with her, as she had at another ball where Aunt Eggy and Empress Bibi had gotten "blootered," as Aunt Eggy would say.

"Help me up, Bibi. I canna dae it myself with these auld knees!"

Birdie watched as Empress Bibi pulled her great-aunt unceremoniously to her feet. Aunt Eggy let out a long, drawn-out moan as she stood up, shoving her green hair and the ostrich plumes back to the top of her head.

"Egg Lady, now that you are standing properly, you must show me this cat wearing a coat. I demand to see it," Bibi stated.

Aunt Eggy placed one hand on her lower back and glowered at the Persian empress. "Bibi, my name is nae Egg Lady And we dinnae put coats on our cats. *Ye heard it wrong.*"

Bibi stared down her nose at the old Scottish woman who was only slightly tinier than herself. "Are you correcting me, Egg Lady?"

"I was. And I will dae so again when ye are wrong, which is vera often, Bibi *Ibi*," Aunt Eggy said as her Scottish accent deepened with her ire.

The empress stared at her a moment. "Very well. I shall allow this correction."

Aunt Eggy pursed her lips and patted her hair. "I believe Princess Charlotte said it was a *baby* in the gentleman's tailcoat, nae a cat."

Birdie groaned.

Empress Bibi looked even more confused and astounded. "Why would a baby be at a ball, Egg Lady? And it is wearing a tailcoat? You English make no sense."

Aunt Eggy stiffened. "I am a Highlander, nae an English woman. There is a difference," she said in a firm, low voice as she noticed they were attracting stares.

Birdie cleared her throat before the two tiny old women could start to argue further. She introduced the empress to Princess Charlotte, realizing her mistake only a moment later as the empress stared at Princess Charlotte in silence.

Princess Charlotte stared calmly and quietly back at the much shorter Persian empress.

"You are the daughter of the Prince Regent whose father the king is unable to rule?" Bibi finally asked as she wiggled her eyebrows and tried to look down her nose at the princess, who was taller than she.

Princess Charlotte nodded solemnly.

Bibi made a humming sound of satisfaction. "I am a *Supreme* Imperial *Empress*. That is higher than a king or queen *or Prince Regent*. It is you who should bow to me first. Then I shall acknowledge you with a nod of my head."

Birdie snapped open her white ostrich feather fan and began fanning it rapidly as she stepped between the women. She knew neither would be bowing to the other.

"Princess Charlotte, you have caught our attention with this most fascinating news! Did you say a *baby cat*? I beg your pardon to tell me is it *a kitten*, perchance?"

Princess Charlotte's eyes went from Birdie to the Persian empress and then back to Birdie again. Her tight smile relaxed. "Indeed, Miss Darley."

Birdie forced a big smile as she looked from her great-aunt to Bibi Habibeh. "There! Do you see? 'Tis a *kitten* he holds in his tailcoat." Her smile floundered at her own words. She spun back to the princess. "But why is he holding a kitten within his tailcoat here at the ball?"

Princess Charlotte snapped open her fan once again and began waving it in front of her face as she turned slightly away from the Persian empress. "I was told that when the gentleman in question arrived this evening that a coach wheel or perhaps even one of the coach horses had stepped on the baby cat's tail. The animal was mewling loudly and the coach driver was about to put it out of its misery when the gentleman stepped forward to retrieve it." She nodded her head profusely. "The gentleman used his handkerchief to wrap the baby cat's tail."

Birdie's mouth fell open and then shut rapidly. "Thunder an' turf, how very curious." She frowned slightly. "All those ladies surrounding him do not seem to have noticed that he has an injured kitten against his chest. They are simply intent on vying for his attention," she said in a disapproving voice.

"Och, dearling, those ladies are his sisters," Aunt Eggy interjected suddenly from beside her.

"*All* of them?" Birdie asked with surprise and doubt.

Aunt Eggy nodded and grinned. "All eight of those lassies are Adairs, just as the gentleman holding the kitten is! He is called *Ten* for a reason, seeing as he was the tenth child born. He was born just after his twin brother! The poor mon has eight sisters older than he that he is noo responsible for since he has inherited the title of the Earl of Fairfax after his poor, dear Da and older twin brother passed on." She made a *tsking* sound. "Och, but I cannae imagine it." She shook her head sadly. "I heard Captain Adair resigned his commission due to his new title. 'Twas Baron Warwick de Walton that pulled him off the battlefield. He has far tae many sisters that depend on him." Aunt Eggy made a humming sound. "I see only seven of his sisters. Where is Octavia, I wonder? She doesnae like these balls. I saw her earlier watching the dancing from behind one of the columns." Aunt Eggy peered around looking for the young lady.

Birdie frowned as she glanced over at Ten Adair. She had not been able to see the man's face, but she knew who the gentleman was now. She had not seen him in a very long time, but she disliked Ten Adair tremendously. He was far too...*too pretty,* she thought. Too charming. Too friendly. Too annoyingly cheerful. He was always smiling and sending women into fits of longing over his dark hair, green eyes, and that dimple when he grinned just so. One could certainly not miss the rugged-looking dent that formed the dimple in his chin.

However, he had shown his true self when they met at Graestone Castle a year ago. He had been abominably rude to her when Birdie had visited her sister Lula and Baron de Walton at Graestone. War de Walton was now Lula's husband, and Ten Adair was a very close friend of War's. Now he was a friend of her sister Lula's as well.

Still, Birdie did not like him. Not at all. She frowned as she stared at him. He still had his hand protectively over his coat, presumably where the kitten was.

Kitten or not, she found him sarcastic and condemnatory, and at the same time, far too jovial. He had never agreed with anything she had said when she met him at Graestone Castle and seemed to find amusement in everything. On top of that, he was always staring so disapprovingly at her.

He was irritating.

Extremely irritating.

Her frown deepened.

And he disliked her good friend Freddie Rockingham, who had been at Graestone as well. Anyone who disliked Freddie, well, she would dislike that person of a certainty for their poor opinion of Freddie.

Freddie Rockingham, the young, new, golden-haired Duke of Trenton, was a catch that had drawn the attention of all the mamas looking for a match for their daughters. Captain Rockingham had suddenly and most unexpectantly inherited the title of Duke of Trenton after first his father and then his older brother's deaths. Recently, the death of his only remaining older brother put the title on his head. His last remaining brother would have inherited the title if he and his ship had not disappeared. The young Captain Frederick Rockingham, however, had refused to leave his regiment. He had become an instant hero for his passionate entreaty to stay and serve with his men. Somehow, his colonel had procured permission for him to stay with his regiment. At least until his brother's death and the loss of the ship could be verified.

His entreaty to stay with his regiment declared him the bravest of men by the Morning Post, of course.

Many understood, however, that a duke would not be on the front lines. His title could not be risked by his death. He could still keep the uniform, but do nothing else but wear it as a symbol of bravery to others.

Birdie hoped that this was true and that Freddie was kept away from the battlefield. She had known him as simply Freddie ever since she was a very young girl when he had come to Aldbey Park to unsuccessfully court her oldest sister Julia. Birdie had sighed over his golden looks from a very young age.

Birdie's eyes strayed away from Ten Adair to look for Freddie. She had been watching him all evening, before Ten Adair and his kitten had stolen her attention away.

She spotted Freddie on the dance floor.

The pretty, young debutante he was dancing with was staring unabashedly up at him. She was sighing and giggling with excitement.

This time, it was Birdie who sighed with impatience.

Birdie's great-aunt's voice chatting away to Princess Charlotte and Empress Bibi faded away.

She moved to the edge of the dance floor. She stood there, furiously tapping her ivory-slippered toes as she watched him.

She crossed her arms over the satin bodice of her breasts with her white ostrich fan hanging limply from one of her wrists. She was tapping ahead of the tempo of the current piece being played by fourteen of the most excellent musicians being directed by Mr. Gow, or was it Mr. Oliver? She was not sure which.

Birdie frowned slightly; it did not matter.

It was a shame actually, because had she been truly listening to the music, she would have realized that it was a current favorite of hers, as well as the Prince Regent's favorite. It was Prinny that was hosting the ball, after all, but there was no sign of him. *I'll Gae Nae Mair to Yon Town* was immensely popular, and it was well known that it was the Prince Regent's favorite.

Birdie sighed again as she kept her eyes on the tall figure in the scarlet coat of a dragoon captain leading his partner gracefully around the dance floor. Freddie was *so* very pleasingly handsome.

"Do not fret, my dear Miss Darley. He'll ask you to dance soon, I would wager. You must have patience."

Birdie was startled, but then smiled as she turned to the princess. "Thunder an' turf, but I will wait as long as it takes, Princess Charlotte. And you are so kind to notice my impatience and offer soothing words. 'Patience is bitter, but its fruit is fulfilling,' they say, so wait I must if I can summon my patience," Birdie answered fervently with a quick grateful glance at the Prince Regent's only child.

"I believe it is 'patience is bitter but its fruit is *sweet*,' Miss Darley."

Birdie stared at her a moment as she thought. "Indeed, 'tis the same thing, I should think. Still, I thank you for coming to stand at the lonely edge of the dance floor with me." She grinned at the princess.

Princess Charlotte looked toward the dance floor. "I am not truly being kind by coming to your side. I fear I simply could not sustain a conversation with the Persian empress Bibi, who is a *Supreme Imperial Majesty*, any longer." Princess Charlotte stared at the couples dancing past. "I must confess I escaped rather abruptly from her presence."

Birdie grinned. "And her eyebrows? Or the smell of hashish?"

Princess Charlotte responded as only a princess could; she offered a serene, barely lift of her lips. "Again, how I do admire your honesty, Miss Darley." She held her ostrich feather fan in front of her face as she lowered her voice. "I must say, I do wish I had been at the Lansdowne ball to witness those two small, elderly ladies smoking hashish." The princess fanned her face to hide her grin as she looked over to the dance floor. Her eyes found and followed a dashing, dark-haired man in uniform.

Birdie smiled and then turned away as she began nibbling idly on her thumbnail. She resumed intently watching Freddie's figure on the dance floor. He was easy to find, for the top of his glorious golden head in all its splendorous waves shone under the magnificent chandeliers.

Princess Charlotte leaned toward Birdie and whispered with a certain contained excitement that only the royals seemed to possess. She pointed subtly to a dark-haired young man. "There is my Captain Charles Hesse. Is he not the most dashing of men in all the Light Dragoons? He wears his red coat in such a masculine way." She fanned herself vigorously as her eyes stayed on the captain. "I do not mean to say that your Captain Rockingham does not look most attractive in *his* red coat, Miss Darley." She lightly touched Birdie's arm. "Please excuse me. I must go speak to Captain Hess."

Birdie spared a quick nod and curtsy for the young princess, but equally as quickly, she turned her eyes back on Freddie Rockingham in his red coat. He had yet another young debutante on the dance floor. How many of the young ladies had he danced with this evening? She had lost count. The young hopefuls had swarmed him, batting their eyes and giggling and blushing profusely as they stared up at his blue eyes, tall stature, and his Greek, godlike head of golden hair artfully combed forward on his forehead in dramatic waves. He also wore long, thick sideburns that followed the lines from his perfectly shaped ears to his perfectly sculpted jaw.

Birdie looked down at her gown. Her gown *was* rather simple, no matter what the princess had said about it being lovely. She did not like overly ruffled or embellished gowns, unlike her sister Lula who loved odd colors and as much frippery as she could put on something. Birdie was also small and dark-haired and not at all slender or pale like the young debutants that had won a dance with the golden-haired, handsome duke. She felt that she did have rather nice blue eyes, however. They were like her mother's eyes, an almost lavender-blue color. Like her mother, her hair was black, not blonde, which was so desirable to the men of the *Ton*, it seemed. As well, her hair was not neat and straight like the debutants, but had a mind of its own and was often escaping the coiffure that she had so labored to force all the waves of it into.

Birdie watched Freddie dance past her, giving her a broad, white-toothed grin as he held his latest partner. He twirled his partner just then, far too close to one of the columns.

A young lady was standing there, tucked beside the column watching the dancers.

Birdie's breath caught.

She knew what was coming.

It happened very quickly.

CHAPTER THREE

F REDDIE'S ARM STRUCK the young lady standing beside the column.

The young lady tried to recover from Freddie's elbow, but could not regain her footing. With flailing arms and a loud, "Oops!" her elegantly slippered feet flew out from beneath her.

She landed in a puddle of pale green silk and chiffon on the edge of the ballroom floor. One of her slippers had flown off and was nowhere to be seen. Her carefully arranged coiffure was tilting precariously to one side and one of her delicate, pale green hose had fallen down the leg of the missing slipper. The hose had slid down to puddle around her ankle and over her heel. A dainty, floral ribbon garter, which had held up the hose, lay on the floor.

The couples who were dancing past shortened their strides as they tried to move around her with looks of horror on their faces. This caused the couples behind them to bump into them until the whole dance floor was in chaos and very much behind the tempo of the orchestra.

Birdie picked up her skirts and hurried to the young lady.

She knelt next to her. "Let me help you up," she said hastily as she watched the dancers glaring down at her and the young woman with horror and disdain as they tried to dance past the girl on the floor. "Hurry, you must stand up!" She turned to the young woman and froze. "You are smiling," Birdie stated in confusion.

The young woman nodded as she indelicately pulled the single, dangling hose off of her foot, pushed her skirts back down over her legs, shoved at her hair, grabbed the errant garter, and accepted Birdie's help to get back on her feet. "I do it all the time, I fear. I seem to be prone to falling out of my shoes." She shoved the hose and garter into Birdie's hands and then tiptoed quickly with one slipper on and one slipper off, out onto the dance floor after her missing slipper.

Birdie looked down at the hose and garter in her hand and then out to the girl darting around the dance floor after her slipper. She watched in dismay as the dainty shoe got kicked aside by one dancer after another. The missing slipper made its way to the center of the ballroom floor with the young woman turning in circles trying to find it.

Birdie bit her lip, took a deep breath and was about to plunge into the fray in pursuit of the slipper when someone inadvertently kicked it again. This time, it came sliding back to the edge of the floor, away from the dancers.

Birdie quickly made her way to the slipper. She bent down and snatched up the lovely pale green shoe before someone could kick it away again.

Birdie stood up and managed to catch the young woman's eye. She raised the slipper covertly in her hand to show her that she had it.

The two young women smiled confidentially at one another as the young lady hurried off the dance floor out of the way of the couples.

The young lady was laughing as she hopped on one foot to put her slipper back on. "I fear I do not know your name to thank you properly," she said to Birdie. She stood up with her two slippered feet once more solidly on the floor.

"Miss Birdie Darley," Birdie said, and smiled with a quick curtsey.

"I am Miss Octavia Adair." She curtsied back to Birdie with a broad smile. Her smile went from her lips to her eyes, which were a bright grass green. "I owe you my thanks, Miss Darley. Please, after your help, you must call me Octavia."

Birdie laughed. "Very well, and you must call me Birdie." She leaned closer and whispered, "Do you not wish to put your hose back on?"

Octavia made a face. "I cannot seem to keep them on. My legs are so thin, you see, and the hose belongs to one of my older sisters and is thus stretched out. The garters do not help either. Here." She took the hose and garter from Birdie's hand and quickly looked around, her eyes settling on a tall potted plant beside a column. She shoved the unmentionables into the dense leaves of the plant. She turned back to Birdie with an embarrassed, shy smile. "Do not tell anyone. I think it shall be months before my hose and garter are discovered, if at all."

Birdie could only grin at her. "Are you hurt? Tare an' hounds that was quite the fall!"

"She does it all the time," came a deep voice at her side.

Birdie turned to see Ten Adair, the Earl of Fairfax, grinning at his sister with the dimple in his chin on full display. His eyes crinkled at the edges with full force.

Octavia gave a shy but adoring smile up at her brother. "Brother, this is Miss Birdie Darley. She came to my aid, quite heroically!" She turned to Birdie. "Miss Darley, my brother, Ten Adair, the Right Honorable Earl of Fairfax."

Birdie gave him an abrupt curtsey, and he bowed his head briefly in return.

Ten's gaze went back to his sister. He rubbed at the dimple in his chin as he tried not to laugh.

"You fell again, Octavia? You are far too clumsy, sister."

Birdie frowned. "Lord Fairfax, how can you be cheerful about this? Your sister fell!"

Ten's grin only grew. "She is used to falling. And making a spectacle of herself, I fear. By the smile on her face, I can assure you that Octavia is fine, Miss Darley." He shrugged. "She is young. Like an ungainly colt."

Birdie's elegant black brows rose above her bright blue eyes as she bristled with indignation. "She is young? Is that the observation of her *caring* brother or a condemnation of all ladies of a certain age? And may I add she is naught much more than a year older than yourself."

Ten took one step closer and grinned tightly down at Birdie. "Age is not always an indicator of *maturity*, Miss Darley," he said as he arched a brow meaningfully at her.

Birdie gasped in indignation.

Octavia stepped between the two of them and whispered sharply, "Speaking of making a spectacle, brother, pardon me, but have the two of you been introduced before this evening? You seem well acquainted of a sort."

Birdie and Ten scowled at one another.

Octavia looked from one to the other. "Very well then, I have introduced you to one another. You should both consider that you have been introduced to a most marvelous person. Now stop scowling at one another this instant."

Ten's lips lifted into a rueful grin. "Actually, sister, Miss Darley and I met at Graestone Castle."

Octavia's mouth opened and then closed quickly. "At Baron de Walton's ball? Oh, it was positively romantic! I should be most pleased to someday receive a marriage proposal as Miss Lula Darley did from the baron! My heart positively fluttered out of my body when all his men said that they were going to keep Miss Lula as well." She sighed dramatically before suddenly spinning to Birdie. "She is your sister!"

Birdie nodded. "Yes, Lula is my sister and Baron War de Walton is my brother-in-law. He is a most *excellent gentleman*." Birdie frowned up at Ten before noticing Aunt Eggy scurrying toward them.

"Och, dearling, ye shouldnae be speaking tae a gentleman unless I am with ye." Aunt Eggy stopped and caught her breath when she saw who Birdie was speaking to. She smiled at the young girl standing next to her great-niece. "Hello, Miss Octavia, and dinnae ye look pretty, and I see ye arenae fairing any worse for yer tumble!" She turned back to Birdie. "Yer mither said I am tae chaperon ye, so that is what I must dae!" She lowered her voice to a mumbling grumble, "Though it seems a glaikit thing. How are young couples tae see if they like one another?" She shook her head and then grinned and primped at her hair and black bombazine gown as she smiled up at Ten.

Ten reached down and lifted her gloved hand to his lips. He bowed. "Lady Egidia Ross, it is very good to see you this evening, and may I add how lovely you look? Your green hair is most remarkable!"

"Guid evening, Ten, er Lord Fairfax!" Aunt Eggy curtsied very carefully. She patted his chest as a blush stole up to her wrinkled face. She studied the stunningly handsome young earl with the charming dimple and green eyes that were hard not to stare into.

"Where is the kitten we saw ye with earlier? I can see that it is nae being held against yer chest." She patted his broad chest again, this time with both hands, and sighed as she stared at the perfection of his shoulders.

Ten grinned. "The kitten is currently with my sisters. Unless you wish to check my, er, *tailcoat* again with your hands?" he asked with a teasing grin.

Aunt Eggy flapped her fingers at him. "Dinnae waste yer charms on me, young Ten. I have known ye since ye were a young lad running through the Highlands when ye came tae visit yer mither's family in the summer." She shook her head. "I dae miss yer mither sae. And yer father. Ye have filled yer father's shoes quite well, my boy. He would be most proud." She turned to Birdie. "He looks particularly handsome this evening. Wouldnae ye agree, dearling Birdie?"

Octavia looked back and forth from her brother to Miss Birdie Darley with great interest. The two of them were glaring at one another again. They seemed to dislike one another intensely.

Her always good-natured, joking, and teasing brother was looking for once like a serious earl. He was even frowning!

"Dearling Birdie?" Aunt Eggy repeated. "Wouldnae ye agree he looks handsome this evening?"

Birdie's eyebrows rose at her great-aunt's remark. "It would be highly irregular for me to answer that question, *as I am sure you know*, Aunt Eggy. I am not a naft, numpty lass. Tare an' hounds, to comment on his countenance would be most irregular and indiscriminate, an infraction on polite society, an infringement of rules. A transgression and trespass on all that is expected of a polite young lady, which of course, I always strive to be. If I am wrong on that, I shall kiss a crooked cricket, Aunt Eggy."

Ten's eyebrows rose as the corner of one side of his lips threatened to tilt up into a grin.

Aunt Eggy snorted and made a dismissive motion of one hand to stop Birdie. She knew that Birdie would very likely keep going, getting more dramatic in her rant. "Och, since when does that bother *ye*, dearling?"

Birdie frowned and pursed her lips. "Aunt Eggy, would you please help me escort Miss Octavia over to a chair? She has had quite the spill, after all. We must needs be solicitous and see to her comfort." She mumbled under her breath, "Unlike her bowfin, glaikit, gallus brother."

Aunt Eggy quickly took Octavia's arm and pulled her away. "I dinnae need yer help, dearling Birdie. I can escort Octavia. Ye two must dance. Ye cannae stand there together. There would be talk, and poor Octavia has given enough reasons for chatter." She glanced over her shoulder to Birdie. "Stop waiting for that idjut Freddie tae ask ye tae dance and dance with the man in front of ye."

Octavia hurried away with Aunt Eggy. She turned her head and stared back with avid interest at her brother and her new friend. She had never seen her brother so riled. "Oh! Lady Egidia, my, er... I must retrieve something."

"Aye, aye, ye stuffed yer unmentionables in the leaves of that potted plant. I amnae blind. However, best ye leave them in the foliage, dearling."

Birdie started to say that she too would help Octavia to a chair, but it was too late. Aunt Eggy had bustled Octavia off through the crowd. She turned slowly back to Ten Adair with a reluctant look on her face.

Ten gave his full attention to Birdie after watching Aunt Eggy lead Octavia away to sit down. He straightened his spine as he stared down at her. His eyes raked over her from the top of her midnight hair to her lavender gown that fell from under full bosom to drape every shapely curve of her petite body to the tips of her white satin slippers with their lavender bow. His eyes returned to her hair. He stared at the single white ostrich plume in the raven masses of curls. The white feather stood up as if signaling to one and all in the ballroom that here was an unattached young lady.

He looked away from her and tugged at his cravat. Rules of decorum dictated that he ask her to dance. His sister's indignant fall had already created gossip. Lady Egidia Ross was correct.

"May I have this dance, Miss Darley?" He held out his hand and waited.

Birdie scowled. "You do not want to dance with me. Why bother to ask?" she whispered emphatically.

"We neither want to dance with the other. Yet it is the proper thing to do," he whispered with a stiff, polite grin. "People are watching, Miss Darley."

Ten continued to hold his gloved hand out to her. He arched an eyebrow as his grin grew into a challenge.

"Thunder an' turf! I suppose I am forced by convention to accept," she murmured under her breath.

As was proper, she moved to his right and put her hand in his. They went and stood with the other couples readying to dance the quadrille. They faced each other in silent displeasure.

Once the music began, they moved stiffly through the first movements of the dance and then stood awkwardly still, facing one another as the movement went down the line, requiring the others to take their turn in the intricate steps that showed off one's—*hopefully*—graceful form.

"You are the last person in this ballroom that I would expect to come to the aid of my sister," Ten said politely.

Birdie's chin rose immediately. "Since we are being so honest, I must confess that *you* are the last person in this ballroom that one could expect to come to the aid of *any* lady, or gentleman, for that matter." She arched one delicate brow at him. "Though I did come to your sister's aid, you should know that if you came to any misfortune, I surely would not come to your aid."

"I can assure you that I can think of no circumstance when I should ever require aid, Miss Darley," he said crisply, and then grinned. "Particularly yours."

They walked toward one another in the line of couples, placed their palms against the other, and turned in a circle.

"I believe that I heard that Baron War de Walton had to come to your aid. He rescued you off the battlefield, in fact."

Ten returned to his place in line. His jaw was tight. He forced a *devil-may-care* grin on his lips and would not be bated by her. "You do not know the whole story of that day," he began in a low voice. They walked forward and slowly circled one another. "I had gone back to carry one of my injured men off the battlefield and was returning to look for a second man when the cannon blast struck me. War de Walton found me and forced me off the field." They turned and then slowly circled one another in the other direction. "War had gotten word that my father and twin brother had died. He reminded me that I had eight sisters relying on my return. I managed to find my second man before I returned."

Birdie's smile dropped at this news. She must remember to ask Lula's husband about this incident.

The careless grin remained firmly in place as he went back to the line and turned to face her. The dance floor was certainly not the place to tell her the horrors that he had met so often on those battlefields, but the challenge in her eyes had goaded him.

Birdie sighed loudly at seeing his grin, though she registered that it did not reach his eyes. Her voice lowered as they met again, repeating the dance steps. "My condolences on the loss of your father and brother. I did not know." She paused, noting he maintained a tight grin. "You carried an injured man off the field of battle. Impressive. But you are smiling. Are you never serious?" she demanded. She sighed in annoyance when he just arched a brow at her while his grin did not falter. "Did you also carry the second man off the field as you did the first, even though you had just been injured?" she asked in a challenging voice.

His grinning lips flattened then. He spoke in a soft voice. "I carried what was left of him off the field. His horse was standing guard over him. If not for that horse, I would never have seen my man. That horse was the only warhorse left alive on the battlefield. The animal was injured, but still stood loyally by his fallen rider. The horse only let me lead it off the field once I picked up his rider. It was a…difficult situation." His brow arched. "And when needed, yes, of course, I am serious."

Birdie went quiet. She watched the swirling, painful emotions in his green eyes, though his grin stayed in place. "Did the horse recover from its wounds?" she asked quietly as she walked around him as the dance steps required.

His green eyes flashed to hers and saw the genuineness there. She was a horsewoman, so of course, he should expect her to ask after the horse. It pleased him that she cared about the animal. His own smile became genuine as well. "Pride is doing just fine."

"Pride?" she asked.

"'Tis the horse's name."

"An odd name, that, but perhaps not really. Pride goeth before a fall, as they say." She frowned. "*Lud*, that was callous of me, for Pride did not go when his rider fell. Thunder an' turf, I do beg your pardon." At his tight nod, she asked, "Could you not rescue any other horses?"

"No," he said curtly, and looked away as it was his turn to

circle her.

"Horrid," she whispered. "Horribly, hugely, horrid."

He looked down his nose at her and then away. "Do you always use alliteration when you give your opinion?" He did not wait for her answer. "You know nothing of what happens on a battlefield, Miss Darley. You can have no opinion of that which you do not understand."

Birdie sniffed in annoyance. She too, looked away from him.

They met and twirled and performed the required steps, maintaining their stiff displeasure of one another with barely a touch of their gloved hands.

Birdie noticed that he in particular did his best to not touch her at all.

"'Tis obvious that you dislike me," she stated.

"Indeed," he murmured. "And you dislike me as well."

"Indeed," she murmured back. She tilted her head at him as they moved left and right and turned in time to the music. "I rather thought you rakes love *all* women."

Ten almost missed a step at her statement. She thought him a rake? He touched her hand this time as they turned around one another. "Rakes do not love women. The opposite, in fact. They have no regard for women."

Birdie was quiet for several bars of the music. "How very interesting. I shall have to remember that," she murmured to herself.

They remained silent as they stood facing one another until it was their turn in the line to dance again or the music ended, whichever came first.

Birdie glanced at his fine, navy waistcoat embroidered with swirling vines of a lighter blue. She could see the top of the waistcoat he wore beneath his finely tailored navy tailcoat. The tailcoat was classic in its simplicity. Masculine due to its wearer, not due to any embellished shape of the coat. This man did not need any padded or puffed embellishments on the coat's shoulders to make him look broader or his waist and hips leaner.

"Yes?" he inquired. "Does my form please you?" He gave her a wicked, slow grin. It showed off his intriguing dimple to perfection.

Birdie's blue eyes flashed at him. She arched her raven-colored brow. "You are incorrigible. I was simply wondering how you fit the kitten in your tailcoat."

Ten turned away from her to see the other dancers. The quadrille was complete and some of the couples were beginning to leave the dance floor while others stayed, waiting for the next dance.

"It seems we are done here." He bowed to Birdie and she curtsied stiffly back. Before the next tune could begin, he gave her his arm and escorted her from the dance floor.

"Thank you," she murmured as she placed her fingers lightly on his arm.

"As for you wondering about the kitten fitting in my tailcoat. It is quite small. As I told your great-aunt, though you may have not overheard, the kitten is currently being held by one of my sisters and is no longer in my tailcoat. Obviously." His voice was casual as he came to a stop and pulled his arm away from her hand. He bowed his head and gave her a polite smile that did not reach his eyes.

She gave him a small curtsey in return.

From over her bowing head, his gaze was drawn to a soldier in a captain's uniform walking toward them. He knew the man. It was Frederick Rockingham, and his gaze was intent on Birdie.

Birdie straightened up and turned to look behind her at what had captured the earl's stern look. Freddie Rockingham was walking toward her. He stood out in his red coat with his stiffly pomaded and artfully coiffed golden hair. She smiled at him with pleasure.

"Miss Birdie!" Freddie said charmingly. "You are the dearest friend in all of London to wait for a dance with me." His glance went to a smiling young lady staring meaningfully at him at the edge of the dance floor. He turned slightly away from Birdie and said in a quick aside to her, "I vow I shall save my last dance for you! I have promised this one to that young lady yonder, and then there are still several more to dance with. I am quite sure that you don't mind waiting." He turned from Birdie without waiting for her answer and waved to the young lady.

Birdie watched him start to walk away. She clutched her fingers together as her shoulders sank.

"I say, Rockingham." Ten called Freddie's attention back to them. "I must inform you that Miss Darley has been spoken for, in fact, for every one of the dances this evening. Pon rep, but all the young bucks wish to dance with her. I was lucky to get one dance. So sorry, chap!"

Freddie turned and stared at Ten in silence. He walked back to them. "I do believe she promised me a dance, Fairfax."

"Tut, tut, tut!" Ten raised one finger as he grinned tightly at the younger man. He lowered his voice. "I don't give a tinker's damn what you believe the young lady promised you, Captain, or should I call you *Your Grace?*" He arched his brow. "No, I think not," he said quietly as he looked at his clothing. "You are still in uniform, so it *must* be Captain." He raised his chin and steeled his jaw. "You begged to stay with your regiment, I hear. How very heroic of you." He spoke in a razor-sharp, fast voice. "Don't make a cake of yourself. You have shown yourself to be a *neck or nothing young blood of the fancy.* Accept that the young lady is in high demand and you have lost your dance *and* your chance to escort her to the dining room for supper." His voice lowered to a growl. "Move off now, *Captain.*" His grin became wolfish as he held Freddie's hostile stare.

Birdie watched in astonishment as Freddie's glance went to her and then back to Ten Adair. After a moment, he bowed his head to Birdie, spun on his heels, and strode away.

Birdie whirled back to Ten and stared up into his glittering green eyes.

"Why?" she breathed out. "Why did you do that? *Lud*, I have been waiting all evening to dance with him! Or have him escort me to the dining room so that I may sit next to him at supper," she seethed in a low, stricken voice.

"I suppose that I could *possibly, perhaps,* escort you to the dining room," he said reluctantly as he watched Frederick Rockingham lead the young debutante onto the dance floor.

"*Possibly? Perhaps?* How kind of you," Birdie said scathingly. "No, I think not. I wanted Freddie to dance with me, to escort me to the dining room, and sit beside me at supper."

Ten's green gaze left Freddie's retreating back to look down at Birdie. He stared into her angry, violet-blue eyes.

"I cannot imagine why. He's a fool," he said indifferently.

Birdie bristled. "He is not a fool. Freddie Rockingham is the Duke of Trenton. You were most rude to him, Lord Fairfax."

Ten swore under his breath. "Rockingham has not *formally* been given the title of Duke of Trenton. He is still only a captain and thus is beneath me." He ran a hand through his dark hair. "Damnation, but his brother Adam has not even been declared dead and some are already calling young Freddie *Duke,*" he said with disgust. "Though Adam's ship has not returned, it does *not* mean that the ship went down and he with it. Those of us who knew Adam well called him Rock because he was strong of mind and body and dependable. We also knew that he could sail through any storm. *Young Freddie* needs to be patient," he said curtly.

"Freddie is very aware of that, I assure you. He hopes for his brother's return, but it looks less and less likely as the years go by. After his father and eldest brother were killed in a carriage accident and then the second-born brother, Adam, went missing at sea, can you blame the king or parliament for wanting this settled?"

Ten studied the emotions on Birdie's face. He raised his chin as he tugged at his cravat.

"I hate these blasted things." He stopped trying to adjust the knot and exhaled loudly as he studied her face. She was staring off after Rockingham. "You fancy yourself in love with him," he stated.

Birdie bit her lower lip and looked back up at him. "What if I am?" She straightened her shoulders and stared unabashedly back at Ten Adair, the Earl of Fairfax.

He rubbed his chin between one finger and his thumb. "Then you are a fool as well, Little Bird," he said quietly. He continued to rub at his chin as he stared down at her. Before she could answer, he held up his finger. "Consider what I just did a favor in repayment for Octavia. Rockingham will look at you differently now. You are now a woman in demand. A woman that he must needs fight for. *As well he should.*"

"I do not require that he fight for me," Birdie said with annoyance.

"Indeed, *you should.*" He yanked angrily at his cravat again. "A man must fight for his woman because he is a man, and she is to be protected, cherished, *and desired,*" he said in a deep, gruff voice. "Not left to stand on the edge of the dance floor, waiting and hoping that he may deign to dance with her." His jaw tightened as he looked down at her. He bowed his head curtly. "I bid you good evening, Miss Darley. I have sisters and a kitten to attend to."

Birdie closed her lips and made a quick, stiff curtsey in return. She watched Ten Adair walk away. She had not noticed before, but he stood heads taller and broader than the other men in the room. His dark hair was not styled and pomaded, but was naturally in disarray and slightly longer, just over his ears and collar in back, for he obviously did not care to beautify himself for anyone.

He also walked with a certain coiled power in his large strides. Men quickly moved aside without a word from him.

He and Baron War de Walton were certainly not the typical men of the *Ton.* Aunt Eggy called them *warriors. Men out of their time.*

Her gaze followed him as he went to his sisters who were gathered around Octavia. He accepted the kitten from one of them with a genuine smile. She watched as he gently lifted the tiny thing and touched his nose to the kitten's. His green eyes crinkled up at the corners in genuine happiness. Then he cuddled the little kitten to his chest as he gave his full attention to his eight sisters' conversations.

CHAPTER FOUR

A VOICE AT Birdie's side and a thwack on her arm from a rather vintage fan broke into her study of the man and his kitten.

Suddenly, once more she heard the sound of the orchestra and realized couples were dancing and guests were chatting.

"Birdie dearling, Queen Charlotte bids yer presence. Ye are off dreaming of something, but I wouldnae haiver aboot, best hurry tae her. She seems most insistent. I cannae think why she wants tae speak tae ye? Can ye?"

Birdie grimaced at her tiny great-aunt Eggy, who had returned to her side with Princess Charlotte. "The queen? She wishes to speak to me? Of course I have no idea why," Birdie said in a rush and then exhaled deeply. She turned to Princess Charlotte standing beside Aunt Eggy. "Princess Charlotte? I beg you to excuse me."

The princess gave her a sympathetic smile. "One cannot say no to the queen."

Birdie grinned, curtsied to the princess, and then made her way through the crowded ballroom, weaving between the people dressed in their finest gowns and tailcoats. She knew the queen would be waiting at the other end of the ballroom seated on a dais where she could watch over the crowd of guests. Birdie had avoided this end of the ballroom for that very reason.

She stopped at the bottom of the dais and looked up at Queen Charlotte.

The queen was dressed in a sumptuous gown of palest gold. Her hair was styled in an intricate coiffure of braids and curls that rose high atop her head. The masses were powdered in gold to match her dress, as were the voluminous, tall, and stately golden-feathered plumes. The effect was stunning and certainly very regal. There was no mistaking this was *The Queen*.

Queen Charlotte's eyes found Birdie's. Birdie watched as she rose slowly and gracefully from her seat. Although, in Birdie's mind, she called it a throne. The queen motioned for Birdie to come up to her.

Birdie's legs trembled beneath her lavender skirts as she walked with trepidation up the two steps to the dais and stopped. She curtsied deeply to the queen and then waited with her head bowed.

"Come closer, Miss Darley. I would speak to you." Queen Charlotte's voice was no-nonsense, commanding yet polite as only a queen would be who knows her commands will be carried out without question.

Birdie rose and walked forward to stand with the queen.

"You must tell me what you have found out," Queen Charlotte demanded quietly while watching the people dancing on the ballroom floor below her.

Birdie took a deep breath. "Your Majesty, I have been investigating the terrible tragedy of the horses that have been taken, just as you asked. I have discovered that the horses are being *stolen* from all around London. They are being *smuggled* out of the city for a most *dire* purpose." She lowered her voice, and added in a whisper, "They are being smuggled across the channel to France! *To replenish Napoleon's army after his dire loss in Leipzig.*" She cringed. She was waiting for the queen's anger at such terrible news.

The queen stilled and then nodded once as her face paled. "It is more nefarious than I feared." She looked at Birdie. "'Tis a dangerous mission I have sent you on, Miss Darley. I think it too dangerous for a young lady."

"Your Majesty," Birdie quickly interjected, "I am up to this task, I assure you! I finally got close enough to discover how and where they are smuggling them out of London! I was even able to recover four horses!" At the queen's shocked look, she quickly added, "The smugglers never had a hope of seeing who I was nor catching me." Birdie did not add the part about the mysterious man who had intervened to help, or that she had been dressed as a boy.

"You cannot get involved! You were only to gather information, Miss Darley! You do not have the help of a man such as your stepfather, Lord Hawke, as your mother did." She looked away from Birdie and pursed her lips.

"Your Majesty, Napoleon needs horses. His army was decimated in Leipzig. This smuggling of our horses *will not stop* if his intent is to re-amass his army. I must do all I can. For the horses, at least."

The queen declared frostily in a harsh whisper, "Yes, his army has been decimated. You are very correct in that, Miss Darley. Though Leipzig was the final blow, his losses started well before that." Her lips thinned to a harsh line as her eyes narrowed. "He is back in France now. We cannot afford for him to rebuild his army *if* that is indeed his plan." She frowned. "He has nothing left. So he steals our fine English horses, which will become still more casualties of this war."

Birdie took a breath. "Napoleon has begun a remount program. Half of the horses he is accumulating are conscriptions. They have been *voluntarily* given, taken, or stolen, and some purchased. They must be over six years old, and trained to ride, so of course he is getting desperate and needs our horses. He also needs heavy draught horses and will pay dearly for them."

The queen sighed in exasperation and some worry as she tapped her enormous fan sharply on the palm of her hand. "This makes some sense. First, it was two of Lord North's finest riding horses, then it 'twas the Earl of Ridgefield's best hunters encompassing half his stables. Lady Nash's *entire* stable was emptied of horses in one night." She waved her hand once. "I could go on, but I shan't. The situation is most dire indeed." She narrowed her eyes and pursed her lips as she stared at the elegant guests milling about the ballroom enjoying themselves.

"Most dire, indeed," murmured Birdie in agreement.

The queen continued, "It is the man who is *behind this* that I *must* have information about. A man that knows the best horses in London and where to steal them from. He is a member of the *Ton* or our own military. I am sure of it!" The queen turned her intelligent and sharp eyes on Birdie, studying her as if deciding on something. "I do not like you being so involved."

"Your Majesty?" Birdie swallowed tightly. This is what she was afraid of. The queen would tell her to stop. She spoke carefully. "'Tis not just the *Ton* losing their horses. The paint and brick warehouses have also lost horses. *Thirty* horses were taken from the Black Eagle brewery's dray horse stable. That is almost half of their stable! Those are the finest heavy horses in London that deliver barrels of beer to *all* the taverns. Your people will not be pleased if they do not get their beer."

The queen nodded. "'Tis very true."

"Virtually every business here in London relies on horses in the making and delivery of their products," Birdie explained. "We all rely on horses for our own transportation. Lud, there are fifty thousand horses here, imagine!" She swallowed and summoned her bravery. "These thieves are hitting anywhere there seems to be an abundance of horses and *I do not believe they are done*. They will keep stealing more for Napoleon's remount program!" She lowered her voice further as the queen frowned with worry. "Won't you please let me continue to help in this effort?" She spoke as respectfully as she could.

Birdie watched as the queen took a long, deep breath. She turned her regal eyes from her guests and stared curiously down at her. "You have had no offers for your hand," the queen stated matter-of-factly. "You should let the men beat you in those horse races you insist on competing in. Men do not like to be beaten, you know."

Birdie's lips tipped down. Why was the queen talking of this? "Those men are terrible riders. It would be wrong to let them pretend to beat me." Birdie bit her lower lip. She had spoken without thinking, as she was wont to do too often.

The queen pursed her lips as her brows rose at Birdie's words. "You presume to judge their riding skills, Miss Darley?"

Birdie shrugged delicately. "I must." She took a breath and tried to explain since she had spoken so openly to the queen already. "How else can I master my skill if I do not always do my best and if I am not aware of others' skills at horsemanship? Must I feign incompetence to spare a man's pride?"

The queen grunted and almost smiled. She studied Birdie critically. "You are somewhat lovely in a petite way, Miss Darley. Though your face shows that you are out in the sun far too often and you have black rather unruly hair, and I think perhaps with your figure, you may be eating too much. Still, you are rather pretty. One cannot miss that those lavender-blue eyes of yours are full of intelligence."

Birdie opened her mouth to say something about why her looks or her weight should not matter, but quickly changed her mind. She bowed her head. "Thank you, Your Majesty," she murmured. "I have been investigating this for many months. I should be despondent to stop. I must beg you to continue to let me help, if I may be so bold to ask that of you?"

"Miss Darley, of course, you may ask this question. You Darley women are certainly not demure and content to sit and sew and drink tea and attend balls." She tapped her fan on the palm of her hand again as she narrowed her eyes on the people in the ballroom. "We only briefly discussed the horses being stolen in our first meeting before you went to visit your sister at Graestone Castle nearly a year past. Just these last months I have asked you to listen to any gossip of the *Ton* that pertains to more horses being stolen. You have done well, Miss Darley." She let go of her fan, letting it swing from her wrist on its jeweled chain. She began adjusting the long, satin gloves on her arms. "However, this is *not* what either you *or I* had expected. *The French!* Stealing *our horses? How dare they?*" she seethed. She took a deep breath and continued to look away from Birdie as she glanced all around the opulent room.

"It is horrid, to think what the horses are being stolen for. *War…*" Birdie said quietly. "Perhaps to ease your qualms, one of your men can assist me? Or one of the prime minister's men? He must be aware of this, I should think."

The queen held up one gloved hand to stop her. Each one of her fingers was covered in large, ornate, bejeweled rings. "I will trust no one from inside the palace *or* the prime minister's office." She leaned toward Birdie and whispered, "I believe we are dealing with *treason.*"

Birdie watched as the queen lifted one of her ringed fingers to her nose, flipped open the top of the ring, and sniffed loudly through one nostril.

Birdie smelled the faint aroma of tobacco.

The queen continued. "We *women* are quite adept at finding out secrets. Are we not?" She arched an eyebrow and studied the ballroom in silence for several moments. "I will allow you to keep helping me on this." The queen snapped the ring shut and turned her sharp eyes on Birdie. "I chose you because you are a *Darley*, a *courageous* young lady not unlike your mother. It was she that found out and exposed the crime at Tattersalls. An astounding act, that was. Like her, you are a young lady who knows *horses.* But of all the Darley ladies, I believe you to be a young lady who enjoys action and bravery. Your mother knows how to match and breed horses to get the finest Thoroughbreds. Your eldest sister, Lady Julia, enjoys the precision of training them. Your other sister, Miss Lula, wants to care for them and treat their injuries. You, however, I believe you simply…" She shrugged and opened her hands. "*Enjoy* them. I have seen you outside of Tattersalls throwing caution and decorum to the wind as you show off Aldbey Park's horses. I have also seen you join a race on your horse alongside men with the same bravado and vigor. *You,* Miss Darley, are exactly what I need!" She looked away from Birdie and clenched the fingers of one hand. "I must not reject your help. *I cannot.*" She lowered her voice as she turned back to stare at Birdie with intelligent eyes. "You have discovered so much, as well as the reason for these crimes. Now, first and foremost, you must *not* endanger yourself with any of the smugglers. You must not get close. *You must only watch and listen!* Can you get me information about the man I believe is behind this? *He is the key!*"

Birdie took a steadying breath. "I believe the man you suspect is innocent. I have found nothing that would prove the claims against him to be true, Your Majesty," Birdie answered in a low voice, matching the queen.

"Nonsense, girl." She waved one hand out toward the ballroom. "I see the way you stare at him. However, you must put your feelings for the man aside and look without clouded eyes. He is part of this, but what part he plays I do not know. I can only say that when he was well, the king mentioned this man's name and warned me about a military secret. The king is not well enough now to ask further, so I must proceed carefully on my own. This man has served us well in the past." She pursed her lips and looked away.

Birdie frowned sadly. "I am so sorry about the king's terrible illness. I pray he recovers soon."

The queen pursed her lips as she stared out at her guests. "Yes, yes, very prettily said, and I thank you." Queen Charlotte smoothed the very brief hint of sadness that had crept onto her face. She resumed her regal air and lowered her voice to a confidential whisper as she raised her open fan in front of her face. "I believe this man has something to do with the terrible tragedy, as you say, of the horses being stolen for the French army. Is this the military secret the king referred to, and this man is orchestrating it?" She snapped shut her fan and turned to Birdie.

She stared sternly down at her. "I do not have actual proof and will not act on this man without that proof." She pointed her closed fan at her. "This you must get me. You know the man. You are close to him, as is your family."

Birdie opened her mouth to say something, but closed it when the queen stopped her with a quelling look. "You said you recovered four horses. I am quite sure that you returned them to their rightful owners, yes? Question those owners, or their stable help. Someone must have seen something, heard something." She tapped her fan on her palm again. "You are staying in London for the season, yes? In your stepfather's house in Grosvenor Square." She nodded sharply once. "'Tis just yourself and your great-aunt Egidia Ross, who is your chaperon. Your mother and stepfather, the Duke of Leids, are busy with your baby brother, I hear, and remain at Aldbey Park." She nodded again. "Your sister Julia and the Persian prince are moving into their new estate, very close to Aldbey Park. Your other sister Lula is busy at Graestone Castle and wedded to Baron Warwick de Walton this past year. A fine match, that." She raised her chin and stared proudly down her nose at Birdie, who looked very surprised. "Yes, I see you may wonder that I am aware of *all* that goes on in my kingdom, except for this horse business! I must know if this man is behind this treasonous activity! Grosvenor Square is an ideal location for you to move around London and watch and report *to me.*"

Birdie nodded slowly once. "Yes, Your Majesty."

The queen stopped what she was about to say as her eyes sharpened on something else.

"Ah, there is your most delightful great-aunt Egidia." She lowered her voice to a whisper. "I see that she is accompanied by the Supreme Imperial Empress Bibi Habibeh. This very evening the empress once again reminded *me, the Queen of England,* that her title is higher than mine." She sniffed as she stared with narrowed eyes at the short, wide empress. The queen's gaze went back to Aunt Eggy. She nodded and smiled serenely at her.

Aunt Eggy made a partial bobbling curtsey, complete with a

soft groan as her hair and ostrich plumes tilted dangerously forward once again. The empress hauled Aunt Eggy hastily back to her feet by her elbow.

The queen glanced sideways at Birdie and whispered, "I do hope your great-aunt and the empress were not eavesdropping on our very private conversation, Miss Darley."

"I should hope they were not, as well, Your Majesty."

The queen made a humming noise in her throat. She turned back to Aunt Eggy and stared at her in a calculating way.

"Lady Ross," Queen Charlotte said without raising her voice any louder. "I recall that you had shockingly pink hair the last time that I saw you. I see that you are sporting rather alarming bright green hair. 'Tis the color of pea soup, this evening."

Aunt Eggy shoved at her hair to move the feathers momentarily out of her eyes. She smiled and said, "Aye, a guid evening tae ye as well, and 'tis a vera fine ball, Yer Majesty. I am sure I will enjoy the soup."

The queen smiled politely at Aunt Eggy. She opened her fan and raised it in front of her mouth as she spoke aside to Birdie. "I suppose at their ages, neither of them can hear well." She lowered it and smiled at Aunt Eggy again. "I do believe they are waiting to walk with you into supper. I rang the bell for the guests to start toward the dining room so that I may have a moment with you." She stared with great interest at Aunt Eggy and Empress Bibi. She turned back to Birdie with a satisfied smile. "I am much relieved, for they appear to be too involved with Lady Ross's. hair and plumes to be aware of the particulars which we discussed."

Birdie looked over to Aunt Eggy and Empress Bibi Habibeh. Aunt Eggy stood there fidgeting with the tiny bun of her green hair, trying to push it back to the top of her head. The bun, along with the plume of feathers, kept sliding down onto her forehead. Empress Bibi was fussing around her head trying to help, but only making matters worse. As she watched, Aunt Eggy began slapping Bibi's hands away as Bibi tried to part the plumes blocking Aunt Eggy's eyes.

Birdie turned back to the queen with her lips held tight to stop herself from grinning. Or worse, laughing. She cleared her throat. "I believe you are correct, Your Majesty."

"I am always correct, Miss Darley. Believe *that*."

Queen Charlotte waved her gloved hand, complete with all the large rings on each finger, to dismiss Birdie.

"*Find me the proof, Miss Darley*. Of his guilt or his innocence."

Birdie swallowed tightly and nodded. "And rescue the horses as well, Your Majesty?"

The queen's sharp gaze came back to Birdie from where she had been watching the couples dance. "You Darley women are indeed willful creatures. You do not need my approval for that. But you must stay away from any danger!" She did not wait for a reply but gave a lift of one eyebrow and a haughty stare as she waved her hand again in dismissal.

Birdie nodded hastily and curtsied. She spun around and hurried to her great-aunt Eggy and Empress Bibi. Without a word, she grabbed both of their elbows and kept going.

Of course, she would rescue any horses she found.

The old wagon horse did not deserve to be sent to the battle-field.

None of those horses deserved to be "a casualty of war."

But how was she to find out the man behind these crimes, and could it truly be the man the queen had suggested?

CHAPTER FIVE

Outskirts of London
Two days later

"TARE AN' HOUNDS!" Birdie whispered to her horse as she peeked around the corner of the building to the dark street beyond. "This may be the proof I need, Mo." She hugged its big head close to her.

Her arm was wrapped around Mo's head as she slowly stroked the horse's face with her gloved hand while peering out of the alley and down the street. She stepped back and led the horse around patches of snow to the other end of the alley and out to the street there. She put Mo's reins over a hitching post near a streetlamp where a boy was watching over two other horses. She gave the lad a coin to watch over her horse as well.

She stroked her horse's head again, letting her fingers trail down the white stripe on his dark head. She hugged its neck briefly. "I shall be back shortly, Mo Graidh," she whispered.

The boy watching the horses in the cold night stared at her curiously. He stomped his feet while keeping his arms wrapped around himself for warmth. "You named yer horse Mo Gray, my lady? He's a bay color, don't ya know?"

Birdie stopped. "'Tis a Scottish saying, and not really a name." She stared at her dark red horse with its black legs, black mane, and black tail. The horse had four short white socks of varying, mismatched heights along with the white stripe on its face. Mo was not an elegant Aldbey Park Thoroughbred, but instead a bit stockier with a head far too large for his body. She had picked the horse for herself on purpose. This was the last of the foals that her father had bred before he had been killed. Mo was quite the ugliest of all the Thoroughbreds at Aldbey Park and would of a certainty, with his coarse and odd looks, not been able to be sold. This only made her love him more dearly. She smiled back at the boy. "Yes, I know that he is a bay. Thank you for watching over him, he is exceedingly dear to me."

The boy called to her just as she was turning away, "A Scottish saying, is it? What does it mean then?"

Birdie did not answer. She was already tiptoeing back to the other end of the alley.

Cold mist rose from her breath as she watched two men just down the street in the shadows away from the lamplight. They were hastily unhitching a pair of horses from a coach as they looked furtively around. Their coat collars were turned up against the cold, concealing the lower halves of their faces as they moved around the horses on the snow-laden cobblestone street.

Birdie pulled the fur-lined hood of her warm cloak up over her hair as she took a step out of the alley to approach them.

A strong hand on her arm stopped her, pulling her back into the shadows.

"Tut, tut, tut," came a deep, quiet voice. *Do not even think it.* Such a brash little bird you are."

Birdie knew that voice. She scowled back at the man in the navy greatcoat and matching top hat holding her arm. "Let go of me or I shall have to strike you with my crop," she said in an angry whisper. "And I do not care if you are the *Earl of Fairfax*, Ten Adair!" She raised her crop as if she was ready to hit him with it.

"My, my. How terribly rude and so full of zeal you are. But alas, not frightening." Ten attempted to grin charmingly down at her, baring his perfect white teeth in the strain of the effort. He reached out and pushed the crop she held in her hand back down to where she had held it hidden within the folds of her long skirts.

"You mockit, manky, mingin fop," Birdie mumbled under her breath as she turned back to look at the street. "If you must annoy me, be quiet then. And turn that dimple of yours on someone that your charm works on! I find it off-putting."

Ten's grin tightened, showing the even row of his white teeth as they gleamed in the darkness of the alley. "Why were you going to approach those men? For that matter, what are you doing in this area *at all*, alone, and at night of all times? You are quite far from Grosvenor Square."

Birdie did not look up at him. He hovered far too close to her back as he tried to look over her head out to the street. She moved slightly away. "'Tis none of your business."

"Waiting for your Freddie?"

She did look back at him then. Her eyes narrowed in indignation and anger. "What if I am?" she challenged.

His grin tightened further. "Well of course, then I should be obliged to inform your mother and Lord Hawke. Of course, your great-aunt Egidia should be told. Your sister Lula and my good friend Baron de Walton would be interested as well. I believe your other sister, Julia, and her husband the prince would also be most interested to hear what you are doing waiting in a dark alley. Alone. At night."

Birdie watched him, tapping one toe in irritation.

Ten was nonplussed as he pulled off one of his gloves and stared down at his fingernails in the dimness of a single street-lamp. He was suddenly quite interested in inspecting them. "Perhaps the *Morning Post* as well?" he added casually.

Birdie smiled calmly at him. "I dislike you terribly, you know."

Ten dropped his hand from where he had been pretending to inspect his already very clean nails. He stared at her glaring up at him. "The feeling is mutual, Little Bird," he growled without a smile or the easy grin that was typically on his face. He pulled his gloves back on with jerky, angry movements. "I believe we already settled our mutual *dis*-affection for one another at the ball."

Birdie narrowed her eyes. "That is all very well then. We agree we dislike each other. Now go *away,* Ten," she whispered firmly.

"*Lord Fairfax* to you, Little Bird," he snapped back at her in a low voice.

"If you are disposed to call me *Little Bird*, when my name is Miss *Birdie* Darley, I may of a certainty call you *Ten*," she declared in a curt whisper. "Besides, we are not in a ballroom and I know very well that my sister Lula calls you Ten. I am no *naft, numpty,* empty-headed miss. *Now go away.* 'Tis no business of yours what I am doing."

"I must presume that you are not waiting for Rockingham, Miss Darley. Any man that asked you to meet him in an alley should be shot, *particularly* if that man is Rockingham. I cannot believe that even such a one as he would stoop to such improper actions," he said. He leaned close to her ear to get a better look over her head at the men she had been watching in the street. He lowered his voice to a casual whisper as he studied them. "I noticed that you sat with your great-aunt and the Persian empress as well as several older gentlemen at supper the other night at the Regent's ball. You did not sit with your Freddie. And I observed that you ate little to nothing."

"I ate nothing because the only serving dish within my reach held boiled tongue and stewed celery, which I do not care for," she whispered angrily. "As for Freddie, you are the cause of any chance I had of being escorted into supper and thus sitting next to him, and by the by, *I did not notice you at all*, much less *observe* you."

"Hmm. Tut, tut, tut, so sad, Miss Darley. Now then, why *are* you here? You would be ruined, as I am quite sure you know," he murmured as he continued to watch the men down the street. At her stubborn silence, he glanced at her and tried again. "Come, Miss Darley. Do tell, what business do you have watching those two men unhitch those carriage horses?"

Birdie shrugged one shoulder to move him away from her. "If you must know, I believe they are stealing those horses," she whispered firmly. She glanced at him dismissively. "But of course, you, *a glaikit mon*, would not know of such things, being the dandy and posh prig that you are. I know men like you; they cease to wear their prosperity with any modesty."

Ten arched a brow and stepped back from her. "'Tis an ignorant summation of my character you have. You most certainly do not know me." He let her comments slide over him beyond that retort. This was a far more pressing concern, for he had been watching the men the entire time from the alley across the street. He had been shocked to see her watching them as well. "What makes you so positive that they are stealing those horses?" he demanded in a steel-like low voice.

Birdie kept her eyes on the men in the street. They were almost finished unhitching the horses. They did not appear comfortable around the horses much less adept at the task of removing the harness.

She sighed dramatically in annoyance at his question. "My summation is due to the fact that those horses belong to a Mr. Pargetter who runs a livery stable for licensed coaches. My family is familiar with the man who trained those two horses in harness for Pargetter's equipage. Johnson trained at my family's estate of Aldbey Park for several months in our stables before going to work for Mr. Pargetter. Neither of those men down the street is Johnson or Mr. Pargetter."

Ten snorted softly. "Very likely they are his liverymen, of course," he whispered insolently from somewhere above her head.

Birdie made an impatient sound as she glanced up at him and then away. "They are not. I heard them say they were Hackney Coach Commissioners." She poked her elbow into his abdomen to move him away from her. "If they are indeed commissioners come to inspect the coach and horses, why are they *unhitching* the horses? As well, they do not seem familiar with how to correctly unhitch one at all. They are bungling about in their task. Thus, I am scrupulously skeptical and suspicious of their spurious purpose. I can only believe that they are in the act of attempting to steal," she whispered curtly.

She heard Ten snort softly and repeat some of her words in a sarcastic murmur. "Scrupulously skeptical are you?"

Birdie would not tell him how she came to be at this spot. The two thin coach horses that she had stolen back from the smugglers were from Mr. Pargetter's livery stable. The black pony and the wagon horse had been stabled across the same mews as Mr. Pargetter's horses. Mr. Pargetter had been very grateful for the return of them. When she went back to visit him, he had answered all of Bridie's questions, including the name of the tavern, aptly named The Horse and Groom, on this very street where his coachman stopped for his supper each night. She had witnessed these two men lurking about the tavern.

The two men also looked rather like the smugglers from the other night from what she could see of their build and clothing.

Birdie did not believe in coincidences. They had to be the same men.

"Yes, I am scrupulously skeptical," she said in a curt whisper.

"And *suspicious* of their *spurious* purpose?" he asked with laughter in his voice. "Could you not come up with any more words beginning with the letter 's'?" he whispered wryly. "You are an odd little bird."

She felt Ten Adair lean closer to her, presumably to get a better look around the wall of the alley. She poked him with her elbow a second time. *Harder.*

Ten ignored this second jab of her elbow. He wanted to have a better look at the two men. He leaned even closer, reaching his arm and hand over her head up to the brick wall of the building. In doing so, it brought his hips up against her taught, round buttocks.

"Step away from me, sir! You forget yourself," Birdie whispered angrily. "You are being far too familiar."

Ten grunted and moved slightly away. She was a petite thing, but all legs for her shapely buttocks fit him perfectly. He cleared his throat. "Do not flatter yourself. However, you are correct. That was most *dishonorable* and *disreputable*, indeed, *dubious* of me. I do beg your *dismissal* of my *discourtesy*."

Her only response was a snort. She had heard the teasing tone of his voice.

His voice lowered to a murmur as his gaze stayed on the men. "It *was* wrong of me to tease you. It was forward of me, but unintentional, I assure you. I just want a better look at those two men." He grunted again. "Where is the coach driver, or his livery servant?" He wondered aloud to himself. He had not been asking Birdie.

"When they told the young livery servant that they had come to inspect the coach and the condition of the horses, they gave him a coin and told him to go have a pint. An inspection is required four times a year to maintain the coach's license, as I am sure you *must* know, or not," she added impishly.

"I am aware of the regulations required to keep a coaching license. Still, you cannot assume that they are not who they deem to be," he said in a haughty whisper. "Speculation is the enemy of truth."

Birdie let out a muffled laugh and whispered condescendingly, "The only true wisdom is in knowing you are wrong and know nothing." She snorted softly in triumphant laughter as she watched the men. "Why then are they *unhitching* the horses? 'Tis not a commissioner's purpose, and that is no *speculation*."

Ten ignored the tone of her voice. "You quote Socrates incorrectly. The saying is, 'The only true wisdom is in knowing you know nothing.' *Not that I am wrong*." He cleared his throat. "What of the coachman?"

She threw a glance at him over her shoulder as she whispered in a calm voice, "It pleased me to add in the part about you being wrong." She turned her eyes back to the street. "The servant had been watching over the coach while the driver went off to have his supper."

Ten stilled and looked down at the young woman who stood with her back to him intently studying the men. "How long have you been here? Never mind that, *why the devil are you here?* It cannot be out of concern for this man Johnson or the theft of Mr. Pargetter's horses." The low hiss of his voice had been filled with astonishment and barely controlled anger.

"You are not entitled to know my concerns," she said haughtily over her shoulder. When his dark brows rose at her answer, she added, "Your anger and condescension will certainly not induce me to make known to you my business here." She turned back to watch the men.

"You being here is in contravention of all polite codes," he said in an arrogant voice.

Birdie shrugged and grinned without looking at him. "I am indeed incautious and indiscreet."

He shook his head. "You are too ripe and ready by half with no regard for your safety."

Birdie glanced briefly back at him. Even in the darkness of the alley, she could see the look of anger and suspicion on his face. She could not tell him the truth about why she was here. She needed to make sure that he did not ask that question again. The queen wanted this kept quiet.

Birdie made a scoffing sound. Without turning away from watching the men and horses on the street, she said in a low whisper, "Ripe and ready by half, am I? Are you accusing me of always being up to something?" She made a soft humming sound in her throat and grinned to herself. "Indeed. So says the man who brought a kitten to a ball."

"The kitten needed rescuing," he said in a disgruntled low voice. "Anyone who would not have done the same is inhumane. Rockingham, for instance. Walked right past the mewling kitten."

Birdie spoke quietly and rapidly in a firm tone. "I am quite certain that Freddie did not see the kitten else he would have surely rescued it himself." She glanced over her shoulder at him and raised her eyebrow. "Why are *you* here, by the by? Have you an interest in Mr. Pargetter's horses and those men who are obviously stealing them?" When he remained stubbornly silent, she added, "I cannot believe that you are interested in the fair offered at the Horse and Groom. Were you on your way to your men's club? Boodles or Brooks, or Whites, perchance? St. James Street is several streets over. Or are you on your way home from your club after having imbibed too much? Have you lost your way then?"

Ten huffed out a breath and laughed softly. "Yes, I have lost my way. That is it, *precisely*. You are so wise to the ways of a man's world."

"I know how men are. I had a father. He was a man, so I know how men are."

Ten's mouth fell open to respond, but he could think of nothing to say in answer to that. He stated, "You have a stepfather in the Duke of Leids. One of your sisters married a prince and the other a baron. They are also men," he said wryly.

"Yes, but they are *good* men," she said simply.

Ten realized that she was intimating that her father, who had been murdered, had not been a good man.

"The Duke of Leids and the men my sisters love and have married are very good men," she added softly.

Ten's lips tilted up into a crooked grin. "I must agree with you on that." He tapped her on the shoulder to get her attention. "Miss Darley, you must tell me what you are doing—"

"Hush, you," Birdie whispered quickly with a glance back at him.

He grinned again, with that charming, lady-winning, dimple-showing, gleaming-white-teeth, *wolf's grin* of his.

"Why are you grinning like that?" she asked him tartly.

"Because you just *hushed* me. I cannot remember allowing

anyone to *hush* me." His grin widened as he arched his brow at her.

She ignored him. She put a gloved finger to her lips before he could ask her anything more. She motioned silently toward the men and the horses.

Ten narrowed his eyes and frowned at her.

Birdie met his frown and increased it with a fierce scowl of her own. She then directed his attention once again to the men in the street. They were pulling on the horse's bridles in an attempt to lead the horses down a nearby dark alley. The long driving reins were trailing behind on the ground and each time one of the horses stepped on a rein, it caused the bit to pull on its mouth. The horses inevitably kept halting. Finally, after much whispering back and forth to one another, the men managed to gather the long reins up in their hands and disappeared with the horses down the alley.

"Well, I'll be damned," Ten growled as he watched them go.

Birdie rolled her eyes and turned to him. "You say that because you have just realized that I, a mere woman, am correct when you doubted me. I win." She stared a moment at his furious face. "*Lud*, you are a contrary, glaikit man. Just admit that you were wrong and I was correct."

At a sound from the street, he stilled. A man was walking down the street, coming in the direction of the alley toward the other men. He was in a hurry as he walked, but he was looking right and left, checking the alleys. He wore a short top hat and had a scarf wrapped around his neck and face to ward off the cold night air, or perhaps to hide his face altogether. Only his eyes showed.

Ten glanced at Birdie and put a finger over her lips. He motioned toward the street. She nodded once and let him pull her deeper into the shadows.

Just as the man was walking closer to the alley where they were standing, Ten's body went rigid.

Birdie pulled him to her. "Pretend we are embracing," she

whispered hastily. She pulled his head down beside hers.

He quickly pushed her against the wall, shielding her from the street with his broad chest and shoulders as his arms came around her as if in an embrace.

They stayed there, listening to the footsteps come closer.

Birdie held his head near hers as his arms tightened around her.

She could hear him breathing softly against her cheek and her ear.

She could feel the softness of his lips so near to her skin and smell his spicy scent.

She felt his body against hers.

She felt his strong thighs against her own thighs and hips.

She felt his broad chest against her breasts.

She felt…all of him.

He felt as hard as the wall at her back. He held himself taught. As if his power and strength were coiled tightly, held in rigid control until ready to spring into action when and if needed. She was stunned. She had never imagined Ten Adair, Earl of Fairfax to be anything but a charming fop. This man who held her was not a dandy.

They both froze as the footsteps came nearer.

"This won't do," he said urgently to Birdie. "He may be able to see us. We cannot pretend."

She felt Ten go rigid as the footsteps stilled as the man paused to peer into the dark alley where they were.

"Forgive me," he murmured.

Before she could react, he covered her mouth with his lips and was kissing her.

"Moan softly," he whispered against her lips. "Put your hands around my neck." He let out a lusty groan of his own as his mouth moved over hers.

His full, soft lips sensuously took hers over and over. He pressed his body fully against hers and held her tightly, securely, within his arms, molding her to his body while his mouth made a full-on assault of her lips.

Birdie did moan then as her arms tightened around his neck, keeping him close.

He groaned again, swallowing her soft whimper of pleasure.

Birdie sighed against his lips.

She felt a tingling in her breasts where they were crushed against him.

She tasted the sweet mystery of his breath.

She was aware of the hotness of his mouth against the cold chill of the night air.

She felt the soft lap of his tongue tracing the bow of her lips.

She reveled in the way he explored and tasted her.

The sound of his deep, throaty groan pierced through her body from the tips of her breasts straight down to her woman's core.

She had never been held in a man's arms much less been kissed before. She was transported, breathless with wonder and heat. A bolt of exciting lightning ripped through her body and settled there, between her thighs like hot, liquid honey.

Everything else but the feel of him, the taste of him, faded away.

As suddenly as he had slammed his mouth to hers, he pulled away. He looked out to the street and then down at her. "He is gone."

Birdie stared up at him with wide eyes. "Tare an' hounds," she whispered with awe as she touched her lips. She realized then that he was not affected by their kiss at all. He was busily looking out onto the street.

"My apologies, Miss Darley," he said with stilted embarrassment as he glanced back at her. "'Twas most dishonorable of me, but I could think of nothing else."

Birdie tilted her head at him. She had a small smile on her face. "I am flattered that kissing me is forefront on your mind." She knew she was teasing him, but could it be true that the charming, always grinning, roguish Ten Adair had a secret sense of morality and honor in him and was truly ashamed of kissing her? She doubted that, but then, *what other secrets could he be hiding? What traits could he be pretending to own?*

He turned and arched a brow at her. "Do not be flattered. I meant that I could think of nothing else that would make sense to that man who was checking each alley. 'Tis natural for couples to find dark, secluded alleys for a private, amorous moment. I assume that you were waiting to do just that with Rockingham, for you kiss with much experience."

Birdie opened her mouth to deny that, but abruptly closed it. She could think of nothing to say, else she gave herself and the queen away. Her anger and pride got the best of her, however, and as she was wont to do, her fiery passion arose.

"I kiss with much experience?" she whispered in a furious voice. "How insulting! How insolent, and impolite! How ignorant and impudent you are!"

He grinned charmingly. "You could take it as a compliment? Or should I say, as you are wont to, you could take it as appreciation, adulation, acclamation, admiration, approval, or perhaps even applause?" He tapped his chin and tried to think of more words but could not. He pointed to her as he circled his finger. "Was that enough words for you? I believe I came up with six to your five."

She frowned furiously. "You win," she murmured softly under her breath.

"There is nothing to win. Calm yourself, Little Bird." He walked back to the end of the alley with her close behind him.

Ten narrowed his eyes as he looked out to the street and then glanced back at her. "I am going after them."

Birdie stood up straight, her ire gone. "My thoughts exactly. We should hurry. The early bird eats the worm, after all."

Ten did not look at her. He was looking up and down the street. "'Tis 'the early bird *gets* the worm,'" he hissed absent-mindedly.

"No, 'tis the early bird that *gets to eat* the worm. If the bird simply *gets* the worm, what is he allowed to do with it, for is that not the intimation? It must be that he gets to *eat* the slimy object of his desire else what is the reward for being *early* after all?" She left no space for a breath much less the time for him to comment, but continued on. "Why are you looking about? The street is empty. We must needs hurry or we shall surely lose the worm, or *worms* in this case."

Ten spun back to her. "Why are you discussing worms?" he said incredulously. "I am in earnest about this endeavor and I am most seriously displeased with your frippery and lack of caution. You are a proper young lady, *or supposed to be.* Truly, you being here *at all* is in contravention of *all* polite codes for your sex!" His jaw tightened as she simply grinned up at him.

"Again, we are not in a ballroom," she chided him. "Nor a drawing room nor parlor nor assembly room. I do not have to abide by these *codes*, as you say, for my sex. I can be myself. 'Tis quite exhilarating, so why are *you* discussing worms?"

"You are incorrigible," he hissed with both brows raised. He struggled to regain his control.

"I find it most interesting to see the Earl of Fairfax, the rake and rogue who charms all ladies with his far-too-handsome countenance and fascinating dimple, who finds humor in all things actually able to lose his calm demeanor."

At her words, his lips lifted into a sardonic grin. He took her by the shoulders and pressed her up against the wall as he leaned down into her face. "Far too handsome? Fascinating dimple?" He arched a brow down at her. "Remember your heart is with Rockingham, Miss Darley," he said firmly as he stared down into her eyes. He frowned and pulled back. "Now, you will stay here. *Right here*," he commanded.

Birdie glared up at him, undaunted by the authority in his voice and in the set of his lips and hard jaw. "Why? Because I am a woman and you fear I cannot manage in this situation? I will have you know that I came prepared."

Ten took several breaths as he looked up into the dark night sky, praying for patience with this young woman. She was a stubborn, willful creature. He exhaled and looked back down at her. "Prepared, are you? I doubt that."

Birdie held up her crop. "If I am wrong, I shall kiss a crooked cricket. Behold—" She stared into his eyes as she twisted the handle and lifted the crop for him to see. Down at the bottom of the short whip, a knifepoint rose from a secret, hollow shaft.

His jaw tightened as he saw the glint of the blade in the lamp-light. "You are a vicious little bird, indeed."

Birdie smiled tightly. "*Indeed.* We are wasting time. We must hurry else we will lose them. I assure you, I shall be fine." She tried to turn and step away from the wall, but his large self, indeed, his broad shoulders and chest, blocked her.

"I am rather convinced that you could manage some damage." He smiled wryly down at the tip of the sharp blade before his glance went back to her. "However, I do not want you hurt. You are...you are a *tiny female,*" he said in exasperation. He tugged his top hat down securely onto his forehead as he glared at her. "You can have nothing further to say on this."

"*Tiny female?* Oh, you *bowfin* man!" she fumed. "*Mac na galla!*" She sputtered some more of the favorite Gaelic words of her Scottish great-aunt Eggy under her breath. "Mauchit, mingin, manky, mockit glaikit mon!"

Ten looked up to the heavens once again as he calmed him-self before looking back at her and retorting with a wolfish grin. "Do not for a moment think that I do not understand what you are saying. *Mac na galla,* eh? Well, I assure you that I am not the son of a *female dog.* My Scottish mother, rest her soul, would be horrified at your words. Indeed, such foul names you are calling me, *eun beag.*"

Birdie narrowed her eyes up at him. "And what did you just call *me?*"

Ten smiled innocently as his dimple deepened. He shrugged. "Little Bird."

Birdie exhaled in annoyance. "I dislike you terribly. Have I told you that?" She pushed at his hard chest with one shoulder and marched past him into the street. Ignoring his look of surprise and anger, she walked with her crop held at the ready like a sword. She heard him following behind her.

"Indeed you did tell me that, and 'tis *most* assuredly mutual. Retract that knife blade." He raised his hands and stopped where he was in the middle of the street when she whirled around to face him with the sharp blade now pointing at him. "Tut, tut, tut. Retract the blade, *for now*," he said firmly.

Birdie let out an exasperated sigh and whispered to herself, "Such a cocky blaegeard!" She turned back around and began walking once again.

Ten chuckled softly, for he had heard her whispered recrimination of him. He passed her easily with his far greater strides. He stopped in front of the pitch-black alley, which was down the street and on the opposite side. The alley had an arched, brick entrance, just wide enough for a carriage. He looked down the length of what he could see of it and then turned back to put a finger to his lips.

"'Tis a mews," he whispered. "I can make out stalls on either side." He looked again and went completely still. "I can hear them."

Birdie went right past him into the darkness of the alley.

Ten reached out and clamped his large hand around her upper arm, pulling her back to him. The quickness and strength of his movements surprised her so much that she slipped on a patch of snow and fell against his chest. He quickly set her away from him, but still, he held her firmly.

"What are you intending to do, rushing in there as you were?" he demanded in a grating whisper as he stared down into her eyes. The cold mist from his breath in the chill night air rose between them.

Birdie tried to shrug out of his hold and gain more space between them, but he held her fast. "If you must know I intend to question those men," she hissed.

"*Question them?*" he sputtered incredulously. He narrowed his eyes. "I find it curious that your concern is not with the horses and returning them to Pargetter," he said suspiciously. "Was that not your business here?"

Birdie paused and pulled back as much as he would allow. "Do not bother yourself with my business. I did not ask you to involve yourself in this!" She could not look him in the eyes and found herself grateful for the cover of the dark mews. She stared instead at the dimple in his chin. She could see it, even in the shadows of his face. "Of course, I will retrieve and return those horses." She stumbled through her answer. "Indeed, yes. That too, of a certainty."

She watched as his square jaw tightened. Her eyes were drawn momentarily to his lips.

"I will detain and question the men. After I do so and deem it safe, I will help you retrieve the horses," he growled.

Birdie spared a glance at his eyes. They glittered down at her from where the nearest streetlamp sent a weak beam of light. It slanted just across the top of his face, under the shadowy brim of his top hat, illuminating those green eyes of his.

"But—" she started to object.

"Do as I say," he said in a low voice. "You are a proper young lady. You will allow my intervention."

"Tare an' hounds—" She started to object again and pull away, but he cut her off.

"My way, or you leave," he gritted out. "I know not what these men are capable of or what weapons they carry. You must stop being a stubborn, argumentative fool and listen to me on this. That is if you want to get those horses back for Pargetter. *My way or you leave.*"

Birdie's lips fell open in shocked fury. She had not asked for his help! She was astounded at the arrogance of this man.

Before she could argue, however, he let go of her arm and thrust her behind him.

She watched as he moved away into the darkness of the

mews in total silence. She shivered once. The man melted into the pitch black with nary a sound, like a panther, a large and very lethal panther.

It struck her then. The man had a *secret side to him.*

He had also not answered her as to why he was here.

CHAPTER SIX

B IRDIE STOOD THERE for several moments, listening to the silence and stillness of the dark mews and thinking.

Of course, the insufferable Ten Adair had *commanded* her to stay here.

Particularly if he was the man behind these crimes. He would not want her to see him talking to *his* men.

Or did he truly wish to help her? And why? *What was he doing here?*

She pictured the man that had fought the smugglers the other night along the channel. That man was big, muscular. His voice had been deep. He had been a rugged type of man, she thought.

She shook her head. That man had not been Ten Adair, the Earl of Fairfax. Ten Adair was a known rake and rogue, a charming gentleman who smiled and flirted with all the ladies of the *Ton*. He was a man who did not take life seriously or come to the aid of anyone, even his own sister. Yet, here he was, *insisting* on helping her. *Why?*

She pushed herself away from the wall and walked down the dark alleyway of the mews. Slowly and quietly, she looked left and right.

She could see the outlines of the stalls that faced out onto the alley. The stalls nearest the street were closed up. Their lower stall doors and top windows were firmly latched. She tried to open one and could not. She saw none of the typical buckets or grain sacks beside the stalls. Nor harnesses hanging on the walls beside each of the stall doors. There were no horses here.

Where were the two horses owned by Mr. Pargetter that she had just witnessed being stolen and brought here?

She walked cautiously further down the dark mews. Several of the stalls here were opened to the mews, their doors hanging crookedly open on broken, rusted hinges. She passed one empty box stall after another. It appeared this end of the mews had been abandoned for a rather long time. She peered inside a few of the stalls, beyond the thick cobwebs and filthy old straw on the dirt floor. Instantly, she could smell the horrid stench of musty old hay and decay.

And death.

In a corner of one stall was a sad mound of something that may have been once a foal or perhaps a dog.

She hurried on, cautious but observant, as she went silently down the dark alley.

Several rats skittered ahead of her across the cobblestones. Others ran in and out of empty, broken, and discarded crates laying against the brick walls of the stable building. Colorless piles of old grain sacks, rags, discarded horse rugs, and pieces of broken, stiff, leather tack lay in other piles here and there, all covered in bits of snowy drifts.

The mews was abandoned, with only the ghosts of past horses and once-bustling activity. She hurried past the rest of the dark boxes, only giving a cursory glance as her steps quickened. The place was cold and damp. It also had an air of death and decay, and something else, something sinister.

She finally found Mr. Pargetter's coach horses in the very last two stalls. She looked around before approaching. Ten Adair was nowhere to be seen or heard, nor were the two men.

She led the two coach horses out of their stalls. The bridles were still on them, though the reins had been tied up around their necks. She untied the reins and gathered them into her hands and then began to quickly lead them back down the dark alley.

"Ten?" she whispered as she walked, looking left and right. Where was the infuriating man?

Suddenly, she heard voices. The noise grew louder as if from down a long hallway. She peered into one of the stalls where the door was hanging wide open.

It was not a horse stall, but a dark corridor leading to what must be rooms for grooms and liverymen.

She peered into the shadowy corridor as the voices grew closer and closer. Suddenly, she saw four men fighting, their bodies slamming into the walls. Two of them were trying to make their way toward the mews. One of the larger men was punching them, trying to stop their retreat.

That larger man was Ten Adair!

She could make out the broad shoulders of his greatcoat. He appeared to be fighting all three men at once.

"Stop, I say! *Stop at once!*" Birdie called out loudly in her most commanding voice. She held up her crop with the knifepoint at the ready.

The men did not even pause but kept coming down the aisle. They were punching, twisting, and striking at Ten as he slammed his fists into any who were near enough.

A single man was running toward her, down the corridor.

She watched as Ten caught him, picked the man up, and heaved him out of the broken door.

Birdie jumped back.

The man flew across the mews and landed with a crash against the stall door opposite. He got up and quickly ran, limping, down the alley and out into the street.

A second, taller man came running out of the door after the first. This was the man with the short top hat. His coat collar was up, totally concealing his face, and he wore a scarf wrapped around it as well, further covering up all but his eyes.

Birdie saw him turn back. He was about to throw a knife at

Ten. She reached out and slashed her crop at him just as he was about to release it.

He let out a yelp and dropped the knife as he cradled his now bleeding wrist and ran on, faster, out of the mews.

Ten and the third man came crashing out, slamming into the walls and the broken door as they punched and wrestled one another. Ten slammed his fist into the man's face, sending him stumbling backward in the direction of the front of the mews.

The man twisted about, regained his footing, and took the opportunity to flee, disappearing into the darkness.

Ten leaned against the building, gasping for breath in the chill air. His eyes landed on Birdie, standing there staring at him with wide eyes.

He took several breaths as he stared back at her. She was holding the reins of the two carriage horses. Even in the dim light, he could see that her pale eyes were wide. The hood of her blue cape was thrown back and her hair had come free from whatever bun it had been in. The midnight locks were trailing over her shoulders in inky black waves and curls.

Her face looked unnaturally pale and her lips unnaturally bright red. Her bowed lips were open slightly as her breasts rose and fell with her heavy breathing.

He thought she must be terrified. His gaze remained on her.

She was not frightened. In fact, she looked…exhilarated. Excited. Stimulated. Her eyes remained on his.

He shoved away from the wall, holding her lavender-blue gaze with his own as he stalked toward her.

"Are you hurt?" they said as one.

Both stilled.

Ten took a step closer to her. He gazed intently into her eyes as he cupped her cheek gently while placing his thumb under the tender skin of her chin and tilting her face up. His eyes roved over every inch of her face, looking for any signs that she had been hurt in the scuffle.

"You are unhurt, *eun beag*?" he asked again in a husky voice.

Birdie stared up at him, finding that she had no voice suddenly. The sharpness of his green gaze seemed to slice straight into her body. A new, raw, feminine awareness uncurled within her, causing a heavy throbbing within her breasts. She could feel the warmth of his chest, where he stood so close to her. It served to ignite a blaze within her very core. His gloves were gone and his large hands were bare. Even his fingers felt warm on her face. His cravat was pulled free and lay hanging in a tangle on his chest and his hat and greatcoat were gone. His dark hair was in wild disarray. He looked vivid, powerful, masculine, and intriguing.

"Little Bird?" he asked. His voice had turned to deep velvet.

"I am quite well," she murmured. "That was most...*invigorating.*" She was stunned. The way he had said her name just then. It had not sounded like his typical sarcastic, condescending use of her name. Instead, it had been like a secret caress between lovers in the dark.

Ten stared into her eyes in the dimness of the mews. "Invigorating?" he asked silkily as he raised one brow and grinned at her.

"Indeed, it was," she repeated in a whisper. She was very aware that he still held her face in his large hand. She studied his face and found only a slight mark on his bottom lip. Staring at his lips caused a fissure of lightning to run through her, settling there between her thighs like hot, liquid heat as she recalled those very lips on hers. Her toes curled just looking at him. Her fingers clenched with wanting to touch his lips and the mark there. "Are you unscathed?" she asked in a husky voice, for her throat had suddenly gone tight.

She had never really looked at a man's lips before. Not even Freddie's.

Ten Adair's lips were full, alluring, and quite mysterious.

Seductive even.

Enticing, perhaps.

With the merest shadow of dark bristles surrounding them.

A sigh shimmered from between her lips, knowing she had

tasted those lips, just as he had tasted hers.

Ten was quiet for a moment. Relishing the fine silk of her skin under the pads of his fingers. The fact that she did not seem bothered that he was standing so close and touching her face was intriguing to him. He let his thumb slide down her neck and found the pulse there, beating rapidly. He brought his thumb back up and trailed it lightly over the perfect red bow of her top lip before sliding it back under her chin.

"Ten?" Birdie forced her voice past the unusual feeling within her chest. She would not, could not, allow it. "Are you unscathed? Did they hurt you?" She involuntarily licked her top lip, following the trail of where his thumb had been. She swore she could taste the salty traces of his thumb on her lip.

His grin tightened as his eyes followed the little lick of her tongue. "Like you, I am quite well," he whispered in a rough voice.

He found that he did not want to let her go. He leaned closer, holding her chin as his gaze roved over her face. She was the most unusual, curious, and brave young woman he had ever met. Besides her sister Lula, that is. Lula was a unique young woman, but clearly meant for his friend War de Walton. What was it about these Darley women?

His thumb caressed her lush bottom lip again. Its perfect shape fascinated him. He blinked several times as he felt the breath tremble from between her lips. Her eyes widened momentarily and her nostrils flared ever so slightly, but he saw it just before she regained her composure. She lifted her chin slightly as a look of challenge rose on her face.

"*Ten?*" she asked. "Are you positive that you are well?"

"Indeed, I am well."

He watched as a small, knowing, and mischievous smile bloomed on her face. "I win," she said with a glint in her eyes.

"You win?" he repeated with confusion.

"Yes, against those men. I helped you. You wanted me to stay behind. You thought I could not be of any use, but I was. You were wrong. So, *I win.*"

"You are indeed a competitive little bird," he said in a low voice as he studied her face with renewed intrigue. "You make little sense." His lips tilted up slowly in bemusement.

"I rather thought you did not like me," Birdie said in a quiet, pert voice. "Yet I think perhaps you *do* like me, Lord Fairfax."

Ten stilled. Her voice had been teasing, yet still, she did not pull away from his hold. Instead, she stared up at him, unafraid, undaunted.

Daring.

He let go of her abruptly and stepped back, well away from her. "I do not like you. We are not even well acquainted or indeed, friends," he stated adamantly in a quiet voice. He bowed his head. "I must give you my apologies, Miss Darley. I only wanted to see for myself that you were indeed unhurt." He rubbed at the dimple in his chin and scowled in confusion. "I am not sure what the blazes came over me. That was most improper. My apologies once again, indeed." He took another step back away from her as a look of annoyance came to his face. He frowned fiercely at her.

Birdie tilted her head at him, noting his discomposure. The always nonchalant and jovial Ten Adair was disquieted. Not only disquieted, *but there was also a distinct look of disgust on his face, for her.* Anger bubbled up within her. "Please, do not think an apology is required, of a certainty. Apologies are only owed when a friend causes vexation to a friend. As *you said*, you and I, sir, *are not friends* and even if we were, why, I am not so easily vexed."

She took several breaths, noting the tightness coming over his jaw. She quickly turned away from him to look back at the two carriage horses. She took several calming breaths as she fussed with gathering the long driving reins. She needed time. Time to let whatever that was that had just happened pass. He had held her face and touched her lips and stared down into her eyes in such an odd way. And she, she had been unable to pull her eyes from his. She had to let *whatever that was between them,* go. It was different than the kiss in the alley. This was deeper, more intimate. It had burned through her. It was unsettling and new.

She took another deep breath and turned back to him.

He was walking out of the dark corridor that he had fought the men in. He had his greatcoat back on. She managed a casual and calm voice when, inside, her whole body seemed to still be vibrating as if in a carriage on a rough path. That spot between her thighs seemed to be getting hotter. She felt a dampness there, even in the chill of the night.

"Did you manage to speak to any of those men?" she asked with strained brightness. "Were you able to glean any information from them before you got into such a mill and chased them away?"

Ten began retying his cravat as he stared down at her with a hard expression. His movements were hard and jerky. "I hate these things," he said deep in his throat. "*No*, to answer your question. I did not glean any information from those men," he said as he pulled on the knot of his cravat. "Only a good study of their countenances. The tall one had the lower half of his face concealed by cloth, however." He finished tying an elaborate knot and then dropped his hands as he stared at Birdie. "Blond hair, blue eyes. As I said, tall, perhaps my height. I would add that he was not too terribly muscled. Probably a few years younger than myself. He was no smuggler, I would wager. The other two looked purse-pinched." He put his hands on his hips and stared sharply at her. "'Tis a havey-cavey business, this. I am in earnest when I tell you to *stay away from it.*" Anger tightened his face as he tried to control his rage. "Indeed, I am still quite unable to account for the matter of you being here *at all.*"

Birdie narrowed her eyes on him. *Stay away from it,* he had said. Of course, he would say that. He would not want her to know *his* business.

"Thunder an' turf. I should wonder then that you took the trouble to come down this mews *at all.*" She stared challengingly back at Ten, throwing his own words back at him.

"*I was a fool for indulging you,*" he gritted out. He ran a hand through his hair in frustration as he looked down the mews toward the street with narrowed eyes. "I did want to question those men, however," he said in a low voice, "but you distracted me."

"Well then, instead of standing here *indulging* me with your presence and letting me *distract* you, should you not be chasing after them?" she asked curtly.

She stood there, stubbornly staring at him as his sharp gaze returned to her. A grin rose slowly on his lips. It was a dangerous grin.

There was a formidable glint and sharpness to his green eyes as his gaze remained on her.

"And you? Should you not be returning those horses, *Little Bird?*" Ten said tightly. He touched his forehead with one finger as if touching the brim of his missing top hat. With another grin, he spun about and strode away in the direction of the men.

CHAPTER SEVEN

"ARE YE SURE ye want tae walk in the park on this cold afternoon?" Aunt Eggy asked Birdie one morning a few days later. "Ye do a lot of walking. To Hyde Park and the Serpentine, to Berkley Square. Ye are vera adventuresome."

Birdie nodded firmly as she pulled on her pale blue gloves and tightened her blue cloak. She pulled on a lavender felt bonnet trimmed in white fur and then pulled the hood of her cloak over that. Her cloak was warm, lined in the same white fur as her bonnet.

She could not tell her great-aunt that she went where people congregated, like all the men at the Serpentine, watching the skaters there. The conversations were sometimes fruitful when it came to the theft of the horses around London.

The other day she had seen Freddie at the Serpentine having a very intense conversation with an older man. Just as she was about to reach them, someone had bumped into her. It was hard enough to cause her to fall. Several people rushed over to assist her back to her feet, and when she looked for Freddie or the man that he had been talking to, they were both gone. The man that had bumped into her was nowhere to be found either.

"I enjoy it, Aunt Eggy."

"Ye are wearing sensible shoes?" Aunt Eggy asked. "Not shoes like those yellow boots yer sister Lula likes tae wear? Not your riding boots? Alexander Hawke has paid a fortune for a fine new wardrobe for ye. Ye no longer have tae dress like a stable boy or a poor country miss."

Birdie grinned and stuck one foot encased in a half boot out from under her violet skirts. It was a short, navy, kid boot with pale blue laces. She hiked her skirts up further. She had worn her thick woolen hose as well. "I am not wearing breeches under my skirt, though I considered it. Still, I shall be quite warm, I assure you, Aunt Eggy! 'Tis just a stroll around Grosvenor Square today. The park itself is snow laden."

Aunt Eggy stared at her niece. "It occurs tae me that ye never call me Aunt *Eggs* anymore, dearling. Ye used tae noo and then when ye were in a playful mood."

Birdie stopped tying her bonnet. She looked at her great-aunt. "I suppose I am grown up now. Did you like me calling you Aunt Eggs?"

Aunt Eggy looked away and began fussing with her skirt. She did not want her great-niece to see her sadness. "Aye, I did. Ye are correct, however; this past year ye have grown up intae a lady. Ye are the last of my dearlings."

"Aunt Eggy," Birdie said softly. "I am not gone. I am still here, with you." She stopped as she tried to find the words. *"Bid gaol acham ort*, Aunt *Eggs*. If I said it correctly, I hope that I just said that I love you." She hurried over and placed a kiss on Aunt Eggy's cheek. She whispered with her cheek against her great-aunt's thinning hair, "I do love you, so very, very much. *Tha e na urram dhomh*, it is my honor, Aunt Eggy, to have you in my life and I am so *very* grateful." She kissed her cheek again and then her voice lightened as she assumed her great-aunt's Scottish accent. "Noo then, quite yer blethering for me maid is waiting oot in the cold!" She kissed the top of Aunt Eggy's balding head and then straightened the tiny white bun of hair back to the center. Then she hurried off to meet her maid who was waiting outside.

The door shut behind her niece. Aunt Eggy wiped the tears

from her eyes. Birdie was the only one of her nieces that was interested in the old language. She stood there for several moments staring at the door before turning around and looking down the first-floor hallway of the London home in Grosvenor Square that belonged to Lord Hawke and now the entire Darley family. The house was impeccably decorated with elaborate ivory plasterwork. The walls and draperies were of pale blues and greens, and Greek columns were spaced pleasingly along the walls and either side of the tall windows. Even the curving staircase was of white marble as were the floors.

There was a large parlor to her left and a grand dining room to her right. Further down the hall were the library and smoking room. The upper floor contained a long, rectangular ballroom and veranda, as well as five bedrooms and a small tearoom.

The lower floor was the kitchens and servants' quarters and storage rooms, as well as a corridor to the harness room, coach house, and stables.

Overall, it was a sophisticated, yet comfortable, tall house. It felt terribly quiet, however. It had none of the bustle and noise and laughter of Aldbey Park when all three of her great-nieces were home.

Aunt Eggy thought for a moment. Her friend, Empress Bibi Habibeh was still asleep in her bedchamber. She needed to rouse her.

She thought about climbing those long stairs.

Instead, she took a deep breath.

"Mr. Druckbert! Where are ye in this behemoth of a house?" Aunt Eggy paused and listened for the butler. She heard the scuttle of sharp, quick footsteps. A tall, thin form appeared from the lower hall.

Mr. Druckbert had a much-aggrieved look on his face. He stopped and stood, rigid, hands at his sides in his formal black uniform with a white shirt and bow tie as he stared over Aunt Eggy's head. His long, sharp nose twitched once, and then twice in distaste, which made the single gray hair jutting straight up from the top of his head vibrate in time with his nose.

"Lady Ross," he drawled condescendingly. "You *bellowed* for me?"

"I did, *Drunk*bert. Ye dinnae think I would puggle meself oot looking all over this house for ye noo, did ye?"

Mr. Druckbert sighed long and low. "It is *Druck*bert, Lady Ross, not *Drunk*bert, as well you know. And you have only to go to a bell pull *and pull it.* As its name declares. *Obviously*," he drawled.

Aunt Eggy made a harrumphing noise. "I can never find the things!" And then she muttered under her breath. "Yer a bowfin mon, *Drunk*bird. Ye look like a stuffed one of those penguin birds the queen has at the palace."

"I heard that. Your insults are improving, Lady Ross. You used to call me an 'auld vulture.'" Druckbert scowled and then added under his breath, "I may look like a penguin bird, but *you,* you are a *Highlander.*" He raised his chin and stuck his nose in the air. It twitched ever so slightly. "I am not unpleasant, and yes, I know what bowfin means." He held his hands rigidly at his sides. "The things I have been forced to put up with within the Darley house after being in service to the *very* refined and *very* dignified Lady Putrose, *may she rest in peace.*"

"Ha! I *am* a Highlander, and I thank ye for noticing. Enough of yer precious Lady *Pootnose.* Ye should be grateful, Mr. Druckbert. Ye were oot on the cold streets with nary a penny tae yer name when we found ye and gave ye a position." She snorted at the aggrieved look on his face. "Noo then, I need Empress Bibi tae come tae the parlor."

Mr. Druckbert stared down his nose at her. "Might I suggest you go to her bedchamber and tell her this yourself?"

Aunt Eggy gripped her black bombazine skirts in her fists. "Ye stuffed English shirt! Why did I ask ye tae accompany my great-niece and I tae London if ye willnae dae what I ask? I had already come doon the stairs. My auld knees dinnae wish tae gae back up them." She rubbed her right knee. "'Tis a vera tall house, this."

She stared calmly at the thin, bony butler and waited. She knew his pride would rise to the occasion. He wanted to feel needed again at his age. She understood this. As much as they bickered back and forth, and enjoyed doing so, he always wanted to be of help.

Mr. Druckbert's face softened and then his stooped shoulders lifted and straightened. He would never admit that he was older than she was or past his time in service. "Of course, Lady Ross. I shall give her your message at once."

Aunt Eggy watched as the old butler walked in short steps and then took hold of the railing of the stairs and began walking slowly up the grand staircase.

She sighed. "Weel noo, I suppose I have a guid lang hour before he even reaches her bedchamber."

She turned around and went into the parlor to sit by the fire and wait for her friend Empress Bibi. The empress was staying with them while they were in London. Bibi slept late daily, complaining about the cold, damp winter of England. This winter, in particular, had so far been freezing with frequent snow.

Aunt Eggy picked up one of her great-niece's bonnets and began to sew on some pale blue ribbon and satin violets. Seeing that the bonnet could be much improved with more of the tiny flowers, she began cutting some scraps of satin to make more.

"Good morning, my very best good friend Egg Lady!" came Bibi's staccato voice as she scurried into the parlor with a rustle of her full-skirted, pale cream, overly ruffled gown.

Aunt Eggy did not look up from her sewing. "'Tis afternoon, Bibi. Come sit by the fire sae that ye dinnae catch a chill."

When Bibi sat down on the chair opposite the fire, Aunt Eggy said conspiratorially, "We have much tae dae, Bibi!"

"Much to do? Tell me you are not going to make me work!" she said in her high-pitched voice. "I knew you were poor." She pointed accusingly to the bonnet that Aunt Eggy had been working on. "You are making your own bonnets!"

"Och, dinnae be glaikit, Bibi. This is lady's work, 'tis all."

Bibi pursed her lips as she moved uncomfortably in her chair. "I thought we could partake of the argila pipe to start the day."

Aunt Eggy shook her head as she continued folding and wrapping the violet-colored satin into flowers. "My day has long been started, Bibi. Ye sleep tae long! I havenae had a chance tae speak with ye these last days, ye sleep all day!"

The empress snorted loudly as she tried to settle her bulk in the dainty lady's chair. "Egg Lady, I sleep because it is far too cold in your country to do much else." She put her hands on the arms of the chair to push her heavy-skirted bottom backward to better fit herself into the small chair. "I am also lacking the servants I am used to in helping me dress. One lady's maid is not enough." She pouted as she wiggled in the chair with a frown on her face. "Dressing makes me very tired. And this too small furniture that is for your very skinny bones is uncomfortable."

"'Tis not the problem of the furniture being too small," Aunt Eggy mumbled, and then in a brighter voice, "Perhaps some tea and toast for ye? Then ye can start yer day?"

The empress scowled. "I already partook of that in my bed. While under my warm blankets. *Multiple blankets.*" She reached for her elaborate glass bejeweled argila and handily lit it from a piece of kindling in the fire. She put the narrow copper pipe between her lips. She closed her eyes and sat back with a smile as a hazy cloud of smoke billowed from between her lips.

"We must talk, Bibi. 'Tis most important! I have been waiting for days," Aunt Eggy announced as she laid down her sewing.

Bibi opened one eye and peered across at her friend. "Yes, we must discuss the delights we are going to experience during our time here in London. I will not ride another fat pony, however. I cannot get off. You know this. We shall have much entertainment without having to sit on an animal's back. Let us discuss the delights we shall partake of."

"No! We must discuss what Queen Charlotte was saying tae my great-niece! *Tae Birdie!*"

Bibi sat up straight. She put the argila down. "Ah yes. *The*

English queen. I could not hear it all, but it did seem rather ominous. Most curious."

"Aye, I couldnae hear it all either, but it could be *vera* ominous. We need tae help Birdie," said Aunt Eggy as she stared into the fire, deep in thought.

"Egg Lady, it is simple," declared Empress Bibi as she picked up her argila once again and inhaled deeply. "We hire an assassin! I have done it before."

Aunt Eggy looked up with a start. "What are ye blethering aboot?" She pointed a bony finger at the empress. "And well I ken that ye have done it before, but who exactly are ye gaunnie try tae be killing this time?"

Empress Bibi blew from between her lips as she peered at Aunt Eggy through the haze of tobacco and hashish smoke. She shrugged. "The queen, if she is putting your Birdie in danger? Or this man she must get information about? It sounded to me like someone needs killing. It is simple, Eggy Lady."

Aunt Eggy patted her hair and then rested her head back against her chair with an annoyed exhale of breath. "Sards! We dinnae dae that here, Bibi Hibi!" She raised her head and looked at the empress. "I cannae and willnae believe the queen is putting my Birdie intae danger, just asking her tae have a wee look aboot, is all. Why is someone stealing these horses?"

The empress snorted. "Stealing horses is a terrible crime, for any reason. In my country *and* yours, Egg Lady! We both have the same punishment for it as well." She ran her finger across her throat in a slow, dramatic motion. "This I know."

Aunt Eggy shook her head. "We dinnae cut people's throats here, Bibi Babi. But 'tis true that stealing horses is a hanging offense!" She pushed the top knot of her hair back to the center of her head without even being aware it had become a habit. She was deep in thought. "Who is the mon the queen asked Birdie tae find information aboot, I wonder? We must keep a close watch on Birdie so that she doesnae take too much on herself. She will need our help."

"She needs a *husband!*" scoffed Empress Bibi. "That is all she needs! She has finished her dance instructions. She should be dancing and *finding a husband* at these balls and assemblies you have here in London. You should marry her off, and soon. To someone of *your* choosing. You give her too much of her own will."

"She hasnae any inclination tae marry unless 'tis tae that Freddie," Aunt Eggy grumbled. "Only a duke will dae for her. But I must wonder at that. She cannae be sae silly, nor sae blind tae see that he is nae interested, Bibi Ibi." Aunt Eggy turned a sharp eye on the empress. "And if ye dinnae ken, I have chosen *all* of my great-nieces' husbands withoot them knowing it and I will dae the same for Birdie tae!"

The empress frowned as she leaned forward. "I chose your great-niece Julia for my son Pasha, not you, Egg Lady."

Aunt Eggy sat up straight and glared. "Ye dinnae. I chose your son Pasha for my great-niece Julia. Ye didnae want her for him if ye let yourself remember correctly."

The two ladies glared at one another.

Finally, the empress's belly rose and fell with silent laughter. She inhaled from her pipe again. "We shall find the perfect match for your last great-niece. This will be quite entertaining!" She sobered when she caught Aunt Eggy's sharp stare reprimanding her. She quickly added, "I will *help you* find the perfect match. Most entertaining, yes." She offered the argila to Aunt Eggy. "You must learn to say my name correctly, Egg Lady."

Aunt Eggy put her hand out for the argila. She took a small puff when Bibi passed it to her. "I have told ye before that I will say yer name correctly when ye start saying my name correctly!" She took another puff. "Must I tell ye that this isnae for yer entertainment, Bibi? This is for Birdie! Noo then, Birdie willnae tell us anything aboot this if we ask her. She likes her mysteries and drama and loves a grand adventure, which I am sure she thinks this is and relishing it! She willnae want us interfering. So we must plan. There is a ball tonight given by the Marchioness of

Saxham, Lady Prudence Chedworthy. She is a dear friend of Birdie's mither. The three of us have all been invited. We must be sure tae watch and listen if there is any talk of horse thefts. And look for a husband for Birdie!"

"You must ask the staff about the horses, Egg Lady. They hear everything."

"Aye, I have already told Mr. Drunkbird tae casually ask the other households if they have heard of horses being stolen."

The two of them sat in front of the fire making plans and talking conspiratorially as they passed the argila back and forth.

BIRDIE CAME DOWN the stairs later that evening dressed for the ball. Her great-aunt was not waiting for her, nor was Empress Bibi Habibeh. She frowned as she walked down the last few steps. The two older women had both acted very strange at dinner. They had not asked her about her walk, or who she had seen or not seen, while out. If they had asked, she would have told them that indeed, she had seen no one.

The walk had been interesting, however. She had left her maid eating a dish of lavender ice cream on a bench under a tree outside of Gunter's. She had told her that it was too cold for ice cream for herself and said that she would walk across to the bookstore.

Two suspicious-looking men had passed by her and her maid just moments before. One of the men was the same man she had seen at the Serpentine, talking to Freddie. She heard the men discussing horses.

She watched as they entered the bookstore and followed them. She wanted to see if she could discover anything. She found them standing in a narrow aisle of books and went to the next aisle to listen.

Sure enough, they were discussing a stable of dray horses

used to pull brick wagons that would be "most suitable."

Most suitable for what? Birdie thought. She moved closer to the shelf of books, the better to hear when one of the men stopped talking.

"Who is there?" the man demanded.

Birdie heard him whisper to the other gentleman, "There is a woman listening. I heard the rustle of her skirts."

Then she heard them walking down the aisle. She looked around frantically. She knew that she must hide.

Suddenly, an arm reached out and grabbed her. A hand covered her mouth and eyes, shoved her into a closet at the end of the aisle, and shut the door on her.

She heard the muffled conversation of the men and then the door of the shop close.

She had discovered nothing and her effort had been in vain.

That evening, Aunt Eggy had only made a grunting sound when she mentioned the lavender ice cream at Gunter's. She did not tell her that she had not had the treat but that she purchased it for her maid.

Aunt Eggy was too intent on spooning up her pudding to look up and listen to what Birdie was saying.

Birdie stopped in front of the large, ornate, heavy mirror that hung above a table in the hallway of the first floor. She ran her hands down the front of her gown, feeling her long stays that raised her breasts rather dramatically high to her critical eye. The stays also made sure the gown fell in a graceful, flowing way. The lovely, light draping fabric followed her ample curves, tapered into her small waist and then followed the curve of her hips and thighs. She frowned and ran her hands over her waist and hips. She was not slender and stately like her oldest sister Julia. But the gown was indeed lovely. It was not simple, nor was it completely white. Instead, this new gown that had been made particularly for her was breathtaking in its intricacies while remaining understated yet elegant.

The gown had a white crepe petticoat worn over gossamer

pale blue satin. Here and there, embroidered swirls with glass beads of lavender and blue shone like small stars with each swing of the skirt or movement of her legs. It was ornamented at the bottom with rows of puckered net, with a border of blue satin and lavender velvet, in puffs.

A bodice of blue velvet with short blue satin sleeves edged with lavender satin cuffs corresponded with the bottom of the dress. A full puckered border of net at the top of the bodice softly rounded the bosom. The net was interwoven with dozens of the blue and lavender-colored beads throughout that glimmered and shimmered with her every breath. There was a stomacher and belt of white satin edged in lavender velvet, which was secured with a pearl clasp surrounded by more of the celestial-colored beads.

Birdie's eyes rose to her hair. Her maid had let her black curls fall beside her face and then swept them loosely back, pinned into the mass of curls that were piled high atop her head. Woven throughout her curls were several pearls and many, many more of the blue and lavender glass beads in all different sizes, making the midnight masses look like they glittered with stars.

Her stepfather had ordered earrings to match the gown. They dangled from her ears, catching the light in their blue and soft purple depths.

Birdie had never cared about her looks before. With both of her older sisters off the marriage mart, it was her turn whether she liked it or not. She felt the immense pressure of it all and sighed deeply. She had always dreamed that she would simply marry Freddie Rockingham. She had thought herself in love with him from the first time he had shown up at Aldbey Park to court her sister.

A memory of Ten Adair's lips on hers suddenly flashed through her. She could still feel his body molded to hers as he held her. The image of him staring down at her was burned into her mind, with his green eyes sparkling like glass and his thumb gently moving over her lips. All of this sent a fissure of lightning racing through her body. Liquid heat pooled between her legs just as it had that night.

She put her fingers to her lips and closed her eyes as her breasts rose and fell rapidly. She recalled his deep voice saying that a man should protect, cherish, and *desire* the woman he loved.

Her knees suddenly went weak as her breath trembled from her lips. She felt almost unwell. *Is this feeling natural?* She had never had this reaction to a man before, but then, she had never been held or kissed before. Ten was her first.

Birdie placed a hand over her heart, willing its racing to calm. *No,* she thought, *this is not normal nor natural.* Her heart felt like it would pound out of her chest!

Her heart was supposed to be Freddie's.

And Ten Adair clearly disliked her, was disgusted by her, in fact.

She pictured Freddie with his head of glorious, golden hair. Their friendship had always been so easy, so natural, so simple. The thought calmed her.

Slowly, her heart ceased its racing beat. It returned to a steady and peaceful rhythm.

She frowned. She had believed that her heart was Freddie's for as long as she could remember, it seemed. And this past year, she had proclaimed it out loud. Everyone had accepted it, albeit reluctantly. She would be married to Freddie.

A nervous knot formed in her belly.

She wanted an adventure. She wanted to see a sunset somewhere she had never been. To see a horizon that was new to her, not the endless rooftops and crowded, manure-smelling streets of London, like here in Grosvenor Square where Freddie had his residence.

After she had her adventure, whatever that may be, *then* she would marry Freddie. That should please her mother and Aunt Eggy.

They had not pressed her about marriage for some time now.

Not in several months.

Not since her visit to Graestone, almost a year ago when she had arrived on Freddie's arm.

Not at all this season.

At a sound coming from behind her, she turned.

"Aunt Eggy, is that you? Are you ready to leave?" she called out.

When no answer came and she heard the muffled sound again, she walked into the parlor. There was her great-aunt and Empress Bibi. Each was sound asleep with their heads back against their chairs and their mouths open. One of them was snoring, which was the source of the sound Birdie had heard. They were dressed for the ball. She noted that Aunt Eggy's eyebrows were drawn in rather startlingly with black kohl. Empress Bibi's eyebrows were connected this evening with a thinner line than usual, though her eyebrows were thicker and heavier with the kohl than normal. Birdie held her lips together to stop from giggling. They had evidently been helping one another with the kohl.

The empress also wore a large, white satin turban with grand ostrich plumes spouting from the top and loops of gold chains going around the turban itself. Her gown was a pale peach this evening and made up of row after row of ruffles, from her hem all the way up her neck.

To Birdie's shock, Aunt Eggy wore a lace fichu with a heavily ruffled border. It was around her shoulders like a shawl. The fichu was to cover one's bodice. It was not needed when one's gown was as high-necked as Aunt Eggy's black bombazine gown was. The fichu was certainly one of Empress Bibi's.

"Aunt Eggy? Empress Bibi?" Birdie said loudly. "The carriage is waiting for us."

Aunt Eggy snorted and coughed and sat up in her chair. Blinking rapidly, she stared down at her lap as she fussed to straighten her skirts. "Och! There ye are, dearling! We have been waiting for ye!"

Birdie looked at the table beside the empress. "And partaking of the argila at teatime, I see?"

The empress opened her eyes and pulled herself forward to a sitting position on the edge of her chair. "The argila is most relaxing, Miss Birdie. I did not sleep well last night, so I had a nap while we waited for you."

"Indeed?" Birdie said, and grinned.

Aunt Eggy's mouth fell open when she looked at Birdie. "Guidness! Ye look braw this evening, dearling! *Braw!* Ye are no longer a young lassy mucking aboot in the stables, but a beautiful young woman, indeed!" She was so at a loss for words she fluttered her hands and then placed them over her heart at seeing Birdie actually looking like a young lady. "The men will fight over ye, I am sure!"

"I desire no men to fight over me, Aunt Eggy. You know this."

Aunt Eggy tilted her head and stared at her with a sad frown. "Ye used tae call it *planting a facer* and ye also used tae seem quite eager tae plant a facer on someone yerself." When Birdie didn't answer, she frowned. "What of yer fairy tales? Yer hopes, yer dreams?" she asked softly. "What aboot yer dream of marrying a duke? What aboot Freddie? He should fight over ye, or at least dance with ye."

Birdie stared down at her clasped hands. "Plant a facer?" she laughed. "Aunt Eggy, I fear my emotions get fanciful and perhaps are far too swiftly spoken. I do not need Freddie to fight over me, with anyone."

"Dearling, no one is ever harmed by having swift or fanciful emotions." She hesitated a moment. "Or changing their mind." She looked meaningfully at Birdie, but Birdie looked away.

Empress Bibi stood up. She looked critically at Birdie. "You look like a very shapely princess or the most desirable woman in the harem. Men *will* fight over you. You will have no say in their desire to fight to win you."

Birdie opened and then shut her mouth at the mention of a

harem. Instead, she shook her head. "I no longer believe in fairy tales of beautiful princesses and handsome men on their valiant steeds doing battle for their lady's heart." She raised her chin. "Perhaps 'twill be *I* that shall battle for the heart of the man I love." She looked at the two old women staring at her. "We should go. Will you fare well in the carriage, Aunt Eggy? I know you think a carriage is a far too modern convenience."

"Humph. Aye, these modern ideas this young generation is embracing! Horses are tae be ridden. One is nae meant tae sit in a box being pulled behind a horse's arse. What if the braces break, or a wheel, or the horse bolts?" She shuddered and then sighed. "I suppose I shall have tae ride in the carriage since Bibi Babi willnae ride one of the ponies. The carriage will have tae do, but only as long as I am nae sitting with my back tae the horse's arse," she grumbled.

"You should know that Druckbert has instructed the coach driver to place the foot-warming box for tonight's carriage ride, and there are furs for our laps. We shall stay quite warm, indeed. Does this not please you?"

"We can also bring the argila to keep you relaxed, my very best good friend Lady Egg. Now, we must go; we cannot be late for this evening's most exciting entertainment!" declared Empress Bibi in her high voice.

The empress took Aunt Eggy's hand, hauled her out of her chair, and pulled her along behind her out into the hall. Once there, the ladies accepted their cloaks from Druckbert who had been waiting for them. Druckbert had no sooner gently placed the cloak on Aunt Eggy's shoulders when the empress grabbed her hand once again. She pulled her right out the door and into the waiting carriage before Aunt Eggy could resist or grumble about sitting behind a horse's arse.

Birdie had to hurry to catch up to the two old women in the carriage. She pulled the fur over her great-aunt's knees and used her foot to push the warming pan under Aunt Eggy's feet and off they went to the ball.

CHAPTER EIGHT

B IRDIE QUIETLY USED as many of Aunt Eggy's curse words as she could remember.

He was here.

So was Freddie.

Two men. Both of the same tall height. One blond and one dark-haired.

One man she had always dreamed of marrying.

The other she had always disliked.

One of them had made lightning race through her body.

One of them could be a traitor.

She had only to figure out which of the two men was stealing horses and which one would steal her heart.

Save one, turn in the other.

And hope that they were not one and the same. The horse thief was not also the thief of her heart.

She looked away from both men and gazed around the room.

The ballroom was very crowded due to the much smaller rooms in Lady Prudence Chedworthy's home. Her ballroom was on the second floor. It was a long, rectangular room, and the guests had spilled out into the hallway and the balcony overlooking the first floor.

Lady Chedworthy was thrilled when she saw Aunt Eggy. She clapped her hands together and pulled Aunt Eggy close.

"How happy I am to see you! And Miss Birdie! My, you have grown into a beauty, just like your mother and your sisters!"

Birdie smiled and curtsied to her mother's good friend. "I am so very pleased to see you again, Lady Prudence. You were greatly missed while away on your travels. *Lud*, but may I say that you look splendid!"

"Candlelight is kind, my dear," Lady Chedworthy chuckled.

"I do hope your trip abroad to visit your relatives was more pleasure than pain? If it is allowed that I ask such a thing?"

Lady Chedworthy smiled. "It was indeed! Though it was sad news of my husband's death that I brought to them, his family is far more civilized and kind than he ever was while he lived. But I fear I stayed away too long. I missed so much of the goings-on here in London. Your two sisters are wed, I hear! One to a prince, the other to a baron named War! Happily so, yes?"

"They have found the greatest of affection for one another, indeed."

At Birdie's smiling nod, Lady Chedworthy said, "You shall be next, Miss Birdie! You will have a husband as well, never fear! But a good, honest man. A man deserving of your trust, not a man like my *dear* Horace was, rest his soul. I never knew the terrible havey-cavey business he was up to."

Birdie's smile wilted on her face. Two men, but which one was up to this *havey-cavey* horse stealing? Freddie could not be involved in this terrible business. She had known him forever. She must prove him innocent, but could she? Ten Adair seemed most suspicious. Why had he shown up in the alley that night? *Could he be the traitor?*

Lady Chedworthy turned away from her to be introduced to the empress by Aunt Eggy.

Lady Chedworthy was the Marchioness of Saxham and a widow. It was well known that she had never mourned her husband's death. In fact, she had laughed with joy. After finding out about the crimes he had been involved in relating to the murder of Birdie's father, it was a relief for Lady Chedworthy.

She had also helped her mother solve the crime, and for that Birdie was grateful.

She was clearly enjoying her widowhood for Birdie had never seen her happier. Her hair was still a bright red with several fiery curls falling on either side of her face. Her gown was a stunning Greek-inspired confection of layers of net in maroon, red, and rose that left her arms bare. It was gathered underneath her breasts by a large gold pin with a ruby center. The bodice was trimmed with gold silk cord and dangling golden tassels that shimmered and moved with her body. She wore a Circassian-style turban cap composed of rose-colored satin with a rich silk golden cord around the edge terminated on one side with three golden tassels that hung down near her cheek. She also wore several golden armlets above her long gloves. Dainty-heeled shoes were on her feet and could not be missed. The shoes were covered in sparkling gold brocade, each with a ruby-encrusted buckle.

Birdie thought Lady Chedworthy looked like a true diamond and all the crack of fashion.

"Eggs!" came a loud voice. "Demm my eyes, is that you, Eggs?"

Birdie turned to see a very tall woman of a size equal to a large man pushing aside the guests to come to them.

It was the dashing, loud, outrageous Lady Letitia Lade.

Her blonde hair was mostly white now with only swathes of blonde here and there. She still wore the great masses of her hair piled high on her head in contravention of any fashion. Her hair was her greatest vanity, besides her stature and her bosom, which was just as daunting as her large height. Her hair was topped by an enormously tall, bright saffron satin turban trimmed with swansdown. Sticking straight up from the top of the turban were five long peacock feathers, their tips dipped in gold. Her gown was a bright yellow crepe worn over saffron satin with swirls of brightest greens and blues. It had a shockingly low bodice trimmed in a braid of bright blue and green satin, which appeared to be straining to hold her large bosom in. The bodice had a fan of gold-infused lace that started by her shoulders and arched high up the back of her neck. The sleeves were large, saffron satin puffs trimmed in more of the satin braid of blue and green. She wore a large lavalier necklace of gold with blue and green stones in the intricate gold swirls. Dangling earrings of large green gems hung from her ears.

Birdie watched as Lady Lade crushed Aunt Eggy to her ample bosom.

"Eggs, demmed but it has been too long, my old Scottish friend!"

"Yer gaunnie suffocate me, ye giant! I always said yer bosom is a weapon, Lettie!"

Aunt Eggy started laughing as the large Lady Letitia Lade released her and stood back, holding Aunt Eggy's shoulders as she looked down at her with a huge smile on her face.

"Let me bloody look at you. Demmed, but your hair is blue, or is it an odd sort of green over that white hair of yours? And your eyebrows look demmed black!" She chuckled. "Devil take it but I have missed you, Eggs, you cussed bony old stick!"

Aunt Eggy grinned. "I have missed ye too, ye loud-mouthed giant! Have ye been racing any more men in that gallus bright yellow, high-flying phaeton of yours and putting them tae shame when ye win? Or racing them on one of yer horses?"

Lady Lade threw her head back and laughed a loud belly laugh. "You know me so well!" She looked over to see the empress staring at her. "Bibi Habibeh!" Her voice boomed. "Good to see you as well! Is your handsome princely son here with our very own Princess Julia?"

"My son is not here, and Julia is not a princess," Bibi said curtly. "I, however, am a Supreme Imperial Majesty. You must call me Empress Bibi Habibeh, or Your Supreme Imperial Majesty."

Lady Lade roared with laughter. She pulled the empress in for a hug against her bosom as she had Aunt Eggy. "I forgot how demmed funny you are! The last time that I saw you was at your son's wedding to Miss Julia Darley. I am bloody happy you are here at Pru's ball! *Welcome!* I can speak for my friend when I say you are demmed welcome in this house!"

Lady Lade let go of the tiny empress. She smiled down at her as the empress glowered and did her best not to smile back.

Birdie could not help the large grin that bloomed on her face as Lady Lade turned to her, stopped, and simply stared.

"Bloody goodness me! Can this be the young, corky, always-pulling-at-her-bit and up to demmed something Miss Birdie Darley? *Lawks!* I suddenly have the bellows to mend for I cannot bloody breathe. Who is this beautiful stepper?"

Birdie laughed, "Beautiful stepper? *Thunder an' turf!* I am not a *horse*, Lady Lade!"

Lady Lade threw back her head again and laughed uproariously. "There she is! I know no other that says *thunder an' turf* but Miss Birdie Darley! Come here, young gel!"

Birdie was pulled against Lady Lade's bosom, just like Aunt Eggy and the empress, and then released. Lady Lade looked down at Birdie with a sparkle in her eye.

"You have grown into a demmed striking woman, Miss Birdie Darley. As I live and breathe! Damnation but you are a bloody good looker!"

"You look like a prime bit of blood yourself, Lady Lade!" Birdie said with a smile as she gazed at Lady Letitia Lade's gown. "I see you are still winning all your carriage races and can shine everyone else down."

Lady Lade flapped her fingers at Birdie. "You are doing it much too brown. But yes, I am still winning. Foolish men, trying to prove themselves against a woman who lives, breathes, and loves nothing better than horses! Particularly all my unbeatable Darley-bred horses!" She adjusted the many rings on all of her fingers. "I sometimes must wonder if the presence of money in a woman is sometimes more unsettling than the lack of it for men. I have shockingly so much of it that men frequently try to part me from it." She shrugged and laughed again. "They always lose."

Birdie grinned. "Because you are a top sawyer of a horse-woman."

"Indeed! Am I correct that you have been riding in horse races yourself? And beating them into the blazes too, I hear, on your horse Mo? He is unbeatable, they say, unusual looking but beyond brave and a true tryer."

Birdie grinned. "Yes, I enter races now and then. Only riding, however. I shall leave the carriage racing to you. Mo is unusual looking? You are being kind. I know they say that Mo is ugly, but he is the dearest horse I have ever known. I love him so! He will run to the ends of the earth for me, and I believe he would try to jump the moon if I asked, but I never would. I could not risk him over some of the ridiculously dangerous jumps these men put their poor horses to. But truly, Lady Lade, if I just think it, he does it! For me."

Lady Lade smiled down at Birdie. "That is how I started, partnering with one horse that seemed to be joined to my mind and heart," she said quietly.

Birdie gave her a full smile of joy. "Yes, that is it exactly! Joined mind and heart!"

"Someday, you will meet a man that you will feel the same way about. Joined body, mind, and heart." Lady Lade looked off into the past.

Her voice was so soft that Birdie could barely hear her.

"I beg your pardon, Lady Lade?" she asked.

Lady Lade came back to the present with a start. "I was say-ing, be warned, my dear, it takes a strong and demmed bold woman to try her skill against men. Be the best, Miss Birdie, at whatever you choose to do. Then no one can have a word to say against you. Like your mother and your sisters, and with what I hear in the gossip around London, I am demmed sure that you are!" Birdie smiled as Lady Lade smiled back at her and added, "We are two mad horsewomen, Miss Birdie!"

Birdie nodded happily and walked into the ballroom with Lady Lade and Empress Bibi. Aunt Eggy was walking ahead of them. She had her arm linked with Lady Chedworthy's. Both had their heads close together as they chatted quietly.

The women walked to a tea board and each picked up a glass of sweet Madeira wine. The empress pulled her pipe out of her reticule, filled it, and then lit it. She put it between her lips with a sigh of satisfaction as she inhaled and then slowly let out a thin stream of smoke. Then she lifted her glass to her lips and took a long sip of her wine.

"I am very thirsty and this is quite delicious, Lady Prudence Chedworthy," Bibi said as she took another long drink, draining her glass. She set down her empty glass and picked up another as the ladies watched her with their mouths open.

Lady Lade gave a great bellowing laugh as she clinked her glass to Bibi's and then tipped her own glass back and emptied it. She slammed it down on the tea board and picked up another.

"What?" Lady Lade asked as she saw her friends staring at her. "I was bloody joining Bibi."

Bibi frowned at their shocked looks. "You English women do not drink and you do not smoke." She shook her head and scowled. "You do not enjoy life. Even the act between a man and woman you do not speak of. It is necessary for a woman's comfort. Frequent use is healthy. Otherwise, you will dry up, like Egg Lady," she said matter-of-factly.

Lady Prudence started to grin, but then caught herself. "That is outrageously indelicate, Empress Bibi," she said quietly. "Though I am quite sure we all agree that, er, frequent use is…healthy." She looked around at the other ladies with her lips pursed and her eyes twinkling.

Aunt Eggy frowned fiercely. "I amnae dried up, Bibi Ibi!" she hissed in a whisper. "I will have ye ken that my second husband and I used tae enjoy—" she flapped her fingers, "—*that*, vera frequently!"

Birdie looked back and forth between all the women. "What

are you all talking about?" she whispered.

"Lovemaking, Miss Birdie!" Lady Lade explained. "The demmed best part of life! Particularly when your husband knows what he is doing!" She laughed loudly as she fanned her face rapidly with her large and very ornate orange feathered fan.

"Indeed!" chuckled Lady Prudence. "Indeed, indeed! And if they are handsome and have attractive muscles, which makes it so much more enjoyable." She sighed with dramatic longing. "I very much enjoy staying, er, *healthy*," she said delicately with a mischievous grin. "I stayed *very* healthy on my trip abroad, I can tell you."

"I bloody well enjoy staying demmed healthy as well!" boomed Lady Lade.

Several of the guests looked their way at Lady Lade's loud voice.

"Sards, Lettie! *Wheesht!*" Aunt Eggy hissed. "Bibi." She shook her head. "'Tis nae polite conversation." Her face was turning bright red. "Ye cannae be talking like that around my great-niece! Ye naft, numpty woman! Her mither has asked us tae be her chaperons! Chaperons dinnae speak of such things!"

The empress was giggling. "You need some of this, Egg Lady. Here." She pushed the pipe into Aunt Eggy's hands.

Aunt Eggy took the pipe that Bibi offered her and took several quick puffs.

Lady Prudence could not help herself from chuckling as she looked around the room at her guests. "I see many healthy women, and some who I believe could be, er, somewhat healthier, do you not agree, Lettie?"

Lady Lade turned to look around the room as well. "The recently widowed Lady Townsend looks very healthy, if I do say so myself." Her eyes roved over the ladies in the room. "Lady Belton looks terribly unhealthy." She nodded her head in the direction of a pinch-faced woman standing next to her husband. He was very obviously flirting with another lady standing in their group.

Birdie blushed as she stared at all the women. A flash of Ten Adair kissing her came into her mind. She quickly pushed it away as she glanced at the women. Each had a secretive look on their grinning faces, all except for Aunt Eggy who was contentedly inhaling from Bibi's pipe and had a suspiciously glassy look to her eyes. "Aunt Eggy, *Lud*, but I had no idea you were married twice. What happened to your first husband?"

Aunt Eggy lifted her lips and slowly exhaled a fragrant cloud of smoke. "I stuffed him doon the garderobe shaft," she mumbled with her lips around the pipe stem. "Got the idea from a cousin of sorts, from years past. Agnes, she was. That's how she did the deed."

The women all went quiet. They stopped their perusal of the *healthy* guests and stared aghast at her.

Lady Prudence spoke up first. "A garderobe? As in a sort of commode in a castle that is built onto the outer wall? And has a long, stone extension that hangs above the moat and drains into it?"

"What?" Birdie gasped quietly. "You mean you put him in a commode pipe?"

Aunt Eggy shrugged and puffed on the pipe again before answering. "Aye. I did," she said stubbornly. "Stuffed his body doon it. He was a laird and bigger in his own mind than in his treasures. We lived in his auld castle in the far Highlands back in the day. He was a mockit, manky, mingin, mauchit scunner of a blaegeard. The mac na galla deserved it. I'd had enough of his brutal fists. So I stuffed his body doon the garderobe. It lodged there for quite a lang time. Nae a soul knew, the smell just blended with the other bowfin, boggin smells from the garderobe." She took another leisurely, long puff from the pipe. "Eventually, I suppose he ended up in the moat with the rest of the offal." She shrugged again. "Either way, that's what ye dae with a pios de cac."

Silence ensued. After several long moments, the ladies managed to close their mouths.

"Egidia Ross, why have I never known this?" Lady Prudence Chedworthy said quietly. She leaned toward her and whispered, *"You did kill him first?"*

Aunt Eggy shrugged and scowled as she took another puff from the pipe before answering. "I defended meself. He had near drank himself blootered. Had his manky hands around me neck and was near fit tae choke the life from me. I grabbed the closest thing I could reach, which was a fireplace poker, and struck him. He fell and hit his head on the hearthstone. He was dead instantly."

"But, did no one know? No one came looking for him once you, er, stuffed his body down the garderobe?" Lady Prudence asked.

Aunt Eggy shook her head and scowled. "His vile nephew came looking for him. He was determined tae be the next laird since I hadnae gotten with child." She shrugged again and stared back at the ladies through the haze of pipe smoke around her head. "He tried tae kill me tae, but Laird Ross saved me and took me away and we married." She sighed as a dreamy look came onto her face. *"Vera happily tae."* She looked at Birdie and smiled softly. "'Twas Laird Ross's younger brother that married my sister, yer grandmother."

"Demmed, Eggs! I have so much bloody respect for you," Lady Lade said quietly.

Bibi chuckled. "You are not English after all, Egg Lady. You are definitely my very best good friend! I will ask you when I need someone killed instead of hiring an assassin next time." She chuckled again with her body heaving with the laughter she was trying to hold in.

"'Tis nae amusing tae insult me like that, Bibi!" Aunt Eggy grumbled.

Bibi shook her head quickly. "That time was no insult but a *compliment,* my very best good friend."

Lady Lade laughed heartily. "Oh, Eggs! It bloody is, *it is* most demmed excellent!"

"Thunder an' turf, Aunt Eggs!" Birdie whispered with awe. "Does Mother know about your first husband?"

Aunt Eggy pointed the pipe at Birdie. "No, and dinnae ye be telling her!"

Birdie held her hands up, "I vow I will not! Tare an' hounds, I do not want to be stuffed down a commode shaft like a mockit, manky scunner!" She laughed, but then pursed her lips shut and became instantly serious when Aunt Eggy scowled at her.

"Ye must talk of something else." Aunt Eggy peered sharply around at the ladies. She looked down at the pipe in her hand with disgust and shoved it into Lady Chedworthy's hand. "My head feels funny. This made me talk tae much."

Lady Prudence pursed her lips again to stop from laughing. She inhaled delicately from the pipe. "Perhaps we should talk of Miss Birdie's health," she chuckled.

Birdie shook her head vehemently. "Absolutely not," she said firmly. "We may just as well discuss those *amorous chocolates* you never told me about. But I thank you for your concern anyway."

Lady Lade opened her fan and waved it slowly in front of her face as she stared shrewdly at Birdie. "It was *amorous congress* we were discussing that day you eavesdropped on us so long ago, my dear."

Birdie grinned. "I am aware of the meaning now, Lady Lade. Though I do like the sound of chocolates being amorous."

Aunt Eggy giggled, causing the tiny bun on the top of her head to tilt. "Chocolates dae make me amorous, tae be sure!"

Lady Chedworthy offered Aunt Eggy the pipe, but Aunt Eggy hastily pushed it away. "Keep that far away from me," she said as she struggled to right her hair and her plumes.

Empress Bibi shoved Aunt Eggy's bun and the three short ostrich plumes back to the center of her head without even looking. She was staring at Lady Lade. "I should like amorous chocolates, Lady Letitia Lade," she declared.

Lady Prudence chuckled. "As should I, Letitia. Can you arrange that?"

Lady Lade grinned, but she ignored the women. She continued her study of Birdie. "I must ask, have you not had a single bloody offer for your hand these last two seasons?"

Birdie shook her head. "No, Lady Lade, but Freddie Rockingham—"

"Frederick Rockingham?" Lady Prudence interjected. "So, the *on dit* is true?" She inhaled deeply from the pipe as she fanned herself. "He participated in the debacle at Tattersalls!" She blew a puff of smoke from between her lips. "I do not care if he was acting for the queen, the things he put your dearest mother through. *Never.* Not he. He will not do! Not for you, my dear!"

"But…" Birdie began to speak.

Lady Lade tapped her fan on Birdie's shoulder. "Freddie Rockingham is the only one that you have set your cap on?"

Birdie shook her head. "Yes, he is the only one," she said firmly, not allowing herself to think of any other. "Please do not ring a peal over my head, Lady Lade. Mother and the duke are uneasy enough about it for everyone."

Lady Lade grunted. "I can imagine His Grace is demmed displeased! The Hawke would never agree to give his youngest stepdaughter's hand to bloody Freddie."

Birdie said in a vehement whisper, "Freddie was working for the king at the time you speak of, Lady Chedworthy. He was a spy for Tattersalls, not one of the villains, truly! In the end, he was doing a good thing."

Lady Chedworthy made a *harrumphing* sound. "Is the desired end so very important that *any* means is acceptable to achieve it, even a morally wrong one?"

Lady Lade nodded in agreement. "I say it was demmed poorly done of him. Acting as if he was courting your sister and trying to get demmed close to your mother to get bloody information. A double spy acting for the crown *as well as* those demmed evil men at Tattersalls?" She snapped open her fan and waved it. She shook her head. "A bloody double spy cannot be trusted. Constancy is rarely found in the average man, curse it, much less a spy! Loyalty for them can be as demmed infrequent as rain in a desert."

Birdie raised her chin. "Freddie is not average. He is a good man and an exceptional gentleman."

Lady Prudence lightly touched Birdie's hand. "He may have been trying to help your family, but is he truly a good man? Is he a *gentleman*, Birdie dear?" She tilted her head towards a group of guests standing beside the windows.

Birdie glanced in that direction. There was Freddie. Surrounded by several giggling young ladies and their hopeful mamas.

She sighed deeply as she watched him. She turned back to her great-aunt and the other ladies. "If you will excuse me." She was about to go when she turned back to Aunt Eggy and Empress Bibi. "Please do not give us a repeat of what the two of you did at the Lansdowne Ball." She looked down meaningfully at the pipe now in Empress Bibi's hand. She pointed at them and whispered, "Neither of you is to get blootered!" She whirled around and walked in Freddie's direction.

She heard Lady Lade's voice as she walked away.

"Bibi! Eggs! Do tell! What's in that demmed pipe, for it smells suspiciously like cursed hashish, and the devil take it but did the two of you old girls get bloody blootered at Lansdowne?"

Lady Prudence gasped. "Did I just smoke hashish?"

Birdie could not make out what they said after that as the four ladies began all talking at once.

CHAPTER NINE

B IRDIE WALKED THE short distance to the group standing near the tall windows. She hesitated. It would not be proper to insert herself into the conversation that Freddie was holding with the young ladies and their mamas.

She was about to turn around and return to her Aunt Eggy and the others when one of the young ladies and her mama turned around.

"Miss Darley," the woman said in a shrill voice. She pursed her lips as if she had tasted something sour and said nothing more.

Birdie dipped into a quick curtsey. "Mrs. Schellburne." She looked at the young lady standing next to Mrs. Schellburne. "Miss Charity. 'Tis lovely to see you. I hope that you are both quite well?" Birdie smiled at the tall young lady. She was unremarkable looking with thin brown hair and straight, short bangs over calculating eyes. A single long and thin corkscrew curl hung down either side of her face to her chin. She had ears that stuck out and a figure that was thick and shapeless under a dull-colored, matronly gown. Her shrewd eyes sharpened on Birdie.

Mrs. Schellburne smiled tightly and said in a sweet voice, "My dear daughter Chari and I were just wondering if Lord Hawke and your mother are here this evening, Miss Darley? Or that Persian prince who is the assassin?"

Birdie shook her head. "No, Mrs. Schellburne. I am here with my great-aunt Eggy."

Mrs. Schellburne looked quite satisfied and relieved. "That is very well." She gave a secretive glance to her daughter. "Isn't that very well, my dear Chari?" She stared with sharp eyes back at Birdie. "I think you will find that Captain Rockingham's attention is taken this evening. As are *all* his dances. You are too late," she trilled with satisfaction and a hint of triumph. "I hear it is said that you and the captain have a special affection and agreement with one another. Though all are wondering exactly what that agreement *pertains* for the *on dit* is that it certainly does not seem that a betrothal and wedding are in *your* future."

"Mama!" Miss Charity said with a dismissive, nervous laugh from behind her fan. "I told the others that I *wished* that it were true, not that it was true!" She lowered her fan and smiled at Birdie.

Birdie inwardly cringed at Charity's calculating smile. She did have even, clean teeth, which was her only redeeming feature, it seemed, but her smile clearly showed the scheming of her mind. She braced for whatever Charity was going to say next, for she certainly had more to.

Charity batted her eyelashes and coyly continued. "I am sure *you* of all people can understand how *wonderful* Freddie is. He and I have spent *so very much* time together, what else can one assume about you and Freddie?" She smiled in her calculating way again. "Just gossip is all it was. Nothing harmful." She laughed and raised her fan once more.

"It is not gossip if it *is true*," her mother said adamantly. "You said it *was true*, dear Chari."

Birdie raised her chin and stared back at the ladies. Before she could answer, a voice came from behind her.

"Mrs. Schellburne? I was not aware that you were here."

Birdie turned to see Lady Prudence Chedworthy staring haughtily at Mrs. Schellburne. Beside her stood Lady Lade, Aunt Eggy, and Empress Bibi.

Lady Lade fanned her face calmly. "Devil take it, but I do not recall Mrs. Schellburne or her *dear daughter Chari* being on your invitation list when I helped you write the invitations, Pru. I do remember Mrs. Shelby of Moorgate Manor and her two *delightful* daughters, but demme me, not a Mrs. Schellburne."

Lady Prudence Chedworthy kept her eyes on the woman as she smiled and nodded. "I do believe that you are correct, Lettie."

Mrs. Schellburne huffed and looked around the room with her face growing bright pink. "I received an invitation, I assure you, Lady Chedworthy. I was remiss in greeting you at our arrival, that is true. My dear daughter Chari was in such a hurry to come greet Captain Rockingham, you see? He is a dear favorite of my husband, *General* Schellburne."

Aunt Eggy elbowed Lady Lade aside so she could confront Mrs. Schellburne. "Vera eager tae greet the captain, was she? And tae be insulting tae my great-niece, Miss Birdie Darley? Let us see yer invitation then."

Empress Bibi snapped shut her fan and pulled the pipe from her mouth. She stood staunchly beside Aunt Eggy as she pointed her pipe at Mrs. Schellburne and declared, "Send her to the dungeons!" She turned to Prudence. "Do you have one here in this house, Lady Prudence Chedworthy?"

Lady Prudence shook her head without looking away from Mrs. Schellburne and her daughter. "I do not have a dungeon, Empress Bibi, though at times I wish I did." She looked meaningfully at Mrs. Schellburne.

Empress Bibi grunted and poked her elbow into Aunt Eggy's ribs as she continued to stare at the other woman. "Do you have a commode, Lady Prudence Chedworthy?"

Aunt Eggy gasped as her head whirled to glare at the empress. "Bibi Babi! Wheesht!"

Empress Bibi commanded in her best Supreme Imperial Empress voice, "Guards! Remove this woman and her daughter at once!"

Aunt Eggy glared at her. "We dinnae have guards in our

homes, Bibi Ibi! Wheesht noo! Quit yer blethering."

Aunt Eggy turned back to Mrs. Schellburne. "If ye dinnae have an invitation, and because ye were an ill whilly, gommerel, gorach, glaikit, scunner, blethering on aboot me Birdie, yer gaunnie have tae leave withoot a complaint." She glanced at the empress. "At once!"

Empress Bibi nodded sharply in agreement as the two small ladies scowled at Lady Schellburne and her daughter.

Birdie stepped hastily forward. "Aunt Eggy, that is unnecessary, unneeded, and unrequired! 'Tis undesirable, truly. *Please*, let the matter go."

Miss Charity smiled triumphantly at Birdie's words as she turned back to stare confidently at Lady Prudence. "You see, Mother? This is all unnecessary. A silly mistake is all. Lady Chedworthy and that…"—she pointed a finger at Lady Lade—"that *other* person have misremembered the invitation she sent us." Her sharp eyes went back to Lady Prudence.

Lady Prudence's eyes widened and then narrowed at the young girl. "That *other* person, as you say, is my great friend and a dear friend to our *Prince Regent*. She is *Lady* Letitia Lade, which you would know if you had entered my house and greeted me, for she was by my side to receive all our *invited* guests."

Aunt Eggy glared at Mrs. Schellburne. "You will leave and take yer *dear* daughter with ye, *or* ye will apologize tae my great-niece, *here*, in front of *everyone*."

Empress Bibi nodded her head while pointing her pipe at Mrs. Schellburne's daughter. "That one," she said jabbing her pipe at Charity, "is a calculating, cold, evil girl. I know her kind, Lady Egg."

Aunt Eggy agreed. "Och, aye. 'Tis known and nae gossip that *dear Chari* had amorous congress with Lady McLaren's husband." She nodded firmly. "If I am wrong, I shall kiss a crooked cricket, but I amnae wrong!"

Mrs. Schellburne ignored Aunt Eggy and the indignant gasp from her daughter. She looked from the two tiny old women glaring at her with such hostility to Lady Prudence Chedworthy. "Really, Lady Chedworthy, such ill manners they have! Women of their advanced age should have better manners," she said with a haughty look at Aunt Eggy and the empress. She turned back to Lady Chedworthy. "You cannot mean to dismiss my dear daughter and me for not greeting you!" She took a step forward. *"My husband is a general! The* General Schellburne!"

Lady Prudence smiled angrily. "This is my home and I can dismiss anyone I want for whatever reason I want. You were intolerably rude to my dear friend Miss Birdie Darley *and* Lady Lade; for that reason, I have a right to ask you to leave my house." She lifted her chin imperiously, which caused the golden tassels hanging from her turban to shake. "As well, you did not greet me because you very likely did *not* receive an invitation! Neither your ill behavior of Miss Darley nor your entering my home without greeting me are to be excused!" She glanced at Aunt Eggy and Empress Bibi, who were both nodding emphatically. She looked over at Birdie, who was wringing her hands and biting her bottom lip.

"Please, not for me," Birdie mouthed.

Lady Prudence paused. She lifted her chin and stared angrily down at Mrs. Schellburne. "I do not care who the divil your husband is. But I do care that you apologize to Lady Lade and Miss Darley. *At once."*

All four of the women nodded and repeated, "At once!"

"Very well," Mrs. Schellburne said stiffly. She turned to face Lady Lade and Birdie. "We apologize, Miss Darley, Lady Lade." She nudged her daughter's arm.

Charity pursed her lips as if she had just tasted something sour. "We apologize," she said tightly.

Birdie stepped aside as Mrs. Schellburne and her daughter pushed past her with their noses in the air and disgruntled looks on their faces. The group around Freddie had gone silent. All had witnessed the scene.

Birdie's face flushed with embarrassment until a soft hand

wrapped around her upper arm.

Birdie looked at the hand and then the owner of it. It was Octavia Adair. She had a bright, forced smile on her face.

"Miss Birdie Darley! What a pleasure to see you, my dearest friend! Come, will you promenade the room with me?"

Birdie nodded. She did not say anything, but turned away to walk with Octavia.

Octavia led her away from the group.

She leaned her head close to Birdie's as they walked and whispered to her, "What did your Aunt Eggy call Lady Schellburne?"

Birdie forced a calm smile on her face as they walked past several guests. She raised her fan to cover her mouth as she whispered back, "I believe she called her a bad-tempered, stupid, foolish, loathsome, gossiping person."

Octavia's face turned pink. She was silent for several moments as she took that in as they slowly walked the perimeter of the room.

"I think your Aunt Eggy is marvelous, indeed," Octavia finally whispered with awe. "I am not adept at expressing my feelings, much less standing up for myself against these ladies and their mamas when they have a handsome, available gentleman in their midst and become snarling cats fighting over a fish. Miss Charity Schellburne has been horrid to me as well. She openly laughed and mocked me when I stumbled at Gunter's and spilled my jasmine and rose flower ice cream all over my dress. You know how quickly it melts. Such a terrible mess and stain it made. I can still hear her laughing at me." She sighed. "I should love to have an Aunt Eggy."

Birdie grinned tightly. "Aunt Eggy *is* marvelous, and I am most grateful for her. I love her very dearly." She glanced over to where Lady Schellburne and her daughter were walking along the balcony. "I must admit that I am mortified, however, at what Lady Schellburne said about me and Freddie."

Octavia looked at Birdie with concern. "You have an affection for Captain Rockingham?"

Birdie sighed. "Why do you sound shocked?"

Octavia hesitated, but then shrugged. "I am not sure. I cannot imagine it. Do you truly have an agreement of sorts with him?"

Birdie heaved out a breath. "An agreement? You mean has he asked for my hand in marriage?" She shook her head. "We are friends, of a certainty. I have known him forever, it seems, and always thought we would marry. I was so young." She paused. Her voice became unsure and soft. "Though I think perhaps I do not know the man he has become. He is different from the young man he was, and before that, the boy I knew him as."

Octavia squeezed her arm lightly in support. "We have such dreams when we are young girls, do we not?"

Birdie laughed softly. "Oh yes. I did have such dreams. Of a prince on horseback fighting for my heart and then taking me up onto his beautiful, gleaming, dark horse and riding away together toward the horizon to his castle! I dreamed of a grand love. A love so wonderful and true and deep and powerful that it fills you so greatly that you cannot breathe. You cannot live without him by your side! You cannot live without his love. Together, you can do anything because he is your greatest ally, your greatest friend, your lover." She smiled sadly at Octavia. "I was a silly, dramatic young girl believing in fairy tales." She laughed once. "Though I must admit that I foolishly believed and hoped for all that up to a year ago."

Octavia stopped and turned to Birdie. "Never stop hoping, Miss Birdie! My sisters and I all came out, but Mother died, and then before we could take a breath, Father and Thomas, Ten's twin brother, were dead as well. Ten was off in the military and we did not know where he was fighting, so we could not get a message to him. My sisters and I were terrified we would lose him as well. We clung to one another. We did not go to balls or parties or assemblies or even teas. Life just stopped for us. Warwick de Walton found Ten for us and pulled him off the battlefield. He told Ten what had happened and Ten came home to us."

"Octavia, I am so sorry," Birdie said quietly.

Octavia shook her head. "I am not telling you this to make you feel sorry for me or my sisters. I am only saying never stop dreaming! Never stop hoping." She grinned. "I have seven sisters! We are all trying to restart our lives. And I, the plainest of the plain girls, and clumsy as well, left to stand at the edge of the dance floor. But still, I hope and dream." Her grin widened. "My brother Ten tells us to demand a man who will fight for us, who will cherish us, who will be a true friend and a good man. He assures us that he will help us find the man that each of us is meant to be with. I think perhaps Ten is a dreamer. He has no time for happiness now that he is the earl and has eight sisters to watch over and to find husbands for. Yet, he always puts on a charming and cheerful face for the world to see, just as he always has since he was young. He has never shown a serious side to the world. I know, however, that he is lonely, but he will not let on that this is so. He holds his dreams tightly to his heart, I think."

Birdie did not answer Octavia. She was deep in thought, picturing Ten Adair taking care of eight sisters, all older than he. A smile crept onto her lips. It must be terribly vexing for the man. And then a thought came to her. Would Ten need to find more money to support all his sisters? Their gowns did look terribly dated. Was his estate in order, or were his bank accounts in dire need of money? Perhaps, so dire that he would resort to smuggling horses to increase those accounts?

The two of them continued to stroll the perimeter of the lovely room with its gold embossed paper hangings covered in elegant stripes and florals of flocked gold. The gold seemed to glow under the candlelight of the chandeliers. Birdie realized that, of course, Lady Prudence Chedworthy would choose colors that enhanced her own coloring.

Birdie made sure to slow her steps as they neared groups of guests engaged in conversation that was not the typical polite talk of the weather and gowns. She heard no talk of stolen horses.

She slowed particularly when they walked toward a group of men in their scarlet uniforms who were talking quietly about General Schellburne. It sounded like they did not care for the general or the condition of the horses that he had procured for their regiment. Birdie slowed further to listen.

Octavia squeezed her arm, calling her attention back to herself. "Ten says that my sisters and I must stay away from the '*scarlet-coated rogues!*'"

Birdie turned to her with a grin. "*Scarlet-coated rogues*, are they? Surely, not all of them?"

Octavia shrugged and laughed. "They are most handsome to admire, though, are they not?"

Birdie grinned and pulled Octavia closer as the two of them began walking again. "If Ten says you must stay away from the scarlet-coated rogues, then you shall! Come along, let's resume our promenade."

"Miss Darley!" came a voice from behind her.

Birdie and Octavia turned around to see Freddie coming toward them.

He smiled and bowed his head to Birdie.

Birdie gave him a quick curtsey in return.

"Captain Rockingham, may I introduce Miss Octavia Adair?" Birdie said politely. "She is the young lady you knocked down at the Carlton House ball when you danced so close to the column she was standing near." She smiled in strained politeness as she stared up at Freddie's face.

Octavia curtsied, bobbled in her balance, and would have fallen to one knee had not Birdie helped her steady herself. "Your Grace, er, I mean, Captain, er Lord Rockingham, er, Lord Trenton," Octavia mumbled with uncertainty.

"You may call me Captain, Miss Adair," Freddie said, and quickly looked back to Birdie. "I do not recall knocking anyone down."

Birdie bristled and raised her chin. "Well, you *did*. Thunder an' turf! I witnessed the whole thing. She could have been *hurt terribly."*

Octavia's face turned pink. She spoke softly with embarrassment. "Truly, no harm was done. All is well, Captain. It was my fault for being ever so clumsy."

Birdie turned to Octavia and whispered, "It was not your fault, and clumsiness had nothing to do with it! Don't let him be a mockit, mingin, mhodhail skiver!"

Freddie frowned. "Miss Darley, truly, I do not recall this event you speak of. As well, I suspect you are insulting me with your great-aunt's Scottish words."

Octavia's blush grew as she stared at the captain and leaned toward Birdie. "I don't know what those words mean," she whispered quietly. "Are they indeed insults?"

Birdie's arms were across her chest and she was angrily tapping her toe. She whispered loudly back to Octavia with her eyes narrowed on Freddie, knowing he would hear her. "They mean dirty, rotten, rude shirker and *he remembers.* I saw him look down at you where you had landed on the floor."

Freddie's eyes darted to Octavia and back to Birdie. "If that is true, I looked at her with *great concern."*

Birdie scoffed. *"Oh pish!* Not a thimble of concern was on your face, Freddie Rockingham."

Octavia's lips fell open. She straightened up away from Birdie and said awkwardly as she touched his arm, "All is well, Captain! I am unhurt, but thank you for your concern!"

Freddie quickly drew his arm away as he stared at the two of them. He smiled weakly at Octavia before he turned back to Birdie. "There, you see?"

Birdie made a *harrumphing* sound next to Octavia.

Freddie's glance went back to Octavia. He stared at her a moment with his eyes glancing over her simple, high-necked gown, and then he dismissed her with little care for the matter as he turned back to Birdie. He hurried on. "Miss Darley, I heard Lady Schellburne was raising some kind of a breeze to you. I hope you are not overly upset by any remarks she may have made? I should very much like to make it up to you."

Birdie tilted her head at him and arched her brow. "Make it up to me? *Such concern*, indeed. How?" she demanded. "Will you save me perhaps a dance? Will you spare one for Miss Adair, as well, to repay her for knocking her over at the ball?"

Freddie's smile tightened. "I am sorry, Miss Birdie, I have signed dance cards for each dance this evening. But, would you care to join me and several others in ice skating tomorrow? The Serpentine in Hyde Park has been frozen and we have had excellent skating parties there. However, tomorrow we intend to go to the Frost Fair on the Thames! 'Tis frozen as well with this terribly cold winter! There will be several booths set up on the ice with hot drinks and choices of delectable foods, and ice skating of course! Quite a party it will be." He glanced at the young lady beside Birdie. "Miss Adair, you are most welcome as well, of course."

"Oh! I should like that very much," Octavia breathed out.

Birdie's shoulders tightened. "We have not danced once this season, Freddie, nor spent any time together so that we may have a chance to visit. As well, you have not come to call, though I am staying in Grosvenor Square only a stone's throw from your house. Aunt Eggy has remarked on this very thing. She thinks you have forsaken our familial friendship, and that we must be no longer in your favor." She tapped his wrist sharply twice with her fan and stared at him, noting his growing agitation as she continued. "I told her, of course, this could not be true. You would never do such a thing to the Darley family."

Freddie frowned slightly as he pulled at the sleeve cuff over his wrist that Birdie had tapped with her fan. He swallowed tightly and looked beyond Birdie to the group of guests still standing near the windows. He lifted a hand to signal to them that he would be returning to them shortly. "Please tell Lady Ross that I have been most busy and give her my apologies. Tell her I shall come, of course, as soon as I can." He mustered a small smile.

"I am hardly inclined to believe you, for you have made no attempt to explain your absence," Birdie retorted.

Freddie offered an attempt at a charming smile. "Come, Miss Darley, 'tis early in the season yet for balls and dancing. You shall have a chance to dance with me, I promise. Now then, say you will come to the Frost Fair tomorrow? We can visit there. *How often can one say they ice skated on the Thames?* 'Tis frozen solid and prime skating ice, they say! It will be a most splendid time! Of course, you ladies will not skate. The young ladies enjoy watching, or a few will try sliding across the ice in their boots."

Octavia squeezed Birdie's arm. "We shall be there, Captain! I should dearly love to see the Thames frozen and be able to slide on the ice! And I am sure you will find time to dance with Miss Darley and visit Lady Ross as well. Thank you!"

Freddie smiled, bowed his head to the two of them, and spun around. He was gone before Birdie could say a word or even curtsey. She wanted to ask him exactly what he was so busy with that he could not walk across Grosvenor Square to call on her.

"Well, that was very rude of him, I should think," Birdie grumbled. "Aunt Eggy would say that all his eggs are double yoakit and he should gae awa' and boil his heid."

Octavia asked curiously, "Double yoakit? Boil his heid?"

Birdie nodded once. "He is full of rubbish and he should go away."

Octavia made a face. "But you cannot mean that! You want to marry him!"

Birdie was watching Freddie who was now back with the group of guests at the window. There were several young men and young ladies that had joined them. They were all talking and laughing.

She turned back to Octavia. "Do I?" she asked softly.

Octavia had no time to answer as a gentleman came forward. "Miss Darley, may I have the pleasure of this dance?"

Birdie looked up at him. He was not a young man, though not old either. His eyes were kind and he was fair of countenance.

His name and title came to her.

"I thank you for the invitation, Lord Phillips, but I must refuse. Perhaps you would care to ask my dear friend, Miss Adair?" She nudged Octavia forward.

Lord Phillips smiled and bowed his head as he offered his hand to Octavia. The pair walked to the dance floor with Octavia looking back at Birdie with a wide smile on her face.

"That was kind of you," came a voice from behind her.

Birdie whirled around to see Ten Adair staring over her head at his sister on the dance floor. He did not look happy.

"It was my pleasure," she responded as she turned back to watch Octavia.

Ten grunted. "My thanks were not sincere, Miss Darley," he growled.

Birdie turned back to him with a frown. "My pleasure was," she said firmly.

Ten kept his eyes on his sister. His only response was a grunt.

"What is wrong with you?" Birdie demanded. She saw where he was staring. "Do not tell me that you are unhappy that Octavia is dancing?"

Birdie stared up into his green eyes, waiting for him to answer her. He looked down at her. His eyes traveled from the tips of her satin shoes, up her shapely legs draped so lovingly in the fine gown, and then slowly up her hips and waist. His hot green gaze paused at the blue velvet covering her breasts and the glimmering glass beads in the gossamer net that barely concealed the very tops of her breasts. His eyes traveled on, seeming to caress her neck, her lips, her cheekbones, her unusual eyes with their long black lashes. His gaze traveled up to the masses of her raven hair, piled in curls with some escaping down her back and over one breast. His fists clenched. And then his gaze returned to hers.

She saw the sudden dilation of his eyes, the intake of his breath as his nostrils flared.

"Ten?" she asked softly. She did not understand what she saw in his eyes. "Why are you angry that Octavia is dancing?"

He blinked once, twice, three times, and looked away from her. After a moment, his gaze came back to her and his lips lifted into a wolf's grin. "Leave the matchmaking of my sisters to me, Little Bird."

"Octavia is my friend." She started to say more, but he cut her off.

"She is my sister and *you will stay out of it*. I will choose who she may dance with."

"Lord Phillips is a *good*—"

"Yes, he is *good* at drinking, and *good* at charming women into his bed. I will not have her near him."

Birdie gasped and looked back at Octavia with Lord Phillips. "He is *a rake?*" she whispered to herself with horror. "A rogue, a rascal, a rapscallion, a reprobate, a renegade?" Her hands became tight fists at her sides as she narrowed her eyes on the man with Octavia. "Thunder an' turf but there shall be no amorous chocolates for him," she added fiercely under her breath.

Without saying a word to Ten, she began to march onto the dance floor straight to Octavia.

A hand on her arm stopped her before she could reach it.

"Tut, tut, tut, Little Bird. You cannot make a scene. It shall be worse for Octavia if you proceed in this course of action."

Birdie turned to him with a worried frown. "'Tis my fault. I must do something. I have sent her right into the rake's arms! He could take advantage of her, steal her away, have amorous—" she flailed her fingers in the air, "—chocolates, er, *congress* with him. He could get her blootered with wine and take her to Gretna Green. He could lock her in an old decrepit castle somewhere in the Highland wilderness of Scotland where she will have to kill him and stuff him down the garderobe. Or, *Lud*, thunder an' turf and tare an' hounds, what if he takes her to *America?*" she said with horror.

"Enough," Ten growled before she could go on.

Ten continued to watch his sister as he rubbed the dimple on his chin. He looked down at Birdie with an arched brow as he studied her once more from the tips of her satin slippers to her shapely hips, to the glimmering gossamer net that molded so perfectly to the tops of her full breasts, to the shimmering glass beads that dotted her hair like stars. He gave her a crooked grin. "I have an idea, but you may not like it."

"What is it?" she demanded quickly. "We must hurry to intervene!"

"Dance with me. 'Tis a waltz. We shall get near enough to them that I may tread on his foot and cause him to leave the floor, and thus, Octavia. If I step hard enough, I shall break his foot."

Birdie looked flummoxed. "Stepping on his foot hard enough to cause him to leave the floor is not causing a scene?"

Ten grinned down at her. "Have you a better idea? He is a rake and a rogue, and all those other words that you said that began with the letter 'r'. However, plying her with wine and whisking her off to Gretna Green or a rotting castle in the Highlands is not part of Phillip's agenda. And killing him and stuffing him down a castle garderobe? Wherever did you get that far-fetched idea? Never mind, do not answer that." He held his hand out to her as his grin broadened.

She took his hand. "It was not a far-fetched idea and I shall not tell you where I got it from, but it did happen. To someone who deserved it, by the way." She raised her chin. "I shall think of a better plan than stepping on his foot as we attempt to dance toward them."

She walked beside him out onto the dance floor.

"Octavia's white gown is out of fashion with all those heavy ruffles, is it not? I had not realized it. My sisters have not asked for new gowns, but I shall send for the modiste at once." He shook his head. "I cannot forgive myself for not realizing it earlier, but I suddenly could not help but to notice that she does not dress like you," Ten said as he watched his sister dance with Lord Phillips.

"Like me?" Birdie said with surprise.

Ten nodded his head toward her dress. "*Elegant* and feminine. *Alluring*. Your gown shows your figure to advantage. A man is hard pressed to look away."

"*Lud,*" Birdie whispered. "You like my gown? Tare an' hounds, a compliment from the charming Ten Adair, Earl of Fairfax."

They reached an open spot on the floor. She turned and faced him.

"I did not say that I like your gown. I said that it is hard to look away from it."

"From *me*, you mean," she said cheekily.

He arched a brow at her.

She grinned back at him and placed her hand on his shoulder. She paused a moment, waiting, watching his discomfort as his lips twisted up into what was not a grin but a grimace. She slowly and deliberately placed his hand on her waist. Then she took his left hand in her right hand and waited again. She arched a brow at him as he set her an arm's length away, making sure there was the proper distance between the two of them.

With a rueful grin, he twirled her in a slow circle to join the other dancers.

Birdie stared up at him with a mischievous look on her face.

"Was this a ruse to get me to dance with you?" she asked in a teasing voice.

"Why should I have wanted to dance with you unless there was, indeed, a need?" he asked charmingly as he lightly used his hand on her waist to lead her in the dance.

Birdie grinned. "Because in truth you *like* me. You *want* to dance with me. Though you will not admit it."

Ten arched a brow at her. "I do not like you. We both agreed on that. I am doing this for my sister." He twirled her in a slow circle again, which caused her breasts to brush up against his chest and her thighs to rest against his. He quickly set her back from him. Keeping the proper distance.

"Oh pish, you wanted to dance with me," she said with an

arched brow back at him.

"You can arch your brow all you want at me. I can arch mine higher." And he did, showing her exactly how dramatic an arch he could create.

"Tare an' hounds but you can! You win."

"'Tis not a contest, Miss Darley."

"It is always a contest when we women try to stand up for ourselves where a man is involved."

She moved with him within the music and the graceful steps of the waltz. He was a skilled dancer, fluid and elegantly graceful. She could not help her smile when he kept trying to keep her the proper distance away from his body. It made her all the more determined to dance closer to him.

"Are you truly going to hire a modiste for new gowns for all eight of your sisters? 'Twill be an enormous expense," she said as she watched his face.

He scoffed. "I know it will. I am not concerned about the cost. They shall have as many new gowns as they like. I have increased my estate and my accounts to embarrassing amounts with the ships that War de Walton and I own together. Trading down the southern coasts and with America has proven immensely profitable."

Birdie took that in. *So Ten Adair was not in need of cash.*

"Your Freddie is rather busy tonight," he said in a low voice as Freddie danced past them with a giggling young lady.

"Stop that," she whispered. She stepped closer to him. Breathing in the heady, spicy, mysterious male scent of him. *Had she ever noticed Freddie's scent?*

"Stop what?" He grinned bemusedly. "The man's a fool. That you are not aware of it is most concerning. That you choose him is even more concerning."

Birdie did not answer. She made a small humming sound in the back of her throat.

She took another step closer, not quite brushing up against him, but close enough to feel the heat from his body, which made her breath flutter from between her lips. Once more, he quickly set her a rigid arm's length away from him.

She huffed out a breath. "By the by, you look very nice this evening." Tonight, he was wearing a tailcoat of darkest blue with a waistcoat to match with lighter blue and gold embroidered silk swirls. It made his eyes appear even greener. She stared up into those eyes and her breath caught as she danced closer. Under the luminescent, soft, golden glow of the candles in the chandeliers, she could see the gold striations there in his eyes and it made her heart race. It also made her stomach flutter, her toes curl, and her knees weak. The man was just far too good looking.

"Thank you," he said softly with surprise.

They danced around the room as they stared at one another. She had drifted closer to him once again without him realizing it. Though she was petite, she fit perfectly within his arms, against his body, and moved with him as if they were one body. He quickly set her away from him.

"Miss Darley, you must endeavor to keep the proper distance," he spoke in a low voice. "I feel you are purposely not upholding the proprieties with me. I must ask you to be aware of the acceptable space between us."

Birdie tried to hide her grin. She took a step toward him, close enough that her body brushed his, just for one step of the waltz. "You mean I should not come *this* close?" she whispered huskily.

He set her away with a crooked grin. "No, you should not," he whispered.

"I should not look up at your dimple and sigh loudly, or bat my eyelashes, *like so?*" she asked as she sighed and batted her black eyelashes at him in a sultry way.

He arched a brow at her. "Interesting, but no, you should not."

She pouted her lips. "I should not giggle and hang on your every word, your every smile, as I stare dreamily into your beautiful eyes and wish I could run my fingers through the dark waves of your hair like those debutantes do?" She stopped herself. She was coming far too close to what she was actually desirous of doing herself.

He smiled wryly at her as he growled. "Though that is intriguing, I cannot imagine that you are capable of such behavior, Miss Darley."

Birdie straightened her shoulders and scowled. "You can't? *Why ever not?* I can be romantic and teasing and, *and seductive*," she said firmly.

"Oh, you are being a most seductive little bird, but I say that because *your heart is Rockingham's.*" He lightly squeezed her hand. "I have eight sisters to be mindful of. This is something I must take most seriously, Miss Darley. The Adair reputation must be kept without a question as to propriety or convention if they are to achieve their best match."

Birdie's grin faded. "Yes, yes, of course." She was silent a moment as she stared up at him and saw his far-too-serious face. "I promise I shall not be improper, nor shall I make an attempt to thoroughly seduce you or—"

"That is quite enough," he said with a laugh as his eyes crinkled. "Do not practice playing at matters of the heart with me for use on your Freddie."

Birdie stared at him. Stricken. "I was doing no such thing."

He looked down at her, his grin slowly leaving his face as he saw the truth of her words on her face and in her lavender-blue eyes. He had hurt her by accusing her of practicing on him. He could not miss the look in her eyes, the trembling of her lips, the rapid rise and fall of her breasts as she stared up at him.

They danced on for several more bars of music in silence. The only sound was the whisper of satin and silk skirts as the couples around them twirled to the three-beat rhythm of the string instruments.

Birdie felt Ten's hand on her waist tighten. His face was strained, tense, as he stared down at her, his green gaze moving from her own, to her brows, her nose, her cheeks and hair, and finally her lips. He led her around the dance floor as his eyes seemed to study every one of her features with intense seriousness.

Birdie did not understand the strained look on his face nor in his eyes. Nor did she understand what Ten's intent perusal of her face was making her feel. It was as if lightning was bouncing back and forth between them. As if they were standing in a bubble, all by themselves. Her breasts were rising and falling rapidly with her increased heartbeat. It seemed like the blood within her limbs was becoming slow and heavy. All she could see now was his intense gaze.

She was losing herself in him. She could not look away from the depths of his eyes.

Her heart sped up as her breasts brushed his chest. His head lowered slightly towards hers, sharing her breath as his eyes searched hers.

She should not allow this. Was he a thief of horses? A thief of her heart?

No, she thought to herself, he could not be a thief of her heart. He was forever striving for propriety. He had eight sisters, after all. That left him a thief of horses, a smuggler, *a traitor*.

"*Ten*," she whispered.

"Miss Darley," Ten said in a hoarse and husky voice as he stared down at her. He swallowed tightly. "*Euan Beag*," he whispered. His jaw tightened as he blinked rapidly and lifted his head. "Step back. Let me go."

Birdie took a deep breath, realizing that she had moved even closer to him as they danced. She moved back at arm's length as was proper in the waltz. "Let you go?" she asked in confusion as she looked at their joined hands as they danced.

"Your eyes," Ten said in a tight, low voice. "You are *seducing* me with your eyes."

Birdie blinked several times as the breath rushed out of her. Had she truly seduced him with only her eyes? Did a woman have such power?

She looked away from him, breaking whatever spell had enveloped the two of them. Or was it only her that had been wrapped up in *his* spell? She took a deep breath and attempted a calm, polite smile.

"Did you find those men?" Birdie asked into the silence. Her voice was husky, strained, as she tried to lighten the tension she felt emanating from him.

His gaze snapped up from where it had fallen to her lips. He looked around at the other dancers, anywhere but back into her eyes. "I did." His voice was raw. He narrowed his eyes as his gaze returned to her. He set her further from him.

Birdie's eyebrows rose. "And?"

"The two men that I caught have been dealt with."

Birdie waited, but he said nothing further. She huffed out a breath in exasperation. "Did you question them? But of course you did. What did they say? What did they tell you? Are they part of a large gang of horse thieves or crooked coach commissioners that steal horses? Who is their leader? Where do they meet to make their plans? What did they say they do with the horses? Did they mention smuggling at all?" She finally stopped and took a breath.

"Demme my ears!" he laughed softly. "What kind of little bird are you? Are you quite finished demanding answers, Miss Darley?" The charming, dimpled-chin rogue that was Ten Adair had returned. Gone was the intense stare of his gaze.

Birdie nibbled her lips, realizing she should not have mentioned the word smuggling. She could not be sure of him, as of yet. As she worried at her bottom lip, it drew his eyes like an arrow to its target.

His pupils suddenly flared as he stared at her lips, seemingly unable to look away. Tension returned to his face, and in his large hand as his fingers flexed over hers. The fingers of his other hand tightened on her waist.

Once more, she was pulled into his gaze. Birdie's world stopped as her breath caught with the look of sudden hunger she read there. She stared back at him, held there in his gaze as her blood slowed in her veins and liquid heat poured through her.

Ten blinked slowly. "What were you asking me, *Eun Beag*?" His voice was soft, husky, and throaty.

"I would have you tell me of the men," she said softly as she stared into his beautiful eyes.

"The men?" Ten blinked his eyes rapidly several times and cleared his throat. He glanced away from her for a moment. "*Damnation*," he murmured. When he looked back, his eyes were clear. "Very well, Miss Darley," he said politely with a charming smile. "I can tell you that I turned the two men over to Robert Jenkinson, the prime minister."

Birdie missed a step in their waltz at her astonishment at his words. "The Earl of Liverpool." She knew who Jenkinson was. She was just surprised to hear that he had given the horse thieves to *him*. She would have to think about that. She assumed he would hand them over to a Bow Street runner.

"Yes. The earl is our prime minister."

He twirled with masculine grace, holding her within his arms as he continued to look down into her eyes and follow the lulling rhythm of the orchestra.

"Thunder an' turf, Ten! You did not get *any* information at all?" she whispered incredulously.

Ten guided her effortlessly past several couples as he watched her expressive face. "Why do you wish to know all this? You returned those carriage horses that you found in the mews, I assume?"

She nodded her head.

"Then why these questions?" He looked away from her as his jaw tightened. "'Tis an unnatural interest you have, Miss Darley. Continue and you could be hurt."

Birdie took a breath, trying to remain calm. She smiled politely at a couple dancing past them. "You say that because I am a female?" she asked in exasperation.

"Indeed." He looked down at her and saw the stubborn anger

there as she stared back up at him. He smiled and sighed. "Really, Miss Darley, you need not bother yourself with men's matters. Let the prime minister question those men and sort this out. There is nothing of interest for you."

Birdie purposely stepped on his toes. "Oh dear me, beg your pardon," she said with a hint of sarcasm.

Ten's response was to arch an eyebrow down at her and grin, showing his dimple to its full magnificence.

Birdie scowled slightly. "It is said that General Wellesley, Viscount Wellington, sometimes engages females as information gatherers. 'Tis not so unnatural as you would have it." She stared up at him in challenge.

His eyes returned to hers with a flash of ire. His jaw tightened. There was no grin this time. His voice lowered to a dangerous whisper, "Are they still alive to tell their tale, Little Bird?"

Birdie scowled and lifted her chin. "I took care of myself that night in the mews."

"Indeed?" He leaned his head closer to her. "What if I had not been there? I shudder to think what could have happened to you." He shook his head. "I should never have indulged you that night," he gritted out. He looked away from her through several steps of the waltz.

"Humph," she grumbled. She kept her eyes on his ascot and spoke quietly for his ears alone. "The tall man would have thrown his knife at you, but I slashed his wrist with the secret knife in the tip of my crop. *I* saved *you*. Goodness, I shudder to think what may have happened to *you* if *I* was not there. At least you managed to get a kiss from me for your trouble."

"What?" He gasped as his eyes narrowed down at her.

He looked up and saw that they were dancing near the doors to the terrace.

He quickly guided her outside onto the terrace, away from the windows and any listening ears or watchful eyes. He led her to a darkened corner of the terrace. There would be no chance of anyone seeing them if any other couple decided to pursue some intimate privacy.

He held her by her arms as he stared angrily down at her in the soft, faint glow of the candlelight coming from a window of the ballroom. "Are you implying that I manipulated the situation for my own benefit? *For a kiss?*"

Birdie stared up at him quizzically. She had been taken by surprise by his strong reaction. "No! I pulled your head down to me, if you remember? Yes, you made it a real kiss, but I realize that the kiss was only a ruse to throw that man off. *I know that,* and why you had to kiss me. I was only saying at least you came away with something." She exhaled and lowered her voice as she rubbed her cold arms. "Don't you men prize a kiss from a woman?"

He lifted his chin and stared up at the stars in the heavens for a moment as he tried to calm his temper and seek patience with this petite, lavender-eyed, mischievous young woman. He glanced back down at her and pinned her with his eyes for several moments. "From a woman we desire, yes."

She stared up at him. "And you dislike me terribly, so of course, you would not desire me. The kiss was repugnant to you." She frowned and looked over his shoulder. "I did not find it so."

His sharp gaze slashed into her. "Are you playing at being offended, Miss Darley? Never tell me that you are a prim miss that declares yourself seduced with one simple kiss and I am now indebted to offer for your hand." His eyes were narrowed to green slits between his black lashes as he stared down at her in barely controlled fury. "Indeed, it was clear that you had been kissed before, for you were most skilled."

Birdie blinked several times in shock.

"Do not bother to bat your eyelashes at me in an effort to be flirtatious," he said with annoyed frustration.

"I was doing no such thing," she whispered as she turned her face away while still rubbing her arms. The night air was freezing.

His eyes came back to her at the sound of pain in her voice. Were those tears he was seeing, glistening on the tips of her long lashes?

He cleared his throat, unsure what to say. He saw that she was cold and quickly took his tailcoat off and wrapped it around her shoulders.

She clutched his coat to her, feeling surrounded by the scent and heat of him through the fabric. She lifted her eyes to his. She glared at him through her angry tears. "That kiss was my first, you bowfin, bampot, *blaegeard*, and I only kissed you in the way you kissed me."

He stared at her in shock. "I cannot believe you. The way you kissed me…the way you held me…I felt…" He swallowed tightly and rubbed at the dimple in his chin.

He was astounded. He had never shared a kiss such as that one. He had lost himself in her. Lost any sense of time.

All that he had been able to feel was her.

All that he had been able to taste and smell was her sweetness.

Her lips still drove him to distraction anytime he looked at them.

That kiss was perfection.

He had been thoroughly seduced by that kiss.

Birdie stared up at him with great interest. Ten Adair was stunned. "You told me to moan and I did. You moaned as well, many, *many* times in fact. You liked it," she said with a triumphant grin.

Ten straightened his shoulders and mentally pushed the images of that kiss away. "I did not. It did not move me at all."

"You liked it. You *like* me," she whispered as she stared up at him. She noted that his gaze dropped to her lips. "You want to kiss me," she added in a softer whisper as she marveled at the look in his eyes, for her.

He shook his head once in silence as he stared at her lips and then her eyes like a man starving.

Birdie's heart was pounding as she stared back at him. Her whole body was throbbing. She no longer felt cold. *No*, she felt *hot*.

Lightning arced through her, racing throughout her body.

Her whole body felt like it was aflame.

Her breasts became heavy and her core became moist with hot liquid honey.

For this man.

She stood up on her tiptoes and lightly touched her lips to his.

He groaned and turned his lips away from hers. "I cannot," he whispered in an aching, husky voice against her cheek.

But just as soon as the words were out of his mouth, he groaned again and pulled her tightly against him. He turned his lips back to hers and slammed his mouth over hers again and then again.

Birdie could only hold on to his shirt as he ravaged and plundered her lips and her mouth with his own. She sighed when she felt his velvety, hot tongue thrust between her lips and touch her own. She moaned and whimpered with the shock and the pleasure of it as she tangled her tongue with his in a seductive dance.

She loved the taste of him.

She loved the sounds he was making.

She chased his lips with her own, pulling him even tighter to her as the kiss became hotter, faster, deeper, and their breathing became louder with heavy gasps and drawn-out sighs.

It was all tongues, teeth, and lips, and groans of desire. And then he slowed it down to a torturously sweet, incredibly deep, aching kiss. He wrapped her in his arms and held her tightly for this new and gentle annihilation of her senses. She was pressed against him. Her breasts crushed to his chest where she could feel the thunder of his heart beating, or was it hers? She could feel where his hips pressed against her abdomen and the need there. She could feel his strong thighs against hers, where she leaned into him.

The feel of him, the exquisite taste of him, the way he kissed her, filled her body, and made that place between her thighs throb even harder and become more liquid with desire.

"Ten," she gasped against his mouth.

He sighed and rested his temple against hers as they both waited for their hearts to slow their beating and their breaths to cease racing.

"*Perfection*," he whispered in the barest of murmurs. He pulled fully back and stared down into her dazed eyes. He set her away from him. "Forgive me, *Euan Beag*. I should not have taken such liberties. You seduced me," he whispered, and swallowed tightly as he stepped back further. "I cannot offer for you. Please understand. My sisters…"

Birdie stared up at him for several moments. She suddenly felt chilled once again. She clutched at his jacket as anger turned the warmth in her veins to ice.

"Do not suggest that I would expect that you offer for my hand because of that kiss," she said with trembling in her voice. She would not let him hear that tremble. She continued in a stronger voice. "Of course, I know that you would not marry me, nor any woman, I expect. Not when you have eight sisters that you must find husbands for." She took a deep breath and added softly, "I understand."

Ten stared at her. She was taking this surprisingly well. *Too well*, he thought with annoyance. "And *you* would not *marry me*, because you are determined to marry your Freddie," he said with thinly veiled disgust as he stared into her eyes. He took a breath and gazed over her head as the reality of it hit him. "In truth, I know that someday, *eventually,* I must find a woman to marry," he said quietly. "A mature woman who is older than my sisters. A motherly figure for them. A woman of impeccable reputation and calm demeanor to teach and guide them to be proper young ladies."

Birdie froze at this information. "Of which I am not, is that what you are implying?" She scoffed quietly. "Your sisters stopped living when your father and twin brother died. They need to learn to be brave and to be social, amongst other things. Proper young ladies? They are most proper! Wallflowers even. They stay together in a group, avoiding anyone else. They have no inclination to be anything but proper! Except for Octavia. She yearns for more, I think, but she needs to learn confidence and poise." She took a step toward him. "Are you looking for a mother for them or a wife for yourself? The woman you describe sounds like a saint. A *boring* saint. You will have no fear of being seduced by her, of that I am quite sure, indeed. A requirement of yours that she be older than your oldest sister will preclude any flirtation or attraction, or desire even." She smiled sweetly up at him with an arched brow and stepped even closer. She took his coat from her shoulders and pushed it against his chest. "I hope you do not wish for children."

His eyes narrowed once again as he thrust his arms into his tailcoat. It carried her sweet scent. He yanked at his cravat in annoyance as he looked down at her, realizing that she had come close again. He clasped her arms and set her back away from him. "You are doing it again. I cannot afford your playing at seduction with me, Little Bird. I will not allow it. On my honor, *I cannot.*"

Birdie scowled. "I was not *playing at...at seduction*! Tare an' hounds, Ten! Thunder an' turf, you can be an insufferable scunner!"

"Tut, tut, tut, calm yourself, Little Bird." He lifted his dimpled chin and looked over her head into the ballroom. As several couples danced past, he grabbed her hand and quickly led her back through the doorway. With graceful smoothness, he swept her back into the waltz. He said softly as he stared beyond her, "I am *quite certain* that kiss was a mistake, Miss Darley. For both of us."

She felt his hand tighten on her waist as he led her through the dance with strong, graceful steps.

"You are *certain* it was a mistake," she repeated. Her face became sad as she stared up at him. She had been wrong about him. He was a tight-laced gentleman too wrapped up in correctness and proprieties and responsibilities all disguised behind a charming grin, beautiful green eyes, and an intriguing dimple.

He was not a horse thief, nor a thief of her heart. He wanted no part of that night in the mews and had just handed those men to the prime minister without a single question. She was startled to realize that she was disappointed. "Your *certainty* is absurd," she said softly. "Though certainly, you should be uncomfortably *uncertain* in your certainty."

He glanced down at her with his eyes glittering and crinkling at the corners with his amusement. His lips tilted up in a crooked smile as he laughed quietly. "Never say you are quoting Voltaire? A *Frenchman?*" At her stubborn look, he laughed again and said, "The quote is, 'Uncertainty is an uncomfortable position, but certainty is an absurd one.' *That* is the correct quote."

She shrugged within his arms. "I prefer mine."

"You prefer to do as you will, Miss Darley," he said with a tight jaw. "Not surprising for a woman who lurks in alleys and can outride any man as well as win any race she enters against them. And by the by, wears breeches like them as well."

"Indeed, I am incautious and indiscreet. Clearly, I am not a young lady you should desire to marry or have around your sisters. I am most aware of your meaning." She responded with the same curtness in her voice that she had heard in his.

He arched a brow at her as his tight jaw relaxed. "I cannot regret the truth of my words, but I regret the way I expressed them."

She arched her brow back at him. "Truth has an eloquence all of its own. When indeed truthful, it needs no further expression."

Ten was about to retort, but then scowled as a couple danced past them. It was Octavia and Lord Phillips. "*Damnation*, as well, *you have made me forget my duty to my sister.*"

With the angry scowl still on his face, his eyes followed his sister and Lord Phillips as they danced away from him. He had to admit to himself that Octavia looked happier than he had ever seen her, and Phillips appeared to be behaving himself. But then, he realized that Phillips would not dare behave incorrectly with an Adair sister. He knew what he faced if he came up against himself. Ten would kill him, slowly and painfully if that was his want.

"*He knows I would kill him.*" He whispered his thought out loud as he caught Phillips's eye and glared fiercely at him.

"Octavia is so happy to finally dance," Birdie said firmly.

Ten glanced down at her and then back to his sister and Phillips. "True," he said under his breath. "*Forgive me. I was harsh with you. Still, I will not have her dancing with the likes of Phillips, nor will I allow you to make me forget my duty.*"

Birdie turned her face away from the look of fury in Ten's eyes. The music was ending. "The dance is over. *Forgive me for making you forget your duty.* It must be a miracle, for your sister is indeed, undebauched." She pulled free from his hold, curtsied quickly, and walked off the dance floor.

For the next few hours, she introduced any man that asked her to dance to Octavia.

She watched with pleasure as they escorted an incandescently happy Octavia onto the dance floor. To Octavia's credit, she only stumbled three different times with two different men, but she never fell completely to the floor, nor did she lose a slipper or her hose.

That Birdie knew of.

Until she saw Octavia hobble off the floor with her chin in the air and a calm smile firmly on her face. Birdie continued to stare, knowing that something was amiss. As she watched closely, she noticed that one of Octavia's slippers was tucked carefully under one arm, mostly out of view of anyone looking. Birdie happened to be watching at just the right time for, sure enough, the slipper slid down from where it was hidden under Octavia's arm. She watched as Octavia struggled to catch it before it fell to the floor.

Birdie hid her smile as Octavia resumed her nonchalant, ungraceful hobble off the dance floor. She had the slipper once more tucked securely away under her arm until she could reach a seat and put it back on.

Birdie also surreptitiously watched Freddie dance with almost every woman there, save herself.

She could not help but notice that Ten Adair was retained for several dances, which caused an odd feeling within her breasts. When Aunt Eggy saw her watching Ten, she informed her that she believed that each of the women that Birdie had seen him dancing with was one of his sisters. When Birdie questioned Aunt Eggy's choice of the word '*believed*,' Aunt Eggy admitted that she could not be sure if all of Ten Adair's dance partners were indeed his sisters.

Birdie had turned away, no longer watching Ten, but not before seeing the concern in Aunt Eggy's eyes.

CHAPTER TEN

B IRDIE WAS DELIGHTED to see that Freddie was sitting across from her at supper.

She was less delighted when Lord Phillips sat down on her left.

She was not sure how to feel when she saw Ten Adair's name elegantly scrolled on the seating card to her right.

She did not know what to make of the man, and that bothered her, terribly.

She thought of moving the card, but it was too late. He walked into the room beside another gentleman. The two were talking in low tones as they strolled down the length of the table, looking for their seating cards. Ten stopped beside Birdie upon reading his name and paused with his hand on the back of the chair. He turned and continued to speak quietly to the gentleman beside him.

Birdie did not look up at him. She took a sip of her wine and looked at the other tables placed around the room. Several other guests had sat down, while others were switching around name cards to their pleasure. There was an entire table of what appeared to be most of the Adair sisters.

As Birdie held the glass to her lips and continued to glance around the room, she caught the eye of Aunt Eggy and Empress Bibi, who had been escorted to the dining room. They were seated further down the long table. The two of them were grinning like mad women with their heads together as they raised their glasses to her. She arched a brow at them. They had clearly moved seating cards so that they may sit next to one another.

The two wily old women were partly blootered on their hashish and tobacco pipe, and the wine, no doubt. But then she saw Lady Prudence and Lady Lade also smiling at her from where they were standing at the entrance to the dining room. They all looked like cats that had caught the early birds. The very birds that had caught the worms.

"Humph," she mumbled as she set her glass down.

She avoided their eyes as she looked around the beautiful long dining room. It was lovely in the glowing candlelight.

One side of the room was a series of tall windows with elegant draperies in rich, ivory brocade. The other side was made up of white paneling, the architecture of which exactly matched the windows. Within each of the rectangles of paneling were ivory paper hangings with images of birds flying with branches of berries in their beaks. They were flying over individual scenes of couples lying under a tree. As Birdie stared at the paper hangings, she saw that each of the couples was lying entwined in various positions of amorous embraces and undress while cherubs with tiny wings fluttered above their heads, pouring their wine.

Birdie tilted her head, the better to see what the couples were doing, but then quickly looked away as she took another hasty swallow of wine.

"Tare an' hounds! Amorous chocolates, indeed," she whispered under her breath as she took a second quick swallow from her glass. She set her wine down and breathed deeply as she looked anywhere but at the paper hangings.

She inhaled the smell of the beautiful flower blooms arranged on the table. The pure, white flowers were arranged in tall, gold, Grecian urns down the center of the entire table. She was marveling at their beauty and the variety of the blooms when she realized within each urn, there amongst the flowers, was a smiling, entirely naked, golden cherub peeking out at the guests. In the case of the urn nearest her, it appeared that the little, naked cherub was smiling directly at her. She leaned forward. Not a smile, it was a leer. The little cherub statue's mouth was decidedly leering.

"Lud!" she whispered, and looked away as she took up her glass for another drink.

Several golden candelabras were also placed down the center of the table between the flower urns. Birdie studied the elaborate gold candelabra nearest her. She sat back abruptly in her chair. It was another naked, golden cherub, holding up the four stems of the candelabra while smiling mischievously.

"Thunder an' turf!" she murmured in a whisper. She looked down the table at Lady Chedworthy. She was busily chatting away with the guests that were entering the dining room.

Lady Letitia Lade gave her a huge, knowing smile and a wink and sat down in her chair near the end of the table. She tilted her head to the centerpiece of the table.

Birdie's eyes went to the tall centerpiece. *How had she missed that?* It was a three-tier golden tray laden on each tier with a selection of fruits and sugared biscuits. On the top tier stood a cherub made all in white sugar. His anatomy was missing nothing. In one of his open hands was a sugared strawberry. His other hand was to his lips as he blew a kiss while offering his sweets to the guests.

Birdie nibbled on her lips to stop from giggling. Lady Prudence and Lady Lade had a cherub theme for their supper table, obviously. "Goodness," she whispered, and shook her head once.

She could hear Lady Lade chuckling at her response.

As more guests came in to find their seats, Birdie glanced over at Ten Adair and the man. They were still speaking in hushed voices. She realized with a start that it was the prime minister, Robert Jenkinson, Earl of Liverpool, that Ten was speaking to so seriously! She grew quiet as she concentrated on their low voices. They were speaking about the French Grande Armee and their great loss of men and horses at Leipzig. Jenkinson said something about stopping Napoleon for good by exiling him to an island called Elba. After a few more words that she could not hear, they ended the conversation. The prime minister went to find his seat.

Interesting, Birdie thought.

Ten Adair pulled out his chair and sat down.

"Lord Fairfax." Birdie greeted him with a polite smile.

"Miss Darley," Ten said stiffly as he reached for his glass of wine without looking at her.

"Any news from the prime minister on those men stealing horses? Or perhaps Napoleon?" she asked him nonchalantly.

"None, Miss Darley," he answered with charm.

Birdie frowned, knowing that they had indeed discussed Napoleon. What should she make of his refusal to tell her what she did indeed know they were discussing?

She looked down the table and saw Octavia on the other side of Lord Phillips. She was not sitting with her sisters. Birdie watched as Octavia blotted up some drips of wine on her white ruffled gown as Lord Phillips looked at her with disapproval.

Octavia saw Birdie watching her and shrugged hopelessly as she laughed.

Birdie smiled in encouragement at her.

Then she looked across the table at Freddie. She hid her frown. He was listening to Charity Schellburne, who was seated beside him. She was chatting with animation to Freddie.

Lady Prudence Chedworthy took her table napkin, snapped it open, and placed it on her lap.

At this sign, bowls of white soup were served to the guests by several footmen.

Lady Chedworthy took the first dignified spoonful and smiled at the long table of her guests.

They too began sipping spoonfuls of the flavorful soup.

Lady Chedworthy's gaze returned to the prime minister seated at her right. "Prime Minister? Have we seen the last of Napoleon after his disaster at Leipzig, would you say?"

The prime minister set down his spoon as the murmur of conversation stopped around the tables. All eyes were focused on him.

"We hope so, Lady Chedworthy."

Lord Phillips spoke up in a loud voice. "Hope so, eh? He has no military left and no horses! They all froze to death. Never try to march an invasion in the winter. He is done, I say! Hiding in shame back in France."

Birdie said in a calm voice, "He could be taking this time to rebuild his army and find horses. Perhaps to make a last stand. A finale' of the Grande Armee."

Aunt Eggy grunted. "One cannae assume men who have tasted power such as he will just gae away."

Birdie looked down the table at her great-aunt. "'Tis true. Plato said, 'The measure of a man is how he holds his power.' Napoleon will not give it up so easily, I think."

Ten turned slightly toward her. He stared sharply at her in silence. He was rubbing at the dimple on his chin with his thumb and forefinger.

"*What?*" she mouthed.

He shook his head and looked away. He picked up his wine glass, put it to his lips, and drank. After a moment, he set it down and whispered under his breath, "Plato said, 'the measure of a man is *what he does with power.*'"

Birdie arched a brow at him. "'Tis the same."

"No." He grunted in annoyance and drank again.

Aunt Eggy slurped at her soup as she watched Birdie and Ten Adair with shrewd eyes. Her gaze returned to the prime minister. "Napoleon may find more men, but nae horses. I assume those horses that dinnae freeze tae death or starve tae death on the march *were eaten*," she said, pointing her soup spoon in the air with a dramatic flourish.

There were horrified gasps from all the tables.

"*Oh Lud*," Birdie whispered painfully under her breath. "*I had not thought of that!*"

She saw Ten's head whip around from where he had been staring at Aunt Eggy. She bent her head back quickly to her soup.

Aunt Eggy spoke louder. "There isnae a Frenchmon that is gaunnie give up his horse tae Napoleon's military after that bowfin, bampot's last disaster. Where dae ye suppose he will be getting horses noo?"

Birdie did not look up from her soup. *Wily Aunt Eggy*, she thought. How had Aunt Eggy figured out her mission for the queen? She must have been listening that night when the queen spoke to her at the ball! Her mischievous great-aunt had pretended to be hard of hearing!

She narrowed her eyes on her great-aunt. Aunt Eggy just stared calmly back as she shoved the tiny knot of her hair off her ear back to the top of her head and then patted it primly.

Well, why not just say it? Birdie calmly sipped from her soup spoon and lowered it back to her bowl. "He must be stealing them," she said into the quiet, and then waited.

"Dae ye mean smuggling them, dearling?" Aunt Eggy asked her in a loud voice.

Birdie could feel Ten staring at her.

Several of the guests at the tables began talking loudly all at once.

Birdie was just about to answer when she felt Ten's foot lightly press down on top of hers, and then it was gone. She glanced at him. His eyes were narrowed at her. He gave a very subtle shake of his head. She picked up her slippered foot and lightly kicked him in the shin.

His lips lifted into a warning wolf's grin.

He pressed his leg firmly against hers, restraining her, just as she was about to kick him again, harder.

Birdie's eyes widened at the feel of his muscled calf touching hers from her knee to her ankle. The man positively emanated heat.

He scowled fiercely at her.

She scowled back at him, but then batted her eyelashes. At

him. On purpose.

He gave her a charming, roguish grin and moved his leg from hers.

Birdie looked away from him and noticed Freddie was staring at her as well.

Empress Bibi said loudly into the chaos of discourse on Napoleon stealing their horses, "Stealing or smuggling, it is all the same, and whoever is doing it should be thrown in the dungeon, just as I told you, Egg Lady!"

The table became silent once more at the empress's commanding words.

Birdie looked up from her soup, straight into the prime minister's intelligent eyes. She could not help herself. "Is it not a crime if Napoleon is being helped by someone, perhaps even right *here*, in London?" she asked him. "'Twould be a treasonous, thieving, traitor if it were so. A felonious felon, at the very least."

She heard a soft, strangled groan from Ten Adair, but she ignored him.

The prime minister chuckled in a strained manner. "Miss Darley, Lady Ross, Empress, I assure you that Napoleon is not stealing nor smuggling horses from us." He chuckled again and looked around the table at the guests.

Birdie gave a furtive glance at Ten as the guests joined in the prime minister's laughter and began talking again. Ten was sipping his wine and staring at her with his sharp, green eyes. No, he was studying her, she thought. She saw something there in his gaze.

Birdie put her head down and concentrated on her soup. She knew the prime minister was staring at her. So were Aunt Eggy and Ten Adair, who had not looked away from her.

Birdie made a humming sound and concentrated on sipping politely at her soup when what she really wanted was to tip the bowl to her lips and drink it.

It was delicious and made of veal stock with fresh cream and almonds.

She was starving and managed to finish her soup in no time. After her last spoonful, she glanced up to see Charity and Freddie staring at her as they took gentile sips from their soup spoons.

Charity pursed her thin lips in distaste. She glanced at Freddie, batted her eyelashes, and smiled before looking back at Birdie. "You have a hearty appetite, Miss Darley. Quite like my brother Davis, I would say. He is rather overweight." She looked meaningfully at Birdie's bosom.

Birdie's mouth fell open at the direct insult, but she quickly closed it. "Thunder an' turf," she said in a quiet, polite voice. "That was rude, even for your set." And then Charity's brother's name registered. She took a calming breath. Her brother was Davis? "I know your brother Davis well, for I have raced my horse, Mo, against him at Newbury in Berkshire and other locations several times. Davis is not overweight or his horse could not carry him." Her voice tightened as she continued. "He is ruthless, however, and whips his horse as well as any riders that manage to pass him. I also know for a fact that he unbuckled a racer's girth and the saddle fell off the horse during a race. If the rider had not been skilled, that rider would of a certainty been killed under the hooves of all the racing horses."

Out of the corner of her eye, she saw Ten's body go tense as he turned his head to her.

Charity's eyes slanted into narrow slits. "You race against men?"

Birdie smiled. "Yes. 'Tis *common* for men to race their horses wherever and whenever they can, so 'tis *constant* and *continual* that I shall race against them, and I need not your *condoning* of it, nor your *condescension* of my racing or *critique* of my figure." Birdie did it; she could not help herself. She batted her eyelashes at Charity.

Charity's eyes narrowed even further. "Those men let you win, I'd wager. Or 'twas just a lucky chance," Charity said in a nasty voice. She hastily shut her mouth and gave a guilty, surreptitious glance around the table to see if anyone else had overheard her.

Birdie shrugged delicately. "Excellence is never an accident, Miss Schellburne. It is always the result of sincere effort and execution. Choice, not chance, determines your destiny. For we are what we repeatedly do. Excellence, then, is not an act, but a habit." She grinned widely, showing her teeth like a young lioness. "So, you see, those who know, do; those who do not know, insult those who know."

Charity opened her mouth to give a scathing retort when Ten cleared his throat, glanced at Birdie, and then across the table to Charity. He grinned charmingly at her.

"Tut, tut, tut, Miss Schellburne," he said in a low voice as he continued to grin. "It is easy to see the *resentment* a young lady may have for Miss Darley's *remarkable* figure and her *rare* and *renowned* expertise in riding, but one must be civil and not make oneself a *rival*. Even a *respectable* and *reputable* young lady such as yourself. *Rudeness* is never attractive on a lady."

Ten looked at Birdie and took a slow sip of his wine as he continued to stare at her over the rim of his glass. When he put the glass down, he said in a quiet voice to Birdie, "I win," he whispered in a sultry voice as his lips tilted up crookedly. "I had eight words to your six, I believe." He took another sip as he stared at her with his smile showing in his eyes. "And well done, by the by, I believe you used several pieces of Aristotle's quotes altogether. He raised his glass to salute her. "Clever little bird. However, the last is, 'Those who know, do. Those who *understand, teach.'*" He took another leisurely sip from his glass.

Birdie leaned toward him and whispered, "Mine worked better for the situation, and not because I willed it so."

Ten gave her a slow up-tilting of his lips as his eyelids lowered in an almost intimate way. "True. You win on that one," he whispered back in a velvety soft voice.

Birdie smiled with surprise at his words, not to mention the sultry tone of his voice and the way he was staring at her. What was Ten Adair playing at? A frisson of heat hurtled through her.

Charity whirled to Freddie. "Freddie!" she whined in a harsh whisper. "Did you hear what that man just said to me? He called me rude, and, *and uncivil!*" She placed her hand on his wrist to get his attention.

Freddie quickly yanked his arm out from under her hand and looked over at Ten.

Ten pulled his eyes from Birdie. He grinned leisurely back at Freddie. It was full of warning, and from between his narrowed eyes, a challenging, sharp, glitter of green could be seen. Ten arched his brow and waited.

Freddie's cheeks pinkened. "That man is Ten Adair, the Earl of Fairfax, Miss Schellburne." He looked away from Ten to Birdie. "Miss Darley, I understand that your horse, Mo, is undefeated in your races. Quite the jumper, and quick-legged as well." He smiled broadly in an attempt to be charming. "May I add how lovely you look this evening? Your gown is particularly beautiful."

Charity gasped again and sank back in her seat with a furious look at Birdie.

Birdie started to say thank you to Freddie, but she stopped when she heard Ten growl under his breath.

He was staring sharply at Freddie as he slowly and deliberately set down the wine glass in his hand.

"Too late for your false niceties, I would say, Rockingham," Ten gritted out. He began speaking sharply and rapidly in a low voice, "By the by, any word from your *older* brother Adam, the *true* Duke of Trenton? Perhaps you should speak to Jenkinson about him. No? You have never spoken to the prime minister about your brother's absence? Oh yes, you do *everything* through your general. That would be General *Schellburne*, of course. Such an obedient little soldier you are."

Freddie's shoulders went rigid. "*Fairfax*," he snarled as he stared back at Ten Adair.

"*Rockingham*," Ten growled in a low voice.

The two men went very still as each stared coldly at the other.

Neither of the men was going to give in or look away from the other.

Several footmen entered and took the soup bowls away while others marched in single file to place multiple platters of food all around the table.

Still, the two men stared in hostility at each other.

Charity pulled at Freddie's sleeve. "I am hungry, Freddie. Can you stop staring at him now?" she whined. "You are supposed to be paying attention to *me*, not Ten Adair or Birdie Darley!"

Freddie yanked his arm away from her without taking his eyes off of Ten.

Ten noticed Freddie's impatient response to the young lady and silently raised an eyebrow as he stared coldly at him.

Birdie looked back and forth between the two men with great interest. What was this hostile stare they were doing? Was it about Adam Rockingham's disappearance and missing ship? General Schellburne? Or was it about Charity's remarks?

Freddie's rude response to Charity's touch on his arm was also out of character.

As she was staring back and forth at the men, she happened to see the platter that had just been placed in front of her. She groaned quietly and whispered to herself under her breath, "Why do I always get the stewed celery in front of me?"

Ten continued to stare at Freddie as he reached for another platter, the one that had been placed nearest him. He shoved it roughly towards Birdie without looking at it or her. "Here," he grunted.

"Thank you," she whispered back as she stared at this new platter of food.

"My pleasure," he growled to her while he held Freddie's eyes.

Birdie looked over at him and then back to the plate that he had pushed toward her. "My thanks were not sincere," she whispered to him with a laugh in her voice. She stared questioningly at the plate of calf's feet jelly he had pushed toward her.

"My pleasure was," he said in a low voice while still staring intimidatingly at Freddie.

"Don't look away from Freddie, but this one is calf's feet jelly," she whispered softly to him. "I cannot abide it."

"It *is* terrible," he agreed without taking his eyes off of Freddie Rockingham.

Ten reached over to his right and pushed another platter toward Birdie. "There," he grunted as he continued to scowl at Freddie.

Birdie frowned and sighed in disappointment as she stared at a plate of larded sweetbreads.

Aunt Eggy's voice came to them just then. *"Captain Freddie*, I dinnae wish tae interrupt whatever it is that ye are doing doon that end of the table, but will ye pass that plate of Scotch collops doon this way? I dinnae want tae eat whatever this is in front of me. Some foreign dish I think from Prudence's travels around the world."* She shuddered.

The table went quiet at her rude manners. Guests were to eat what was within reach. Reaching over someone or passing dishes was not proper.

Lady Prudence cleared her throat in the silence and announced, *"Why not?* Let us pass *all* the platters around the table and find something we would like to eat!"

Lady Lade let out a booming laugh. "Bloody good idea! Devil take it, but I cannot stand the cursed jellies and this crimped cod's head in front of me! Pass me something bloody else!"

The guests laughed and began passing platters as the conversation around the table buzzed.

Freddie blinked several times as a plate of strongly fragrant boiled sole was held under his chin. He looked away from Ten Adair, down to the platter, and hastily passed it on.

Charity immediately began talking rapidly to Freddie with a relieved smile on her face that she had his attention once again. She passed him platter after platter, keeping him busy as she commented on and critiqued each dish.

Birdie laughed softly as she helped herself to some mashed turnips and baked chicken that had been passed her way. She offered the platters to Ten Adair. "Well done with Freddie! You won," she said softly to him. "Though I did not need your assistance in defending me, I do believe that Aunt Eggy gave you her assistance with staring down Freddie."

Ten arched a brow at her.

Birdie arched her brow back.

He raised his brow impossibly higher as his grin became a broad smile.

"Most impressive," she said, looking at his brow. "But still, I win," she whispered, and arched one of her raven-black brows sharply at him.

"Not a contest, Little Bird. And you did need my assistance."

Birdie nodded once. "I thank you for your help and all those words describing me beginning with 'r'. *Remarkable,* am I? *Rare* and *renowned*? Well done, indeed." She smiled cheekily as her eyes sparkled in the candlelight. "You like me."

Ten shook his head as he piled mashed turnips and chicken onto his plate. "No. I dislike you terribly."

CHAPTER ELEVEN

"AYE, I HAVE known him since he was a boy, just as I have that Freddie," Aunt Eggy was saying to Birdie over their breakfast meal of toast and jam and sausage.

Birdie kept her eyes on Aunt Eggy. Her wily great-aunt looked decidedly guilty. She was very interested in drinking her tea and would not look at Birdie over her teacup.

"Aunt Eggy, I am aware that you have known Freddie Rockingham for a very long time. My question was about Ten Adair, the Earl of Fairfax. I also know that you two were eavesdropping on what Queen Charlotte was speaking to me about. Out with it! What do the two of you know?" Birdie waited, but Aunt Eggy was still drinking her tea.

Empress Bibi laughed. "Are you going to drink that tea all in one gulp, Egg Lady?"

Aunt Eggy put her teacup on its saucer with a clatter of the fine china. "Bibi Babi!" she said. "Mind yer own tea!"

Empress Bibi looked at Birdie. "I think the man with the dent in his chin named Ten is the most handsome man I have ever seen. However, Freddie with his golden hair also catches my eye, but Egg Lady says he is something called an *idjut*." She sighed and took a large bite of sausage.

Birdie put her toast back on her plate and stared sharply at the two old ladies. "You are both avoiding my question!" She leaned forward. "Aunt Eggy? What do you know of Ten Adair? Is he a man that would steal horses?"

Empress Bibi choked on her food. "That is the question you ask?" She looked from Birdie to Aunt Eggy. "She is not asking you, Egg Lady, which man she should marry?" She made a *tsking* sound and stabbed another bite of her sausage.

Aunt Eggy scowled at the empress. "Ye know vera well why she is asking that question Bibi Ibi Babi Ibi, just as I dae." She turned to Birdie. "I cannae and willnae believe it of young Ten. He is as good a man as any I know and wouldnae be stealing horses." She banged her thin, bony fist on the table. "He isnae a traitor! He wouldnae be smuggling our horses tae that Napoleon." She made a harrumphing noise and picked her teacup back up.

Birdie's shoulders relaxed somewhat. "Aunt Eggy? Why do you look so worried then?" she asked quietly as she picked up her knife and began spreading jam on her toast.

Aunt Eggy turned to Birdie with worried eyes. "Queen Charlotte has asked a terrible task of ye, I think. I can see that ye are waring with disliking and liking Ten Adair. I can also see that ye still hold Freddie in high esteem. Ye have had a dream of him for sae long, 'tis hard tae let go. Ye must discover which man tae put yer faith in, my dearling. Ye must find oot which man ye can trust and which man deserves tae keep yer heart. Keeping means tae protect and cherish, tae hold, tae keep safe, tae have yer back, and *tae love*." She frowned sadly. "I must warn ye, a man who plays at being a thief cannae promise tae dae any of that. Though he may tell ye it is so, 'twill be lies coming easily from his tongue, and lies on his lips as he tries tae woo ye with his deceitful kiss. All lies, just like his life."

Birdie was silent as she stared at her great-aunt. She put her toast and knife down. "Do you believe Freddie could be the traitor leading the smuggling of horses, Aunt Eggy?" she asked softly.

Aunt Eggy looked over at Empress Bibi.

Birdie glanced at the empress. She looked concerned and was suddenly very busy eating with her head down.

"What?" Birdie asked with dread. Still, the two old women would not look at her. "What do you two know? What have you heard?"

Aunt Eggy pushed the tiny knot of hair that had fallen over her forehead back to the top of her head. She glanced at the empress.

Empress Bibi nodded solemnly once to Aunt Eggy. "You must tell her, my very best good friend, Egg Lady. She needs to know."

Birdie groaned and looked back at her great-aunt. "What do I need to know?" She clutched at her table napkin.

Aunt Eggy pinched her lips together and turned her sad eyes on Birdie. "Ten Adair is up tae something, dearling."

Birdie frowned. "Why do you say that?"

"One of his footmen told one of our housemaids who he has been walking oot with, who then told it tae one of our footmen who she had set her cap on, who talked aboot it with one of Bibi's lady's maids while the footman was in an amorous moment with *her*, and she mentioned it tae one of the kitchen maids, who told Mr. Druckbert, who told me." Aunt Eggy took several breaths and stared at Birdie as she clutched her thin fingers together tightly.

"Tare an' hounds that is a lot of talking and telling, Aunt Eggs." She stared at both of the old women as they looked back at her with worried faces. "But you said he is *up to something?*" Birdie asked. "What does that mean?"

Empress Bibi cleared her throat and said in a dark, ominous tone, "It means he has been acting…*suspicious!*"

Birdie looked back and forth between the old women again. "Thunder an' turf! That could mean anything." She exhaled heavily and toyed with her toast as she looked at their concerned expressions. "Eavesdropping and employing spies, are you? Is there anything else that I should know that the two of you have been doing? Hopefully, while you have *not* been smoking hashish!"

Aunt Eggy's face turned pink.

Birdie noticed the look of guilt in her great-aunt's eyes. "Out with it, Aunt Eggy," Birdie said firmly.

Aunt Eggy lifted her chin. "Freddie has been disappearing at odd times of the day and night."

Birdie stared at her. She took a deep breath and asked, "Go on, Aunt Eggs, tell me how you came to know that."

Aunt Eggy leaned forward and said earnestly, "His valet mentioned it to his cook, who happened tae mention it tae the butcher, who told our kitchen maid, who reported it tae our cook, who was gossiping with the coachman when she was bringing him dinner, and he mentioned it tae one of our footmen, who told Mr. Druckbert when he brought him the *Morning Post,* and Mr. Druckbert told me." She stopped and took a breath and stared at Birdie expectantly. "That is all we know aboot the two men, my dearling. But 'tis vera worrying, for both."

Birdie looked away from her great-aunt and the empress. She stared sightlessly out the window onto Grosvenor Square. "Oh *sards,*" she whispered. "Indeed, it is."

She had begun to trust Ten.

Now, she knew that she could not trust either man.

BIRDIE WALKED DOWN the stairs to the main hall in her warmest riding gown of deep indigo velvet. She held her short blue top hat that had an airy plume of pale blue ostrich feathers that would drape down from the hat to curl around her cheek. She also held a long pelisse of matching heavy velvet in royal blue. Here and there the velvet pelisse had embroidered vines and flowers done in fine, pale blue silk. The pelisse was also lined in a warm, fine fur and edged all down the front with white swansdown, which was also around the high collar and cuffs.

She was going to ride her horse Mo to the Frost Fair to meet Freddie for ice skating. Though she preferred to ride astride, she knew that she was expected to ride side-saddle when out in public, and not racing, of course.

When Mr. Druckbert had knocked quietly on her door moments ago and told her she had a guest waiting for her in the parlor, Birdie had been surprised. She thought that Mr. Druckbert was there to tell her that her horse was saddled and ready for her.

She had taken a deep breath and gathered her pelisse, gloves, and hat.

She assumed that it was Freddie and that he was actually going to escort her to the park himself, since it was he that had invited her. She walked toward the parlor, but stopped and paused before entering. Questions ran through her head. There was so much that she wanted to ask Freddie.

She pressed her hand to her abdomen, took another breath, and walked into the parlor with a smile firmly on her face.

And stopped.

It was not Freddie who had come to escort her.

It was Ten Adair.

He stood up hastily from his chair and turned to her with his hat in his hand.

Aunt Eggy and Empress Bibi remained seated together on the settee, watching Birdie and Ten with avid interest.

Birdie stared at Ten. She had always thought of him as too attractive, too handsome, and very much what she assumed a rake looked like. But, somehow, he looked more roughly masculine, larger, taller, and more intimidating standing here in the feminine parlor. Those green eyes of his bore into her, causing an uncurling of heat to race, throbbing, throughout her body. This feeling he caused was becoming too common, and it blocked her common sense and critical thinking on the matter of the identity of the horse thief.

"Hello," she said quietly with surprise. Her breath trembled from between her lips. Why had she never really and truly looked at this man?

"Good morning, Miss Darley," he replied with a bow of his head.

Birdie caught herself at the sound of his voice. Here in her parlor, the soft, deep, low tone of it hit her. A feminine awareness of this man caused that same feeling of heat to bloom there, at her most feminine core, once again. Just as it had when he had kissed her. She was surprised to realize how much she liked the sound of his smooth, velvety voice and how simply and easily it caused the reaction in her body.

She squeezed her thighs together, remembered her manners, and curtsied quickly.

Aunt Eggy and Empress Bibi continued to look back and forth between the two of them. They were clearly enjoying watching the scene.

Birdie and Ten stared at each other in silence, both looking quite uncomfortable and unsure of what to say.

Aunt Eggy watched them and rolled her eyes in impatience. "Weel, gae ahead! Tell my Birdie why ye have come!" she ordered Ten.

Ten grinned uncomfortably as he looked down at his hat in his hand. He held the brim of the top hat, rotated it between his hands, and then slapped his thigh with it.

"Skating," he mumbled.

"What?" Birdie asked him. She had been mesmerized by his hat, or was it his thigh? Or where his hat had *hit his thigh*? Her brain had gone soft, it seemed, at the sight, for his legs were muscular and showed to their advantage in his dark breeches and tall boots. The man rode often, she could tell.

He looked up at her then with a crooked grin. He lifted one hand from his hat and stroked his thumb over the dimple on his chin. "Octavia said that Rockingham had invited you skating."

Birdie frowned; her eyes were drawn back to his face and that lady-winning, dimple-showing, gleaming-white-toothed, charming smile he was giving her. "Yes, he did."

His grin tilted further upwards. "I thought I would escort you, if you will let me."

Birdie glanced at her great-aunt and the empress. They were smiling madly as they watched them with avid interest. She looked back at Ten. "I thought that perhaps you were Freddie, come to escort me."

Aunt Eggy snorted in disdain before catching herself.

Empress Bibi lit up a pipe and took a long puff without ever taking her eyes off of them standing in the middle of the room. She bumped Aunt Eggy's elbow to hand off the pipe to her. The two old ladies exchanged the pipe while managing to never let their eyes stray from the scene before them.

Ten cleared his throat and looked down at his hat. He turned his charming smile to Aunt Eggy and Empress Bibi before raising his head and looking back at Birdie.

"Freddie came to collect Octavia earlier," he said gently, and then sighed when he saw her go still at this news. "I rode to the Frost Fair to chaperon and did not see you there with Octavia and all the others." His jaw tightened as he stared at her. "I thought I would come by and escort you myself."

Birdie broke her gaze from Ten's. She looked away from him, ignoring her great-aunt and Empress Bibi's far-too-curious eyes. She walked to the tall windows of the parlor and stared outside. She saw Ten's horse there. It was tall and heavily bodied, well over the normal fifteen hands of typical cavalry mounts. It was dark with a noble head and a calm, wise eye. Clearly, it was an exceptional, finely bred horse. It also showed it was well cared for in its gleaming coat and extremely well-muscled body. A warhorse? Of course, it would be, to carry a man such as Ten Adair. And, of course, he would bring his loyal warhorse home safe from the hellish battlefields. Just as he had his men, or rather, most of his men. Those that he could save.

"He escorted Octavia, but not myself?" she repeated quietly as she continued to study the lines of Ten's horse. A Thoroughbred with some draft in it perhaps? Like her Mo?

She heard Ten walk up beside her.

"It appears so, *Little Bird*," he whispered. "My horse is just outside, and I saw that yours is saddled and waiting for you in the stable way." His voice lowered further. "I should be happy to escort you, *m'eun beag*."

Birdie shook her head, letting his use of m'eun beag, which meant *my* little bird, pass through her thoughts only fleetingly. "He didn't come to escort me, yet he collected Octavia." Birdie spoke softly as she gazed out onto the snow-laden park of Grosvenor Square. She barely glanced at Ten before her eyes returned to the window and his magnificent dark horse waiting there for him. "Your horse is standing so patiently without a groom, waiting for your return. You should go, but I thank you, Ten."

"Pride can wait," he said quietly.

Birdie's gaze snapped to his. Before she could remark, Aunt Eggy snorted into the silence.

"Och no, dearling. I ken what ye are thinking. Ye are nae staying home! Ye should gae tae this skating party!" Aunt Eggy called out to her.

"Egg Lady is correct. You must go." Empress Bibi's voice was shrill in her command.

"Dinnae let that idjut Freddie ruin yer day or yer plans. Gae! Gae with the handsome and kind man who stands before ye. Gae with Ten Adair. Ye shall have a better time of it, I ken!"

Birdie turned and frowned at her great-aunt. She put her hands on her hips, thought better of it, and shook her finger at her. "Aunt Eggy, this bit of eavesdropping you have been doing is becoming quite a bad habit."

Aunt Eggy ignored her. She patted her hair and smiled sweetly up at Ten. "Ye must take my dearling Birdie to the skating party, Ten, er, Lord Fairfax. Dinnae listen tae her feeling sorry for her wee self and having a fit of those blue devils."

Birdie scowled. "I am not feeling sorry for myself, Aunt Eggs!

I am just thinking." She looked meaningfully at her great-aunt. "Remember my promise to my *friend, Charlotte*? The one who needed some information about a man she was most interested in?"

"The idjut?" Aunt Eggy asked.

Birdie groaned and rolled her eyes.

Ten cleared his throat. "Pardon me, Little Bird, er, *Miss Darley*. Rockingham is indeed an idiot," he said in a firm voice. "Do not let the fact that he came to collect my sister in his carriage give you a..."—he glanced over at Aunt Eggy and then back to Birdie—"a sad fit of the blue devils." He exhaled harshly when she remained quiet. He forced his next words out rapidly in distaste as he stared past her shoulder. "The carriage was full, else I am quite sure he would have come here to collect you next."

Birdie bit her bottom lip to stop a smile from spreading upwards. Ten looked so serious, and rather angry too. Was he angry that she may have been sad that Freddie had not come for her? "Freddie lives here in Grosvenor Square, Ten. Why would he not have collected me first?" She arched a brow at him. "I do not have a sad fit of the blue devils. *Tare an' hounds,*" she added in a murmur. She shook her head at him and spoke louder. "Do you not wonder what his sudden interest in your sister is about?" She stared sharply at him, waiting for him to understand. When he did not, she continued in a quieter voice, "I cannot think it is good. It is quite clear after last night that he dislikes you terribly. You must go home and collect yourself. You must not cause a scene for Octavia. I shall investigate this and watch over Octavia."

Ten's eyes widened. He straightened his shoulders and stared at Birdie as her meaning dawned on him. "Damn his eyes! He is going to get even with me by wooing my sister?" he thundered. He paused as his eyes narrowed on hers. "Did you just *order* me to go home and *collect* myself?"

Birdie shrugged. "*I did*. What I say makes sense. Freddie has shown no interest in Octavia before this. Indeed, you must calm yourself, which is why *I* shall go and handle this. You'll make a mull of it and be planting him a facer in a public setting, which will not help Octavia in her pursuit of a husband. You would be making a scene if you do this *brash thing*," she said meaningfully, using his own words. "'Twould be *brash* and *boorish* and *brutish. Brazen* even."

Ten arched one of his brows as he bared his teeth in a tight grin. "Putting my fist into Rockingham's face would be *significant, sound,* and very *satisfying*," he said curtly as his eyebrow arched further.

Birdie grinned, counting off his words on her fingers. She shook her head at him as she held up three fingers. "I win."

Empress Bibi's eyes went back and forth from Birdie to Ten as she whispered, "What are they doing, Egg Lady?"

Ten stood there scowling at Birdie. "And, *and…*" Ten rubbed at his dimple but could not think of another word that began with the letter 's'.

Aunt Eggy took a puff of the pipe and then whispered back as she kept watching them, "I am nae sure, but 'tis most interesting and fascinating and I cannae stop watching." She handed the pipe to the empress.

Empress Bibi grunted in agreement as she took the pipe and stared avidly while puffing away.

Birdie smiled broadly at Ten. "As I said, *I win*," she repeated.

Ten arched a brow at her and gave her his best charming grin. "I could have thought of more words if I had a mind to. I *let* you win," he stated firmly.

Birdie grinned mischievously up at him. "Because you like me."

Ten's grin tightened. "I dislike you terribly."

"I think not," Birdie said lightly. "Go home. I shall handle this."

Ten snarled at her, slammed his hat onto his head, and whirled around to stalk from the room. He stopped suddenly when he realized the two older women were still there, huddled together on the settee. They were staring at him with great interest and overly huge grins on their faces while passing a pipe back and forth to one another. He narrowed his eyes at the smell that emanated from the pipe, but shook his head, not believing the aroma that he had inhaled. He bowed his head to the two old women and then stormed from the room.

Aunt Eggy and Empress Bibi turned from watching Ten leave the parlor to Birdie, who was staring after him as she nibbled on her bottom lip.

"Gae after him!" Aunt Eggy said firmly to Birdie. "Ye ken he is nae gaunnie home but tae the Frost Fair. He is gaunnie tae hit Freddie and Freddie has all of his friends tae help him beat back Ten." She made a *tsking* sound of worry. "'Twill be a bloody mull."

Birdie shook her head. "I know he will not go home. He is not that kind of man." She sighed as something bright filled her chest. "Perhaps 'twill not be a bloody mull, Aunt Eggy, at least not for him. Indeed, I have seen Ten Adair fight three men in an abandoned mews. He actually threw one of them across the alley!" She placed a hand over her breast and felt the pounding of her heart. "He is quite strong and rather intimidating and a very good fighter. 'Twas very invigorating watching him," she said with excitement as she relished the thought of that memory. "I believe he can take on any of Freddie's young friends." She dropped her hand from her breast and pounded her fist into her other hand. "Those bounders won't know what they got themselves into. They will end up with bloody lips and black eyes and perhaps even a broken nose or two! If I help Ten, they will fair even worse!" She made a slashing motion with her hand. "I'll bring my secret crop and I shall wield it!" she said viciously as she pointed up into the air with a stabbing motion. "Though I must make sure that Ten does not harm Freddie." Her arm lowered as she got very quiet. "What if Freddie is an even match for Ten?" She bit her lip again. "Thunder an' turf, I had not thought of Freddie. What if his friends are not useless young men of the *Ton*? What if his friends are strong men that he knows from the military?"

"Quickly!" Empress Bibi said to Birdie as she motioned wildly with her pipe toward the door. "The handsome earl with the dent in his chin may be killed by the golden-haired *idjut* and his men."

Birdie wasted no time. She hurried from the parlor.

Aunt Eggy grunted in satisfaction as she watched her hurry from the parlor. "She loves him."

The empress watched Birdie go as well. She breathed deeply from her pipe and handed it to Aunt Eggy. "She is an unusual young lady," the empress remarked. "All your great-nieces are unusual."

"Aye," Aunt Eggy said proudly. "They are descended from warrior women. The Ross clan was renowned for its strong women."

Empress Bibi smiled. "I shall have strong, warrior grandchildren then, with my Pasha married to your great-niece, Julia. This makes me very happy, Egg Lady."

Aunt Eggy nodded with pride as she held the pipe in the corner of her lips. She looked from the doorway to the empress. "Perhaps we should gae tae the Frost Fair tae, Bibi Babi." Aunt Eggy took a puff and then blew out a ring of smoke. The white haze billowed up and hung above her pink and balding head like a halo. She handed the pipe to the empress.

"Do you think Idjut will hurt the man named Ten, Egg Lady?" Empress Bibi asked as she took several long puffs from the pipe. She tried to blow a ring of smoke as she had seen Aunt Eggy do but did not have any success, even after several attempts. "I would not like that. Idjut is indeed an idiot."

Aunt Eggy took the pipe that the empress handed her and stuck it back in the corner of her lips. "I would rather tae swallow this pipe whole than think of Ten getting hurt," she said around the pipe stem. "But tae see Ten plant a facer or two on that idjut would please me vera much. Aye. 'Twould be most interesting," she said as she puffed thoughtfully on the pipe. Several smoke rings floated slowly above and around her head.

"Most interesting and fascinating, Egg Lady, and most amusing too." Empress Bibi looked at the smoke rings that Aunt Eggy had created so effortlessly with great interest.

Aunt Eggy pointed the stem of the pipe at the empress and spoke calmly. "His name isnae Idjut, Bibi Babi Beh. 'Tis Freddie."

Empress Bibi grunted and then grinned. "I know this, Egg Lady. I *prefer* to call him *Idjut*, just as you prefer to say my name oddly." She stared meaningfully at Aunt Eggy for a moment and then continued. "I shall be rooting for the handsome man with the green eyes and the dent in his chin whose name is the number Ten who has eight sisters to care for. I do like him, very much."

Aunt Eggy sighed long and loudly as she stared at the doorway that Birdie and Ten had gone through. "I dae tae, Bibi. He is a guid mon. The best of them. Even from a vera young age, he was a guid and loving and cheerful little boy and still remains so. He thinks of his sisters first and shall see that they make guid and happy matches." She sighed. "The *Idjut* hasnae become a grown mon yet, I think. Perhaps someday. But nae today. I think my dearling Birdie is becoming aware of this." She smiled secretly. "Birdie doesnae know it yet, but she nae longer dislikes Ten Adair. Now, she wants tae keep him."

Empress Bibi nodded solemnly. "It is clear to see that she loves him. A flaw that dent in his chin is, though intriguing. I find myself wishing I was a young girl again when I look at him." She primly touched her black hair and then her eyebrows, which were connected to one another with a thick line of kohl. "If I was young once more, he would surely have fallen in love with me."

Aunt Eggy snorted and laughed. "Ten Adair is meant for Birdie and nae one else, Bibi Babi. That is just the way life is. They are meant tae keep one another! They just have tae find their way tae one another's hearts, and we shall help them." She stared at the empress through the haze of pipe smoke. "Will ye gae tae the Frost Fair with me, Bibi?"

Empress Bibi sat up with alarm. She spoke in her high-pitched, staccato voice. "Will I have to ride that much-too-fat pony to this Frost Fair? Though I do want to watch Idjut get a *facer*, as you say, you know that I could not get off of that pony before when you made me ride it. It is too wide and too fat for my delicate bottom."

Aunt Eggy made a soft grunting sound. "'Twas nae the pony that was tae wide or tae fat. Though 'twas amusing tae watch ye, *and* yer *delicate* bottom, trying tae get off of it."

"Can we bring weapons?" the empress asked with excitement. "Miss Birdie has her sword in her crop. We should bring something too in case Idjut is a fighter and the man named Ten needs our help!"

Aunt Eggy looked out into the main hall and the display of ancient family weapons hanging on the wall there. She looked back at Bibi and smiled. "I think that is a guid idea, Bibi Ibi. A vera guid idea!"

CHAPTER TWELVE

B IRDIE WALKED OUT of the front door instead of going down to the corridor on the lower floor that led to the stables. She stood on the front steps, put her fingers to her lips, and blew out a shrill whistle.

Instantly, she heard a loud neigh and the clatter of hooves as Mo came trotting from the mews behind their house out to the street. The big horse stopped in front where Birdie was waiting.

Birdie smiled and ran down the steps to greet her horse. She patted his neck and offered Mo a small bit of biscuit that she had put in her pocket. She glanced at the sidesaddle, and with a determined look, she began to undo the buckles of the girth.

The stable groom came running up to her where she stood with Mo.

He stopped beside the horse, breathing heavily.

"Begging your pardon, Miss Darley! He just took off all of a sudden, and I could not stop him!"

Birdie smiled serenely at the young groom. "'Tis fine! I whistled for Mo and he came. It is our game. We have been doing this since he was a yearling." She handed him the sidesaddle, girth, and pad with a cheerful smile.

She led Mo over to a stone carriage step along the street and easily mounted her horse bareback.

Birdie waved and smiled at the groom who was staring at her

with his mouth open and his hands full of Mo's tack. She put her heels into her horse's sides and turned him with her seat. Instantly, Mo pirouetted on the spot and was cantering away in the direction of the Frost Fair on the Thames.

Birdie smiled. The morning fog had been dispersed by the bright rays of the sun. The air was chilly but invigorating. She took a deep breath of the morning breezes swirling past her face as she cantered down the streets.

And frowned.

The snow-packed streets were strewn with a brown, dusty substance, making it possible for the horses and carriages to move safely along the snowy streets.

Birdie crinkled her nose.

The smell in the air was pungent.

It was clear what that substance was. The city had used dried manure on the snow-packed streets. She supposed it was a good use for the fifty thousand horses, plus all the cattle, sheep, and pigs that lived in and around London. The manure was collected near the Smithfield Market area of the city.

She pushed Mo on faster until they came to the Thames where she brought him down to a trot as she looked for the Frost Fair just near the London Bridge. It was here that the river moved slowest and sometimes froze.

The banks on this side of the river were lined with elegant carriages with their occupants watching the activity. In one of the carriages, she spotted Empress Bibi's good friends Sir Gore Ouseley and Mirza Abul Hassan, the Persian ambassador, who was also titled the Envoy Extraordinary and Minister Plenipotentiary. They were watching the skaters as they sipped a hot beverage being served to them by one of Sir Ouseley's footmen.

She rode on and spotted a group of horses, including Ten's horse, standing together with a groom watching over them. She dismounted and handed the groom a coin to watch over Mo as well. As she walked past Ten's horse, she slowed her steps. The animal was even larger than she had thought, for she could not see over its back and wondered if even Ten could. She noted its thick, heavily-muscled body and feet the size of dinner plates. This horse was clearly part dray horse. It was truly magnificent, and intimidating as well.

She noticed with great sadness that it had several horrid scars marring its coat that she had not been able to see from her parlor window. There was a terrible scar just above one eye, and the tip of one ear was missing. A deep, ragged scar ran along the back of its haunches from his tail down its leg. All four of its legs had taken the brunt of the battlefield, it seemed, for they were heavily covered in lines and lines of scars that had healed in thick ridges and bare patches. The horse's knees and hocks and fetlocks were covered in knobs and bumps from old wounds as well.

She started to reach up with one hand to stroke the horse's gleaming neck when the groom called out to her.

"Do not touch that one, Miss! That one is fearsome, to be sure. 'Tis the Earl of Fairfax's old battle horse. 'Tis trained to fight, mind you! I'll not go near it myself!"

Birdie looked at the groom and then back to the horse. The horse's head was down, contentedly chewing at some hay that had been strewn on the ground for the horses.

She smiled at the groom and moved on, not wanting to disturb the horse or the groom.

She made her way along the bank of the Thames where people were gathered in groups talking and laughing and watching the skaters. The women wore warm, heavy, colorful cloaks or pelisses, and bonnets lined in fur with matching fur muffs. The men wore thick, wool greatcoats and tall hats and had scarves wrapped around their necks. Several of the groups were gathered around impromptu bonfires or under makeshift canvas tents.

She slowed her steps as she passed by a group of men engaged in quiet, tense conversation.

"Truman's Stable has lost so many that they plan to build a new block of stables that can be locked. It's a right awful business," one of the men said to the others. "Word is they are being 'procured' by the dragoon generals for the military. But why without payment, and *which* military, I say?"

Birdie slowed even more, but the conversation changed when the crowd of spectators erupted in applause at the skill of one of the skaters out on the ice.

She turned to see what had caused such excitement. She saw several young bucks showing off their skating skills, racing in fast circles and even skating backward. There were several young boys, amateurs, trying their skills at skating, falling and laughing and slipping about. There was also a group of six fashionable young men skating difficult figures with excellent execution, all together, as if following the steps and figures of a country dance. While others, much younger, raced one another up and down the frozen river.

What the spectators had applauded for became clear, however. Closest to the bank where the crowded throng could watch best was a single man with two young ladies. He was skating in circles around the ladies. She watched as he twirled and spun and changed direction and skated around and in between them. The ladies clapped and squealed their delight as he showed off his skill to them as well as to the throng of onlookers' pleasure. Now and then he would grasp one of the young lady's hands and pull them along as they slid in their boots and squealed and giggled with delight. Then he would break off and describe more incredible spins and twirls on the ice, and the throng which crowded the bank would once again burst into applause.

Birdie looked closer.

Of course.

It was Freddie.

Birdie was about to walk closer to the edge of the ice when her attention was drawn to one of the ladies near him.

She wore a pelisse completely made up of swansdown. She even had white booties and a white bonnet with dramatic white plumes. She looked rather like a swan herself.

Birdie could not imagine the outrageous cost of her attire.

And then she recognized the young lady as Miss Charity Schellburne.

Birdie bit her bottom lip and decided to move on to find Octavia.

She looked all around as she walked along the edge of the frozen river.

There were several booths set up right on the ice with vendors hawking coffee, black tea, and cups of hot cider or hot chocolate. There was even gin and Brunswick Mum, a German black beer. There was a booth selling purl, which was a wormwood ale. Others offered biscuits and scones or sweet rolls, hot apples, roast mutton, or beef.

There were crowds gathered around the booths; some were standing, and some were sitting on benches. They were eating and drinking and watching the skaters. More of the dusty manure had been spread so the crowds could meander from booth to booth safely.

There were people dancing to the tune of a small orchestra and more people playing nine-pin bowling.

Birdie thought it all looked lively and exciting and excellent amusement.

She spotted Ten out on the ice sitting on a wooden bench near one of the booths. He was strapping on some wooden skates to the bottom of his boots. Birdie could see that the booth was renting skates to the public, for they had shelves and shelves of wooden skates with curled iron blades. Octavia was standing next to Ten, bundled up in a warm, long pelisse and bonnet, looking around with excitement as she clung to one of the poles of the booth so as not to slip on the ice.

She watched as he stood up and skated around, testing his skates, moving forward and backward and spinning once. Then he skated forward to Octavia with a grin. He offered his gloved hands out to her to pull her along.

Birdie stood still with her breath held. She was captivated by watching him skate so effortlessly backward. He was giving his sister such amusement as she slid along with him, clutching his hands as they both laughed with joy.

As she watched, they disappeared into the crowd of skaters and she lost sight of them.

"Miss Darley! You came!"

The sounds of skates sliding to a stop on the ice made her look to her left.

Birdie took a deep breath and forced a smile on her face. "Hello, Freddie." She looked around, expecting to see a bevy of young ladies following him. "Where are your friends?"

Freddie skated right up to the edge of the river, closer to her. He motioned with one gloved hand up the bank. "Chari and the others are getting warm by one of the fires."

Birdie looked up the bank as well and saw the two young ladies standing with a group of young people near a large fire. "Tare an' hounds, I hope Miss Charity does not catch her swan feathers on fire."

Freddie just looked at her, a bit uncomfortably and nervously. "I am sorry I have not had time for you, Birdie."

Birdie turned back to him. "Why haven't you, Freddie?" she asked quietly.

Freddie looked away. His cheeks turned even redder under his top hat, and his breath blew out in a white cloud in the chilly air.

She watched as he rearranged his scarf around his neck and chin. He held one hand out to her. "Come. You can slide."

Birdie did not speak, but took his hand and stepped carefully out on the ice.

He smiled wryly. "Perhaps this is one thing I can do better than you, Bird," he said with a short laugh.

"What?" Birdie said with surprise as she shuffled along, sliding beside him.

He darted a glance at her. "I know that you think I am foolish and unwise."

Birdie stopped. She was startled.

He stopped as well and stared down at the ice beneath his feet. "You think I should have already accepted the title of duke, even though we do not know the truth of my brother's disappearance. All the young ladies think this."

"You did not hear that from me, of a certainty! *Lud*, you are short on ears and long on the mouth if you believe I said that. All the young ladies do *not* think this. Perhaps Miss Schellburne, but not I."

"Still, I believe you think I am foolish."

Birdie frowned. "I object to intellect without logic, common sense, and critical thinking. Perhaps I feel you are foolish in some of the company you choose to keep, but that is none of my business."

His jaw tightened. "There are things you would not understand."

"Enlighten me then," she retorted firmly.

"Chari Schellburne is my general's daughter. His dearest wish is that I court and wed her. He bids me to accompany her to balls and assemblies."

Birdie stared up at him. She had known him forever, it seemed, yet this man standing before her, she did not know at all. "And, of course, he and his daughter wish for a duke." She paused. "You must do as General Schellburne bids?" She watched his face. He would not look at her. Her voice lowered. "Is there anything else he has bid you do for him? He is an important dragoon general, after all." When he did not answer but only continued to look away from her, she laid her hand over his.

He pulled abruptly away with a hiss of pain as he laid his other gloved hand over his wrist.

"Forgive me!" She stared down at his wrist. The same wrist she had noticed the night before. "Freddie? *Are you injured?*"

"'Tis nothing," he growled, still without looking at her.

"May I see?" she asked quietly.

He shook his head adamantly. "It is nothing, I tell you," he said angrily.

She gentled her voice. "Freddie, are you mixed up in some trouble?" She paused for a moment, studying him. "The horse thefts, perhaps?"

His eyes returned to her then. "Why would you ask such a thing?" he asked coldly.

Birdie remained silent as she stared into his eyes.

Freddie sighed and then gave her a charming smile. "Forgive me. I know you are acting out of concern. You are the dearest of friends, Birdie." He eyes darted to the ice under his blades and then back to Birdie. He leaned down and kissed her lips. His mouth lingered there as he whispered against them, "Do not concern yourself with this."

He drew back and stared meaningfully at her as he smiled once again. He touched her cheek with one finger. "Forget this, *for me?*"

Three of his friends from the *Ton* came skating up with big smiles on their faces. "Come on, Rockingham, we came here to skate!"

Freddie glanced at them, but then continued to stare at Birdie.

She reached up and touched her lips. She had been momentarily shocked at the brief feel of his lips on hers. Even his scent had not stirred her as Ten's did. She also did not like what she saw in his eyes. He was hiding something. She looked down at his wrist and thought of the wound he appeared to have there.

Could it be from that night in the mews when she struck out with the knife in her crop?

"Get away from her, Rockingham!"

Birdie looked up from Freddie's wrist to see Ten come skating toward them. He slid to a stop and turned to stand beside Birdie as he glared at Freddie.

"Pon rep, Fairfax!" Freddie laughed. "Are you bosky? What are they serving in those booths?" He laughed again and looked at his friends with amusement on his face, but then quickly turned back to Ten. His grin fell away and an impudent scowl took its place.

"I know you escorted my sister Octavia to anger me," Ten snarled.

Freddie smiled nastily. "Did it work?"

His friends laughed at that.

Octavia! Birdie thought with a start. *Where was she?* Birdie looked around for Ten's sister and saw her sitting on a bench out on the ice. She was strapping on skates!

"Thunder an' turf! Ten, *Octavia is putting on skates,*" she said quietly with grave concern.

Ten ignored her as he continued to snarl at Freddie.

"Stay away from Octavia, Rockingham, and stay away from Birdie as well," he growled in a low voice.

Freddie narrowed his eyes. "Miss Darley will do *and choose,* as she wants. You can have no say in that."

Ten lunged at Freddie and sent his fist into his face so hard it lifted Freddie off of his feet.

He landed on his back on the ice with a stunned look on his face. His friends stared at Ten with their mouths open. With a look at each other, they charged at Ten.

Ten was punching and spinning as they came at him from all sides. No sooner had he planted his fist in one man's face when another came at him. He punched that one across the nose and then the next man was charging him.

Birdie watched in horror as Ten went down to the ice with the three men pummeling and kicking him.

She reached inside her pelisse and pulled out her crop from where it was stuck down into the calf of her boot.

She waded into the fray without a thought for her safety, swinging the crop at anyone in her way. She swung for their faces as Lady Lade had taught her. The stinging crop sent them back away from Ten.

She stood over his prone form, straddling him with her feet on either side of his hips as she stood there, glaring at the men. She twisted the handle of the crop. The sharp glint of the knife point rose. She stayed ready, looking from man to man as she pointed the crop at each of them.

"Leave, you bunch of mockit, manky, mingin, mauchit, *scunners!*" she said curtly to them.

"*Eun Beag,*" Ten growled.

"Hush," she commanded without looking at him. "If you can't beat them, I must join you."

Ten growled again. "'Tis, 'if you can't beat them, *join them.*'"

Birdie made a face. "Yes, yes, but it makes no sense when said that way. Join your enemy? *Tut, tut, tut,* Ten!" She looked pointedly at Freddie. She gave a short laugh as her eyes raked over the others. "Why would I ever do such a thing?" She turned and glanced down at Freddie again. "You should go too," she said quietly. "Take your *friends* with you."

Freddie rose slowly from the ground, cradling his jaw. He motioned with his head for the other men to go.

Birdie stayed where she was, guarding Ten, until the men moved away. She noted that they had not gotten away unscathed from Ten Adair's fists without several bruises of their own. She spotted one with a bloody lip and missing tooth, another clearly had a broken nose, and the third would have a black eye.

She stared after Freddie as he gave a snide look down at Ten and glided awkwardly away on his skates, still holding his jaw.

Birdie turned slowly back to Ten. She offered her hand to help him up, but he snarled and arched a brow at her. He rose from the ice without her assistance and glared at her.

"What were you thinking? You could have been hurt! I did not need your help! Nor did I need you to bloody *fight to protect* me. A man protects his woman, not the other way around. As you can see I am unscathed. I did not need your help." He grabbed his top hat from the ice and slammed it on his head. "You are incorrigible, indiscreet, interfering, and irrational." He slammed his hands to his hips. "And possibly insane."

"What were *you* thinking? You hit him? And those young men of the *Ton*? Here, on the ice, with hundreds of spectators *watching?*" She glared right back up at him. "How will that affect your sisters' reputations?" She, in turn, slammed her hands to her hips, mimicking his stance. "That was incautious, ill-considered, imprudent, imbecilic, and definitely, inexpressibly insane!" She arched a brow at him. "I won." She stared at him and waited for him to argue further. "Well, what have you to say for yourself?"

Ten rubbed at his dimple as he stared at her with angry, frustrated eyes. "I saw him kiss you," he said in a hoarse voice.

Birdie's hands dropped from her hips as she took a breath. She expelled it harshly. "He kissed my lips only *briefly*. And what right do you have to interfere? You do not know what preceded that kiss." Her eyes raked his face, seeing his flushed cheeks and the angry glitter to his green eyes. The man hated Freddie. "You do not know Freddie as I do."

"*I know him*," he said with controlled fury. He looked away from her as he struggled for patience. "You cannot be serious in choosing him." He seethed quietly as he glared at the lingering skaters that had been watching the scene. They quickly moved off at the look on his face.

Birdie's face turned pink. "You know *nothing of it*, Ten Adair. I have known Freddie since we were young. I am content—"

But he did not let her finish. His head whipped back around to face her. "Stop," he said curtly.

He stepped close to her. His voice dropped as he looked her up and down. He noted that her dashing blue men's top hat was tilted precariously from her fighting to protect him. He righted it and then ran his finger over the light blue ostrich feather curling lovingly around the perfect curve of her ivory cheek. He paused to stare into her angry eyes with equally furious eyes of his own.

"*Content?*" he asked in a harsh whisper as jealousy rose within him. "Don't you dare settle for *content*. A woman like you deserves a man who makes you feel like you are a burning candle. Like hot wax melting before a bloody bonfire each time those seductive lavender-blue eyes of yours meet his. Like you have a blazingly bright bolt of bloody lightning sizzling through your body every time you see him, speak to him, feel his touch. *Just as he feels the same for you*, curse it." He took several breaths as his hands fisted at his sides. He spoke slowly and firmly. *"Don't you dare settle for content.* A woman like yourself deserves more. Rockingham doesn't bloody deserve you, *Eun Beag."*

He stared down at her for several moments as he breathed heavily with his breath coming out in great clouds of white in the cold air. His green and glittering eyes raked over her face.

Without warning, he pulled her into his arms and slammed his mouth to hers with a groan. He kissed her deeply, instantly slowing the kiss to one of tenderness and possession, and instant, intense, intimate passion. Just as quickly as he had pulled her against his taught body for that perfect kiss, he set her away from him.

Birdie was stunned and could not speak. She felt all the things he had described. She felt a blazingly bright bolt of lightning sizzling through her body. She felt like hot wax wanting to melt into a puddle at his feet. The familiar feel of heat settled there between her thighs. And then a smile grew on her lips. He had said, *"a man protects his woman, not the other way around."*

She stared back up at him with wide, astonished eyes. She placed her fingers there on her lips, savoring that perfect kiss.

"You like me," she whispered.

He raised his dimpled chin and looked down at her as he made a growling sound from somewhere deep in his throat. He was about to turn to skate away from her when, suddenly, he froze and looked over her shoulder.

"What the bloody blazes are they doing?"

Birdie whirled around to see what he was staring at.

Her eyes widened at the sight that met her eyes. *"Thunder an' turf,"* she whispered.

CHAPTER THIRTEEN

AUNT EGGY AND Empress Bibi had arrived.
With their weapons.

They were each carrying an ancient battle ax and were sitting astride two wide, short, stout, black ponies. The two old ladies were bundled up in fur-lined, long pelisses, the collars of which covered them to their noses. Both were wearing woolen turbans that sported garish-colored feathers.

"Aunt Eggy?" Birdie asked hesitantly as she stared at her great-aunt in her pompadour pink woolen pelisse and matching turban that she had evidently stuck feathers into. "What are you two up to?"

Aunt Eggy lifted her rusty, dented battle ax. She spoke in a muffled voice from behind the high collar of her pelisse. "Tell her, Bibi Ibi!"

Empress Bibi raised her battle ax. The blade was chipped and dented. It looked out of place with her regal pelisse. The pelisse was heavily embroidered in gold thread on ivory wool. On her head, she wore a bright, sunny, yellow turban with an array of feathers in many colors. "We have come to fight Idjut!" she declared.

Ten stared at the two old women. He rubbed at his dimple as he tried to remain serious, but his smile reached his eyes.

"Who did you come to fight? I cannot hear you from behind

your collars."

Aunt Eggy lowered her battle ax with a stifled groan and pulled down her collar. "The idjut Freddie. We have come tae help ye, Ten. We willnae let him hurt ye."

"What the devil!" Ten exclaimed as he stared at the two old women.

Birdie put her hand momentarily over her mouth to hide her grin. "Aunt Eggy, Empress Bibi, I cannot believe that you rode here carrying those old weapons that I know very well you took off the display in the main hall. You are most fortunate that you did not hurt yourselves or those ponies!"

Empress Bibi's eyes scowled at her from above her high collar. "We are warriors, and these are our warhorses."

Ten let out a muffled snort from behind his hand, which covered his mouth.

Birdie looked sternly back at him.

He pursed his lips and became serious.

Birdie cleared her throat as she turned back to her great-aunt and the empress. "The fight is over," she said calmly.

"We missed it?" Aunt Eggy said with disappointment.

"A war does not make the warrior," Ten said in a serious voice. Still, he could not help the grin that grew on his face at the sight of the two old ladies and their ancient weapons on the old, shaggy ponies.

"Did that idjut hurt ye, Ten?" Aunt Eggy demanded.

"No," Birdie replied before Ten could speak. "He did not get hurt. I defended him myself. I had my crop with the secret knife. It was most useful and the men were clearly intimidated."

Ten groaned.

"Och, were there many against him, dearling?"

Birdie nodded. "Oh yes, there were three of them *and* Freddie. But I managed it."

Ten groaned louder and put his face into his hands.

Birdie glanced at him and then back to her great-aunt and the empress and the ponies they were on.

The two old ponies were standing there with their heads low and their eyes almost closed.

Aunt Eggy adjusted her turban. "Bobby and Flora were vera excited tae ride intae battle, I can tell ye!"

"Yes, Aunt Eggy, I can see that they are indeed very excited."

Ten looked up. "Who the bloody devil are Bobby and Flora?"

"The ponies," Birdie, Aunt Eggy, and Empress Bibi said all at once.

At his confused look, Birdie explained, "Aunt Eggy purchased the two old ponies from the Marquess of Lansdowne. Or rather, she was obligated to purchase them, after she and the empress had *borrowed* them without asking, you see. They had needed the ponies to ride after my sister Julia when she had been taken by some assassins from Persia that had been sent to kill the prince's betrothed." Birdie pointed to Empress Bibi's pony. "The short and stout mare is named Flora McDonald. Aunt Eggy named her after the woman that helped save the life of Bonnie Prince Charlie."

Ten was grinning again now. "Tut, tut, tut, don't let Queen Charlotte hear that, Lady Ross."

Birdie pointed to the other pony that Aunt Eggy was sitting on. "That wide gelding is named Bobbie Burns after the Scottish poet."

"Of course it is," Ten murmured.

"Weel then," Aunt Eggy said as she looked around. "Is there anyone else ye need us tae fight, Ten?"

"No, Lady Ross," he said quickly, holding his hands with his palms toward her to stop her. "There is not. I assure you! Perhaps you would like to dismount and warm yourselves by one of the bonfires?"

Empress Bibi made a long, muffled sound from behind her collar.

"No one is gaunnie hear ye behind that thick collar, Bibi Babi. What did ye say?"

The empress pushed down her collar just enough to expose

her mouth. "I said I am not getting off! I shall fall on my delicate bottom in the *snow!*"

Ten hid his grin. "I shall leave you then. Thank you for, er, coming to my aid with your *battle axes*."

Aunt Eggy nodded regally and turned her pony around. She looked back to see Bibi's pony still standing there, sleeping, while Bibi stared ardently at Ten. She turned her own pony back around, reached for Bibi's reins, and pulled her along with her.

The two stout old ponies ambled slowly back up the bank carrying the old ladies.

Birdie turned to watch Ten skate away into the crowds on the ice until she could no longer see him.

After a long moment of trying to find him so that she could watch him skate, she gave up. She turned away, looking back to the benches to see if Octavia was still there tying on the wooden skates. She did not see her anywhere near the booths or out on the ice.

She decided to walk back up the bank to have a better vantage point to look out over the ice and the skaters there. She could not shake her concern at Octavia trying to skate on her own.

As Birdie began to walk up the bank, she heard the empress making a fuss about something.

She stopped a moment. She also heard men's voices.

Birdie picked up her skirts and hurried up to the top of the bank.

She stopped abruptly and put one gloved hand to her mouth as she stared at the scene before her.

Sir Gore Ouseley and the Persian ambassador, Mirza Abul Hassan, had gotten out of their carriage. They were standing on either side of Empress Bibi where she still sat astride on the short pony. It appeared that they were attempting to help her off the wide little mare.

Her battle ax was being held carefully by Mirza Abul Hassan. He was holding it well away from him as if it were a snake.

Aunt Eggy was shaking in silent laughter, and now and then offering suggestions and encouragement to the two men trying to help the empress off of the short pony.

"I told ye tae lift her right leg and put it over the wee pony, Mr. Mirza!" Aunt Eggy called out.

Mirza Abul Hassan picked up the empress's right foot and tried to lift it at the same time that Sir Gore Ouseley tried to lift her other leg, holding her at the ankle.

Empress Bibi shrieked and fell forward, clutching the pony's mane with one hand. With her other hand, she began swatting at Mirza Abul Hassan and then switched hands to swat Sir Gore Ouseley away from her leg.

"I am your Supreme Imperial Majesty, Hassan!" The empress spoke shrilly in her high-pitched voice. "I have told you that you may not touch my foot! If you desire to keep the title of Envoy Extraordinary and Minister Plenipotentiary, you will not dare touch me again!" She glared at Sir Ouseley. "And you! How dare you touch me, Sir Owley!" She swatted at his hand again when he tried once more to lift her leg. "Stop that, I say!"

Aunt Eggy tried to contain her laughter, but she started snorting.

Birdie hurried forward. "Empress, they will have to touch you in order to assist you off of Flora McDonald, else you shall have to dismount yourself. 'Tis no other way."

Empress Bibi stared red-faced at Birdie. She was breathing heavily, leaning forward clutching the pony's neck in terror. "I will fall," she said through her breaths.

Birdie looked from the empress's leg to the ground. "Perhaps only a foot or two. Either you let these kind men help you or you slide off by yourself." She looked meaningfully at the ground beneath the empress's left foot.

The empress looked down to the ground as well. "Oh," she moaned miserably as she tightened her grasp on the pony's neck. "I cannot! I will fall on my delicate bottom in the snow and slide down that bank onto the ice! I know I will!"

Aunt Eggy guffawed at that. "Och, I should dearly love tae see that," she said through her laughter and her belly rising and falling.

"Egg Lady, this is *not* amusing," Empress Bibi said shrilly. She motioned for Birdie to come forward. Her face turned impossibly even redder. When Birdie came to stand next to her, she waved Birdie even closer until Birdie bent her face close to hers. Only then did she speak in a hoarse, shrill whisper, "I am a Supreme Imperial Empress. No man can touch me, or my *legs*, save the Emperor, my husband." She lowered her voice further. "I must tell you that even *he* has *never* once touched my legs." She stopped and stared at Birdie as she gulped and tried to calm her breathing.

Birdie stepped back as she stared at the empress. "I see. Yes, of course." She frowned over at Aunt Eggy. "Aunt Eggy, *tare an' hounds*, stop that laughing at once." She looked back at the empress, who was still clutching the pony's neck.

Empress Bibi looked down at the snow. "Miss Birdie, I want to get into the carriage, but I am not used to snow. I shall slip and fall down that bank." With her high voice, she sounded like a little girl.

Birdie thought for a moment and nodded her head once. She went to the head of the pony and walked it forward, well away from the bank. "There. You cannot slide down the bank now; all is well!"

Aunt Eggy handed her own battle ax to Sir Ouseley. She rode her pony closer and whispered to the empress, "Dinnae be afraid of the snow, noo. Birdie has made it right. But yer gaunnie have tae lift yer skirts oot of the way, Bibi Ibi, sae that ye may put yer right leg over the horse. I shall make sure that no one can see ye." She moved her pony over to the right side to block Empress Bibi's exposed leg from any curious male eyes.

Empress Bibi nodded. "Thank you, Egg Lady, and Miss Birdie. I thank you most sincerely." She peered at the two of them sharply. "Though this is most evident why a lady and a Supreme

Imperial Majesty should not have her *bottom* on an *animal*, much less sit *astride*. 'Twould have been easier to ride side-saddle. *No!* 'Tis best to *sit* in a sedan chair and have footmen to *carry me!*"

Aunt Eggy snorted. "'Twould take an army of footmen tae carry ye, and then ye would have no army left tae command. Which means that ye could niver be a *warrioress* yourself, Bibi Babi, unless ye change yer *vera poor* thinking this instant."

"Aunt Eggy!" Birdie said with reproach.

Aunt Eggy looked at her with her brows raised innocently. "Did I say anything wrong?"

Empress Bibi glared at her friend and spoke shrilly. "I do not believe you said anything right!"

Aunt Eggy pursed her lips at the empress. "I was vera right."

The empress's mouth dropped open and then closed abruptly. "Never say that, Egg Lady! I could be a warrioress!" She began hiking up her skirts.

Birdie was about to reach up to help the empress get down and then escort her over to Sir Gore Ouseley's carriage when she heard a loud crack rend the air. There came screams, and then another louder crack, and then several more frantic screams.

Birdie spun around to the frozen river. She scanned the crowds who were now running for the bank, south of where she was standing.

She could see that the ice near the Frost Fair booths had cracked and several skaters had fallen into the freezing water.

The brown dirt and dust from the dried manure spread there for the pedestrians seemed to be having the effect of softening the ice.

Birdie watched in horror as people ran past those screaming for help as they thrashed about in the water trying to pull themselves back up onto the ice.

"I must go!" she called back to her great-aunt.

She kept her eyes on the figures in the water as she ran along the bank, pushing past the people rushing away from the river when she spotted Ten. He skated toward the open ice, skidded to a stop, and dropped to lay flat on his belly, dispersing his weight over the fragile, cracked ice. She watched as he reached his hand out to those in the water.

She was about to hurry down the bank to help him when another loud crack and a single scream came to her.

Aunt Eggy called out, "Birdie! *'Tis Octavia!*"

Birdie stopped and looked back at her great-aunt. She saw that she was pointing frantically north. Birdie looked up the river and saw that Octavia had gone through the ice there. Two young boys were lying flat on their bellies over more cracked ice next to the hole. The boys were clinging to Octavia's hands to keep her from falling in further. Each time the boys tried to move, the ice cracked further while Octavia struggled to hang on.

The ice on the Thames was thawing!

Birdie changed direction and ran back along the bank, pushing her way through the crowds until she was past them all and just above Octavia.

"Tare and hounds, *hang on, Octavia!* Hang on, boys! I am coming!" she called out with terror in her voice.

"Birdie!" Octavia called in desperation and fear.

Birdie ran down the bank and slid to a stop.

The ice was cracking even at the shoreline.

She pulled out her crop, hoping it would reach Octavia, but she realized that Octavia and the boys were still out of her reach.

"Birdie! Help!" Octavia cried out again.

Birdie frowned fearfully as she looked around frantically for something to use to reach out to Octavia, but there was nothing but snow. "Hang on! I must find some way to reach you all! *Hang on!*"

Birdie looked up the bank to Sir Ouseley and Mr. Mirza, but she could not see them. Aunt Eggy and the empress were alone, standing there watching her with white, frightened faces.

"Where are Sir Ouseley and Mr. Mirza?" she called out.

Aunt Eggy shook her head. "They went tae help doon the other end!"

Thinking quickly, Birdie put her lips together to whistle for Mo. She waited, but did not hear him neighing to her or even trotting toward her. She ran up the bank to where the horses had been left standing with the groom.

Every single horse was gone save for Ten's horse.

Mo was nowhere to be seen.

She tamped down her rising panic and hurried over to Ten's huge horse. She began to quickly untie his lead as the horse snorted at her and stomped one of his enormous, dinner plate-sized front hooves.

Birdie hastily moved out of the way of his hooves as she continued to untie the lead. "Hush, Pride. That is your name, is it not?" she spoke rapidly. "I desperately need your help and I need you to *behave*. We must save my friend and two young boys." The rope came free. "Come!" she commanded.

She began to lead him away when he stopped, raised his gigantic head, and leaned back against the rope.

Birdie huffed out a breath as she tried not to cry with fear for Octavia. "Please, *please,* Pride," she whispered, and reached out to stroke the horse's big cheek, but he snorted and yanked his head away from her hand. She looked up at his scarred eye. "You can't see out of that eye, can you? I surprised you by reaching for your cheek." She quickly moved to his good side where he could see her better.

Instantly, the horse let up the tension on the rope. "Better now that you can see me? Good. We must hurry, *now,* Pride," she said quietly but firmly.

This time, the horse came willingly. She led him quickly down the bank to the edge of the broken ice. "Stand," she ordered quietly as she took a single step out onto the ice.

A new crack spread from under her foot. She slowly took another step and then another, inching along as she kept her hold on Pride's rope until she was at the end of the lead rope. The cracks were getting bigger and louder, spreading out farther along the ice. She lay down on her belly as she had seen Ten do, spreading out her weight.

"Octavia! I can come no further. I am going to reach out to you with my crop. Can you grab the end of it?"

Octavia groaned and thrust herself toward Birdie's crop. She grabbed it with another groan.

"I, I have it, B-b-b-irdie!" she said with chattering teeth.

"Thunder an' turf!" she said with relief. "*That is excellent!*" Birdie hollered back as she tried to contain a sob. "I shall have you out in a moment! Hang on! *Boys,* grab Miss Octavia's boots and the horse will pull us all along the ice!"

Birdie turned her head back to the immense warhorse. "Back, Pride, back up," she commanded firmly.

Instantly, the huge horse lowered his haunches and began backing up. Birdie tightened her hold on the crop as she felt the heavy pull of Octavia and the boys' weight on the other end.

"Back, Pride, good boy. Back, back," she said as she felt Octavia come over the edge and onto the ice.

Octavia was sobbing incoherently.

"All is well, Octavia, I have you now!" Birdie called out reassuringly.

"The ice is is st-st-still cracking!" Octavia said in terror.

Birdie risked looking back at Pride. "Back, Pride, more! Back, hurry, boy! Back, *back!*"

Inch by inch, the big warhorse pulled them along the cracking ice.

Birdie's bonnet came off, but she dared not let go of the horse's rope nor the crop to grab at it.

The horse pulled steadily until she felt her boots hit the edge.

Suddenly, she saw several figures running down the bank. It was Sir Ouseley, Mr. Mirza, and Freddie.

"Here, Miss Darley!" Mr. Mirza said.

Birdie stood up cautiously and stepped off the ice just as Mr. Mirza, Sir Ouseley, and Freddie helped pull Octavia and the boys to the edge of the river.

Freddie reached for Octavia as she tried to stand. He caught her before she could collapse and quickly lifted her into his arms.

"Take her to my carriage!" Sir Ouseley said. "There are furs and a warmer there."

"Papa!" the two boys shouted as another figure came running along the shoreline. The man scooped the two young boys into his arms.

"Thank you, Miss," he said over their heads.

"No, I must thank your boys! They saved my friend's life."

The man looked down at his sons with tears in his eyes and nodded to her. He picked them up in his arms and walked down the shoreline, kissing each of their faces over and over.

Birdie smiled at them and then turned to watch as Octavia was safely put in the carriage and bundled in the furs. Aunt Eggy and the empress climbed into the carriage and sat on either side of her, wrapping their arms firmly around Octavia.

"Sir Ouseley, we must take her tae our house. 'Tis the closest. We must get her oot of her wet skirts! Tie the ponies tae the back of the carriage. Quickly noo, there's no time tae waste!" She turned to look down the bank. "Birdie?"

Birdie shook her head. "Go! Hurry! Get her warm! I am going to help Ten, and Mo is missing!"

Aunt Eggy frowned but then nodded to Sir Ouseley.

Birdie watched the carriage go. She turned and hugged Pride's neck, caressing his warm fur and whispering her words of thanks to the huge warhorse. She felt him snuffle at her hair and realized her bonnet was still out on the ice, but she did not care.

She turned to see Freddie staring silently at her.

He was looking at her strangely. "Your hair. I never realized how long and curly or how very attractive it is, Miss Darley. I have never seen you without it covered."

Birdie reached up to touch it. The pins had come loose and the black masses of it had all fallen down.

She cleared her throat. "My horse, Mo, is gone, along with the other horses that were being watched by a groom. The groom is also gone. Would you know anything about that?"

Freddie's eyes narrowed. He turned and looked to where the group of horses had been standing. He looked back at Birdie and the huge dark horse standing beside her so placidly. "That horse was not taken. It is a fine specimen. A warhorse most definitely."

"This horse will not let anyone touch him."

"Save for yourself *and Fairfax*, I presume?"

Birdie nodded as she tightened her hold on the horse's rope. She spoke in a low, quiet voice, "You knew this was Ten's horse." She watched his face and his eyes, but he remained coldly indifferent. "What do you know of the horse thefts?"

"I can tell you nothing."

Birdie glared at him. "Telling me nothing and knowing nothing are two very different answers, Freddie."

Freddie's jaw tightened. He looked down at the ground. "I must leave you. I beg your pardon." He bowed his head and started to turn to leave, but Birdie called after him.

"Don't you mean you beg my forgiveness? For you shall certainly be given no pardon. You shall be hanged, Freddie! Thunder an' turf! Tell me the truth! What have you gotten yourself involved in?"

He looked back at her. "Why don't you ask Fairfax?" With those words, he spun about and walked away from her.

Birdie turned to the big horse. She needed to get to Ten.

The horse was far too tall for her to climb up onto his back, however, even if she let the stirrups of Ten's saddle all the way down. She looked at her crop and then to the horse.

"How well-trained are you?" she whispered. She tapped his foreleg with her crop. "Down," she commanded firmly.

The horse immediately arched his long neck and dropped down onto his front knee as if in a bow. Birdie smiled with relief and clambered up onto the saddle on his wide back. "Up, Pride!"

She grabbed his reins along with his lead rope and turned him down the shoreline. She squeezed her right heel and pushed her seat. Instantly, the giant horse lunged off into an enormous and fast canter.

She was at the Frost Fair booths in no time. Several of the booths had sunk into the water with only their roofs showing.

"Ten!" she screamed out into the chaos of wailing and crying families along the shoreline.

They were looking for their missing loved ones in the crowds, praying that they were not amongst those lost to the freezing river under the ice.

Several men had joined hands, forming a long line out to the open ice to help pull people from the freezing water.

"Ten!" she screamed again as she looked all around.

She rode Pride through the distraught crowd at a slow walk along the shoreline, calling Ten's name over and over.

The crowd parted for the huge horse as she turned Pride this way and that while looking frantically for Ten over their heads.

"Ten!" she cried out again.

The crowd was too noisy and she feared that he would not hear her.

"Ten Adair," she called out even louder. "Where are you, Ten?"

CHAPTER FOURTEEN

BIRDIE WATCHED AS Ten suddenly broke through the crowd. His hat and gloves were gone and he was carrying a child wrapped in a blanket. He handed the child to its grateful, crying mother.

"Ten!" she cried out.

She saw his eyes widen when he turned and saw that she was on his horse.

He came straight to her in long, sure strides.

"You are on my horse," he said incredulously when he came to a stop. He looked up at her face and her hair as his eyes widened. "What is wrong? What has happened? Are you hurt?" he demanded.

"Ten, Mo is gone. And Octavia fell in the ice, but Pride helped me get her out. Freddie carried her up the bank to the carriage and wrapped her in Sir Ouseley's furs. She is safe and on the way to Grosvenor Square with Aunt Eggy and Empress Bibi, and Mr. Mirza, but Mo is gone, Ten," she repeated with fear in her voice.

Ten looked up at Birdie in horror. "Octavia fell through the ice!" His voice was full of dread.

"She is fine!" Birdie said firmly. "She is on the way to our house in Grosvenor Square where she will be cared for! But you must listen! *Mo is gone!*"

Ten blinked several times. He looked up to where Birdie sat like a queen on his big warhorse with her black hair spilling over her shoulders onto her royal blue pelisse. "You will tell me more of how Pride helped you save Octavia and Freddie's involvement and who this Mirza is. But first, you say Mo is gone? He did not get loose? What did the groom say?"

Birdie shook her head. "The groom is gone as well. Mo would never just get loose. And he always comes when I whistle for him."

Ten ran a hand through his hair as he looked up to the bank, then back at her with his eyes narrowed. "You whistle for your horse?"

Birdie nodded several times. "Mo has been *taken*. All of the horses the groom was watching were taken save for Pride."

Ten patted his horse's neck. "Pride would kill anyone that tried to touch him." He frowned and looked up at her. "But you—"

"I think Pride may have wanted to attack me at first," she spoke quickly, and then continued in a rush of words. "But I realized that your horse cannot see out of the scarred eye, so I talked to him on his good side. 'Twas easy once I realized this, and we have dealt most harmoniously together. He even knelt down so I could mount him."

Ten stared up at her. "You have ruined my horse."

Birdie scowled. "I shall tell no one what a sweet horse he actually is." She huffed out a frustrated breath. "Now, will you help me find Mo?"

"I am sure all the horses just got loose from the groom," he said tensely as his eyes looked beyond her. "That groom is a good lad."

Birdie stilled and stared down at Ten. "You know the groom?" she asked quietly.

"Yes."

"You trust him then?"

Ten grinned up at her, but his smile did not reach his eyes.

"Of course." He tilted his head up at her as his grin became crooked. "What is it?"

Birdie bit her bottom lip as a feeling of dread settled low in her belly. "Have you been lying to me with your beautiful lips and using your perfect kisses to distract me from the truth?" she whispered.

Ten's grin fell. "What the devil are you talking about, Little Bird?" he said softly.

"It was you, at the race. That big horse who cut me off was Pride! And it was you at the inlet of the channel. You smacked the wagon horse's haunches and made him canter. You thought I was a boy." She stared hard at him. His expression did not change. "One of those men ran away, but did you catch the other two men you were fighting?" He did not answer, but only stared at her. "Did you know it was me?" she demanded in a louder voice.

Still, he did not answer her.

"That night when you showed up in the alley. You *insisted* on helping me. You fought those men too. One got away, but not before I slashed his wrist with my knife. You supposedly went after the others and you supposedly turned them in to the prime minister." Her voice lowered. "And now, all the horses that a groom that *you know and trust* are missing, *except for yours.*"

Ten arched a brow at her. "What are you trying to say, Little Bird? That I am the horse thief?"

Birdie arched a brow back at him. "There is so much to be suspicious of when one looks at this in a different light," she said quietly. And then, even quieter, "One can only be skeptical, scoffing, and scornful at the scurrilous similarities. Suspicious, indeed!"

Ten frowned. "I am offended at your outrageous, obscene, offensive, and most opprobrious insinuation."

Birdie was silent for several moments as she stared down at him. "I win," she said sadly.

Ten bristled. "You do *not* win and you are *incorrect*," he growled.

"What did I say that is incorrect? Tare an' hounds, tell me," she pleaded as she leaned forward to stare down at him. "If I am wrong, I shall kiss a crooked cricket, though I would prefer not to, and I do usually prefer that I am not wrong, though this time, I hope that I am," she said in a rush of anger and frustration.

He shook his head. "What?" He took a deep breath. "Never mind. There is no sense arguing with you. You are the most stubborn, confusing, tiny bird that I have ever met!"

He reached up and pulled her off the horse. He set her on her feet on the ground in front of him. He clasped her upper arms firmly as he stood there, looking down at her. "And to think that I indulged you when I have so many other responsibilities. To my sisters, the prime minister, my country!" he seethed as he stared angrily down into her face. "And here you are accusing me of the theft of these horses! You think me a smuggler for France!" He stared up to the sky and then looked back down at her. "Of course I knew you were not a boy that night beside the channel," he said with a gentle shake. "You are far too incorrigibly beautiful not to see that. However, I did not know it was *you* until the night in the alley, when I began to suspect it had been you." His voice lowered and gentled. "I did not fully trust you and your part in this until I heard what you said to the prime minister at Lady Prudence's table, *m'eun beag.*"

Birdie pulled out of his hold. She crossed her arms and stared angrily up at him. "I am *not your little bird.*" She stared warily at him. "You said *your responsibility to the prime minister*? What exactly is that responsibility? And stop staring at me like that! I know what you are thinking."

Ten grinned his wicked, charming, lady-winning, dimple-showing, gleaming-white-teeth, wolf's grin. His eyes crinkled with his smile as he arched his brow. "You know what I'm thinking, do you? *Then you better slap my face,*" he said in a velvet voice. "Your unbound hair is driving me to distraction and I can only think of kissing you."

"What?" she said loudly. "No, *do not* try to sway me with

your silky words or your perfect, sultry kisses." She shook her head and closed her eyes to the sight of his far too handsome face. When she opened them, she spoke hastily. "You were thinking of telling me that the thief is Freddie. *He* told me to ask *you* when I asked him if he was involved, but he would not answer me, even though I asked him about his wounded wrist. He said to go ask Fairfax, which I can only take to mean that *it is you who is the thief!*" She gasped for breath and stopped her tirade.

Ten stepped up to her and gently held her arms. "It is not I, *Eun Beag*. I promise you that I am telling you the truth."

"You think the thief is Freddie simply because you hate him," she said stubbornly. "And because you like me and do not want me to like him."

Ten stared at her for several seconds. "No. I dislike you terribly."

"Oh pish, you do not. You like me."

He stared quizzically. He let go of her arms and rubbed at his dimple. "Why would you want me to like you, while at the same time you think I am the thief that you have been looking for in book shops, near the Serpentine, at the channel, at a race, and in an empty mews?"

Birdie's lips fell open. "That was you who pushed me into the closet in the bookstore so those men would not discover me? That was you who ran into me when I wanted to see who Freddie was speaking with at the Serpentine? It has been you, each time, *all along?*" She frowned suddenly. "Were you *protecting me or keeping me from discovering the truth?*"

He stared at her in silence as anger threatened to overwhelm him. He took a breath and offered, "The man by the Serpentine and the man in the bookshop were the same man."

She tilted her head at him. "Yes, I know, that is why I followed them into the bookshop. I believe he was also at the race. There are no coincidences. *Coincidence is the unknown result of known causes.*"

He sighed. "You quote Voltaire incorrectly. 'Tis, 'coincidence is the *known* result of *unknown* causes.'" He shook his head and held up one hand to stave off her rebuttal. "Never mind. You have your reasons for changing the words to suit you. I am aware of this." He stared down into her eyes and spoke slowly, "I was *protecting* you, *Eun Beag*. You are involved in a dangerous adventure."

She stared up at him as a sad smile came to her lips. She could not believe him. "If that is so, then you do like me."

He shook his head and grinned ruefully. "No, I dislike you terribly."

"Are you working for the prime minister?"

He stared silently at her, arching his brow as his grin remained in place.

"Who was that man that was in the bookshop and at the Serpentine?"

Still, he stared at her in silence.

She bit her bottom lip, and then blew out a breath, realizing that he was only going to tell her so much. "You won't tell me anything and Freddie won't tell me anything. You think that the thief is Freddie simply because you do not like him." *And does Freddie think the thief is Ten simply because he dislikes him, or does he have other information?*

He continued to look deeply into her eyes. His grin faded as he began to speak, "No, *Eun Beag*," he said gently. "I know that it is Freddie. I believe that it was he that night at the inlet on the channel. I also saw him speaking to the man we both saw at the Serpentine as well as in the bookstore. And if that is not enough for you, I know it is him because I saw you slash at his wrist to save me from his knife that night in the mews, and he has not let anyone touch that wrist since that night."

"*Wait.* Did you just say that you *believe* that you saw Freddie that night at the channel?" she asked with surprise and doubt. "You recognized him? And you recognized him again at the mews."

"I am fairly certain that it was Rockingham at the channel," he answered softly. He watched the emotions crossing her face. "You doubt me." It was not a question. He found that he was surprised that she still felt doubt after what he had just revealed.

Birdie lifted her chin. Shaking herself from her thoughts, she arched her brow at him. "You did not say that you recognized him at the mews."

Ten grinned crookedly and shrugged. "I assume it was him at the mews. You injured his wrist, and Rockingham has an injury to his wrist." He tilted his head at her as he rubbed at his dimple. "You have doubts, yet you like me."

Birdie frowned. He was so sure of himself. And her. *Too sure.* She forced the words from her lips. "*No.* I dislike you terribly as well, just as we agreed that we both dislike the other after Octavia introduced us."

Ten grinned and shook his head. "Your eyes seduce me while your kisses say that you like me," he whispered. He put a finger on her lips just as she was about to deny his words. "When you come to my rescue, as you did in the mews, you are saying that you like me. Even though when you helped Octavia when she fell at the ball, you swore you would never come to *my* aid."

Birdie stared up into his sparkling green eyes that seemed to smile as much as his lips did. Her gaze dropped to his dimple, his beautiful lips, and the wry grin she saw there. She pushed his finger from her lips.

She arched a brow and scoffed as she wrapped her arms protectively around her waist. "I could say the very same for you." She studied his eyes. The man was giving away nothing but his charming grins and his intriguing dimple. "It seems to be important to you that I like you, but alas, I do not." *She could not.* She would not let herself sink further into his green eyes or his perfect kisses. Not if he was the thief and the head of the smugglers. Not if he was guilty of treason.

Ten's grin bloomed larger. "If I am wrong, stubborn bird, then I shall kiss this crooked cricket you speak of. But I would much rather kiss you," he whispered as he leaned toward her.

She put her hand on his chest to stop him, turning her face away from his lips. She closed her eyes from his view, hiding the doubts that had sunk deep into her mind and down to the bottom of her stomach like lead weights.

Ten Adair was far too charming. Far too polished. Aunt Eggy's words came racing back to her. *"Though he may tell you it is truth, it will be lies from his tongue and lies on his lips as he tries to woo ye with his deceitful kiss."*

"Can we find Mo first?" she said dully as she opened her eyes and stepped away from him.

Ten also took a step back. His eyes raked over her face. This was a new Birdie he was looking at, and he did not like the doubt he saw within her gaze. "Mac na galla! I forgot about your horse! How is it that my mind is always muddled when I am with you?"

"Because you like me?" she quipped quietly, and looked away from him once again.

He grinned and arched his brow at her as he threw her up onto Pride's back. He did it as easily as if she was light as a feather, then he managed to jump up onto the huge horse's back himself.

She pointed down the river. "Freddie went that way. If he is indeed the thief, as you suggest, we should go that way as well."

Ten wrapped his arms around her and off they went.

BIRDIE TOOK CONTROL of the huge warhorse.

"Keep your legs quiet," she said with a glance back at Ten. "Let me direct the horse. I have the reins and it will be my seat and legs Pride obeys."

Ten arched a brow. "Pride is a warhorse, Little Bird. Not a pleasure horse for a leisurely ride in Hyde Park."

Birdie could not contain her grin of anticipation. "I am counting on that. I should have borrowed Aunt Eggy's battle ax. 'Tis a battle we are heading into, after all, Ten Adair. Hold on."

"Did I mention that he is an *old* warhorse? A *very old* warhorse? With only *one eye*?" he said quickly.

"Oh pish, he is not that old and he can see brilliantly with that eye."

As the horse cantered down the road along the Thames, their bodies moved as one. Birdie was sitting snuggly within Ten's thighs, her hips fitting perfectly there. The ebb and flow and thrust of their united hips as they followed the horse's giant canter became almost too intimate for Birdie to endure.

She thought she heard a groan from Ten as his fingers squeezed her hips.

Birdie stared resolutely ahead of them as she kept her mind focused on the task. She looked down any side alleys they passed for a group of horses that seemed out of place. She thought it would be fairly easy to spot them, for they all would have saddles still on, except for her Mo.

"Good God," Ten exclaimed.

Birdie brought Pride down to a walk. "What is it? Did you see the horses?"

"No," he said in a low voice. "Look there."

He pointed ahead of them. There was a small group of people gathered around the lifeless body of a young man.

"'Tis the groom," Birdie said in a hushed voice.

"They killed him," Ten gritted out angrily, seeing the blood on the lad's head. "Keep going *Eun Beag*, we are heading in the right direction. I wager the poor lad was chasing them."

Birdie put her heels back into Pride's sides and they cantered away. "The brick factory and loading dock are down the next street," she said back to him. "The man in the bookshop was talking about dray horses that pull the brick wagons."

She felt Ten nod. "Head to the loading dock."

They rounded a bend in the road and then turned down a narrower street that led to the docks. It was bordered on both sides by brick buildings.

"Well, this is indeed ominous and oppressive," Birdie whispered.

"Indeed, 'tis dismal, dire, and full of doom," Ten whispered back near her ear.

"You win," Birdie said in a hushed voice.

"No, I have not won yet," Ten said in a husky voice as he tightened his arms around her waist.

Suddenly, they were met by four large, rough-looking men on horses facing them at the other end of the street.

Birdie tightened her seat and collected Pride into a very slow, collected canter.

One of the men rode forward a few steps. "*You there! Stop,* turn around. You cannot come this way!" the man shouted.

"Interesting," Ten said in a low voice. He held Birdie's hips as they moved together in tight, short movements, following the horse's collected canter.

"Do I detect a French accent?" Birdie asked in a quiet whisper as she kept her eyes on the man.

"You do," Ten whispered back.

The man viciously kicked his horse and galloped straight toward them.

"Hold on!" Birdie pushed with her seat and gave in the reins, opening up Pride's canter. She steered him straight toward the man.

"Birdie!" shouted Ten. "What are you doing?"

"I am riding a warhorse!" she called back with excitement. "I really wish I had Aunt Eggy's battle ax!"

The Frenchman's eyes widened as he realized the size of the horse coming at him in the narrow street.

"Kick that rider off his horse when I say!" she called back to Ten.

"What?" he shouted back.

Birdie asked Pride to bend. "Kick him! *Now!*" she shouted.

Ten kicked the man off his horse just as Birdie cantered Pride sideways away from the man and his horse at the last second. She heard the man hit the brick wall of the building that bordered the street. He cried out and fell to the ground.

Two more men galloped toward her, shouting and yelling. The second man broke away from the third. He seemed braver than the first as he stayed his course, determined to charge his horse at hers.

Birdie sat down heavy in the saddle and brought Pride to a canter in place. At the last moment, just as the other horse would have hit her, she spun Pride around on his hind end.

At that moment, Ten leapt from Pride's back into the other man just as she cantered away. Ten and the man went flying to the ground together, grappling and punching one another. Ten got to his feet, holding the man up with the man's shirt in his fists. He threw him into the brick wall.

Birdie watched as the man slid down to the ground in a heap.

At a loud roar, she saw the other rider coming straight at her with fury on his face.

"Birdie!" Ten shouted in warning.

Birdie cantered sideways away from this rider, just missing the horse and rider in the narrow street.

Birdie pirouetted Pride again, turning on the spot to face the rider. She cantered toward him, then brought him down to a slow, exaggerated trot. She knew that this trot was the trot that knights used centuries ago to intimidate the enemy, *just before they charged.* She loved training the Aldbey Park horses to do this to strengthen their backs and hind ends. She just never thought that she would have a need to use it as it was meant for. As a battle movement.

Birdie grinned. She was not ready for the enormity of this huge horse's slow, cadenced, and heavily exaggerated trot, but she loved it. Her seat bounced out of the saddle with each lift of the horse's legs. She forced herself to move with it and her grin grew even bigger as horse and rider became one.

"Birdie?" Ten warned.

"Hush," she called out in a low voice.

Birdie smiled threateningly at the third man who was coming

toward her. She collected Pride further, trotting him in place as she determined the speed of the horse coming toward her. The huge warhorse proudly arched his neck and lifted his shoulders and chest as he sat down, taking his weight on his hind legs as he trotted slowly in place, ready to spring forward at Birdie's command.

"Thunder an turf! You know what I am doing, don't you? You *great big beautiful horse!*" And then, "Now!"

Pride shot forward into a massive, lunging gallop, straight at the horse and rider. The other horse screamed out, throwing his head in the air as he tried to spin and retreat.

Just as Pride's chest hit the man's leg where he sat on the horse, Birdie halted him. The rider flew of his horse's back.

Ten rushed over and grabbed the man. He pulled his fist back and slammed it into the man's chin, almost lifting him off the ground with the force of his blow. The man fell to the ground, limp, his eyes closed.

The man's horse trotted off down the street, giving Pride a wide berth.

She turned Pride to face the fourth rider. She studied him as she arched her brow.

The man stared wide-eyed at her. He let go of the reins as he slowly raised his hands meekly in the air in surrender.

Ten strode toward him and pulled him down from the horse.

Birdie trotted Pride forward. *"Where is my horse?"*

The man just stared up at her in confusion and fear.

She pointed to Pride's head. "My horse has a very large head. Oh pish! Where are *all* the horses?" she demanded of him in frustration.

The man pointed behind him toward the other end of the street, *"Au quai."*

Ten looked at Birdie and translated, "He said *at the dock.*"

Birdie arched an eyebrow at Ten as that feeling of dread sank in her belly once again. "You speak French?"

Ten nodded and stared at her quizzically.

Birdie's eyes went back to the man. "Who is your leader? Your commander?"

The man just looked at her stubbornly.

"You will tell me or I will let this horse run over you," she said in her best commanding voice, though she knew she could never do such a thing.

The Frenchman shook his head fervently. "Schell. Schellburne!" he said hastily.

Ten smiled grimly up at Birdie. "As I suspected. I thought I recognized him as the man in the bookshop and at the Serpentine." He turned back to the man whose arm he still held. "You are coming with us."

"Ten," Birdie said hesitantly. "There may be many men at the dock. Schellburne's son Davis could be there. He is evil and ruthless. My story about the rider whose saddle was unbuckled during that race? It was my saddle, and it was Davis Schellburne that had managed to unbuckle it after hitting me in the face with his crop."

Ten's face tightened as his eyes narrowed with fury. "He is a dead man."

"No, Ten! We cannot go to the dock. This was only four men."

Ten stopped and grinned ruefully up at her. "*Only* four men?"

This woman had ridden his horse in a way that he had never seen done before. He did not know the old warhorse had it in him, but the horse had not looked old today. He had looked proud and strong. A thought came to him and he scowled.

"Are you also worried that you may discover Rockingham there?"

Birdie froze.

Ten turned away from her with a disappointed frown.

Birdie called out, "We do not have to go to the dock and risk being attacked by more men. Mo will come to me. Let me just whistle for him." She did not wait for his answer but put her lips together and blew a sharp, clear, loud whistle. She stopped and listened.

Sure enough, a high-pitched neigh could be heard and then the splintering of wood and the sound of wooden poles hitting the brick paved street in front of the docks.

Ten tilted his head. "It sounds like he has broken free from a fenced area or corral."

Birdie frowned. "I'm quite sure Mo would have jumped out of something like that when I whistled, not broken it down."

A raucous sound came to them.

Hoof beats.

"*Courir!*" screamed the Frenchman as he pulled free from a startled Ten and began to run.

"He said *run*," Ten said as he looked back toward the dock.

The ringing sound of hoof beats grew louder.

And then louder yet.

Several hoof beats.

Too many hoof beats.

"Ten!"

"I know! Your Mo has gotten free and the other horses are following him!" He ran toward her and leapt up onto Pride's back.

The Frenchman did not wait. He was already running for the open street as fast as he could.

Birdie collected her reins and spun Pride around. She put him into a gallop toward the other end of the street out to the main road, where the Frenchman was headed.

The thundering clatter of what sounded like hundreds of horses could be heard charging behind them.

CHAPTER FIFTEEN

B IRDIE TURNED THE corner and brought Pride to a halt close to the wall of a building.

Ten leaped off of Pride's back. "Move out of the street!" he thundered to the people there. "The horses from the docks are stampeding." He pointed to several carriages and wagons that had stopped, listening to the sound of the approaching thunder of hooves. "Put those carriages across either end of the street! We need to block the horses!"

The wagons and carriages moved quickly with Ten helping and directing them.

The people were used to animals stampeding. It happened often enough at Smithfield's Market when farmers brought their cattle, sheep, and pigs to London to the market. They knew what to do and moved quickly, unharnessing their own horses after settling the wagons in place.

Just then the thunderous uproar became deafening as the horses spilled out onto the street in a full gallop. Several slipped and fell on the snowy street while others jumped over them and kept going.

"Ten!" Birdie screamed in terror as she saw Ten trying to run to her while getting out of the way of the horses. He was caught in the middle of the street.

Birdie quickly turned Pride into the rush of stampeding horses as she tried to keep her eye on Ten.

"Ten!" she called out again. "Ten! I am coming for you!"

She saw him turn towards her, dodging and moving out of the way.

Pride was unfazed as he cantered and trotted and cantered again, keeping up with the surge of horses while making his way to where Birdie was directing him.

Some of the horses ran into Pride, but the huge horse did not waver. He kept going, getting closer and closer to Ten.

"Birdie! *No*, it's too dangerous!"

"*Tare an' hounds*, I am not leaving you, Ten! I *will* rescue you!"

Birdie kept pushing Pride forward until finally, *finally*, she reached Ten.

Birdie held her hand out to him. "*Take my hand!*" she called out loudly.

Ten clasped her hand and jumped up onto the horse's back.

She turned Pride around, this time directly into the onrush of the horses.

"Hold him, Little Bird," he said urgently into her ear as Pride neighed as he moved head-first into the oncoming stampede. The warhorse lifted his head and, once again, used his big chest to take on those horses heading right at him.

The horses turned left and right, avoiding him.

Birdie let out her breath.

Finally, they began to slow down, nickering and calling out as they trotted around nervously within the enclosed street.

Birdie trotted Pride quickly back to the edge of the street.

"Are you hurt?" she asked Ten as she turned to look at him where he sat behind her. She threw one leg over the saddle to better turn to see him. She touched his face and his shoulders and ran her hands down his arms.

"I am fine, thanks to you!"

Birdie grinned back at him. "I came to your rescue on a big, dark horse. That is the stuff of fairy tales, Ten Adair. Though

Pride is scarred and not as handsome as a fairy tale horse, still I think he is far, *far* braver than any of those could be. Have I made your dream come true?" she asked with a soft laugh.

Ten grinned ruefully and arched his brow as he pulled her onto his lap and tightened his arms around her. "Well, in my version, I would have rescued *you*, on *my* big, dark horse, my beautiful damsel in distress."

Birdie shrugged. *"I win."*

Ten could only stare into her beautiful lavender-blue eyes.

"You like me," she whispered as she stared up at him. "In fact, you want to kiss me."

Ten blinked several times. He did, in fact, desperately wanted to kiss her just then, of all the worst times, in the middle of this chaos. "I cannot." He cleared his throat. "I do not." Yet still, he was held captive by her beautiful eyes.

"You lie," Birdie whispered as her smile trembled and began to fall.

Ten scowled as he stared at her. He cupped her cheek and tilted her face up to his. He stared down longingly at the perfect bow of her lips.

His mouth slowly lowered to hers.

He reverently sipped at her top lip and then her lush bottom lip as a sigh of surrender escaped from him. He nudged her mouth open and delicately slid his tongue between her lips, touching hers with his.

Birdie whimpered and melted against his chest as the kiss became deeper, slower, impossibly even gentler, and more intense. He was a bonfire and she craved his warmth, his heat, his body against hers. They shared their breaths as they melded and molded their mouths together.

Birdie reached up and clung to the thick fabric of Ten's great-coat, holding him tightly to her as she moved her lips to better fit his.

Ten gripped her hips with his large hands where she sat on his lap, fitting so, *so perfectly* there.

"Sit still," he murmured against her lips and then growled out a sigh as his tongue plunged back between her lips.

The kiss became intensely intimate, filled with need and longing as their hearts raced and their tongues tangled and danced and moved in an age-old rhythm.

Pride moved slightly, stomping one of his huge hooves on the snowy street.

Ten blinked, pulled back, and gulped. "You seduce me every time I look at you, *Eun Beag*," he whispered as he blinked several more times and pulled back even further. His black lashes lowered, covering the green glitter of his eyes.

Birdie stared up at him, seeing the change come over his now solemn face. She frowned as a shaft of pain shot through her. She had to look away from him. "Where is my Mo?" she murmured as she still felt the intensity of his gaze. She turned back around on the saddle as she moved off of his lap. She looked out into the herd of horses. "Mo!" she called out from Pride's back as she continued to look over the herd of restless horses. "Mo! *Mo Graidh!*"

She noticed that most of the horses were now walking around, while several others had halted completely and were calm.

Ten leaned forward and spoke quietly with his mouth next to her ear. "Pardon, but do I understand that your horse, who is named Mo, is actually named for the Scottish Gaelic name for *my beloved?*"

Birdie went rigid. "Yes. 'Tis *Mo Graidh*."

Ten grunted. "I know what it means, Little Bird. I like it." He squeezed her gently. "I take it your horse is your *only* beloved?" he asked hesitantly.

"Yes," she said curtly. "Do not laugh."

"Tut, tut, tut, *M'eun Beag*," he said in a soft, gentle voice as his lips grazed her hair above her ear. "I am not laughing. Indeed, I find that I am most happy and relieved."

Birdie turned her head and looked back at him. She frowned.

"Thunder an' turf, Ten. You make no sense."

Ten laughed softly and looked at all the horses milling around. "I believe that horse with the unusually large head over there is your beloved Mo. Here he comes. He has spotted you."

Birdie looked in the direction that Ten had pointed. "Goodness, yes! *That is Mo!*" she cried out and slid off Pride's back.

Ten watched as she pushed her way through the horses until she reached the stout horse. She wrapped her arms around its head and cradled it against her breasts as tears ran down her face.

The slow, plodding sound of hoof beats came to them again. Six black, wide, dray horses walked placidly out onto the street to join the others.

Ten narrowed his eyes on the horses, but his eyes quickly went to the narrow street behind them.

"Birdie," he called out without looking at her. "Get on Mo and come here, please."

Birdie let go of Mo's head and looked over at Ten. She turned to look at whatever had caught his interest.

A large man was pulling four men behind him by a rope that bound them all together. The man looked dangerous. He was a large man, tall and broad. He walked, confident and powerful, with large strides. His hair was a sun-kissed golden brown and fell to his shoulders. His face was also kissed by the sun and he wore a dark brown greatcoat with a shoulder cape that made him look even more enormous.

Birdie stared harder. He reminded her of someone.

She got up on Mo and rode through the herd of horses toward Ten as she watched the man.

"Ten?" she asked when she stopped, straining her neck to watch the man. "Who is that? Why does he look so familiar?"

Ten frowned furiously at the look of feminine interest on her face. "That," he said curtly, "Is *Law.*"

Birdie continued to look at the man. "He is the law?"

Ten shook his head ruefully. "No. His *name* is Law. Lucas Amos Winchester."

Birdie could not take her eyes off of him. "He reminds me of War de Walton." She leaned toward Ten and whispered as she watched Law, "Whose side is he on?"

"He is not a thief or a traitor, if that is what you are asking," Ten said as he watched Law. "He has those four men that attacked us all tied together." His eyes narrowed on the four men that Law was pulling along behind him.

Birdie smiled. "He is on our side, then! Why are you so angry?"

Ten gave her a wry grin. "You will see soon enough, I am sure."

Birdie gasped. "Look! There is Freddie! He just came out of the street to the docks as well."

Ten grunted. "I see him."

Law came striding up to Ten with a wicked smile on his face. "*Number Ten!*" he said in a baritone voice.

"Law," Ten said with an arched brow.

"I found some garbage you left lying in the street. Still prefer the uppercut with your right fist, I see." Law pointed behind him to the men he had bound together. They clearly showed the results of Ten's fist. "Glad they didn't mar *your* pretty face, Number Ten."

Law looked over at Birdie then. He let his eyes leisurely rake over her face and down her body.

Birdie sucked in her breath. She was met by a pair of whisky-colored eyes studying her.

"My, my," Law said in lieu of a greeting.

Ten growled. "Miss Birdie Darley, meet Lucas Amos Winchester, better known as *Law*."

The two nodded at one another in silence.

Law openly studied Birdie for several more moments and then turned to Ten. "I take it that the little piece with the lavender eyes is yours?"

Birdie gasped indignantly. "I am not his. That is incorrect, Mr. Lucas Amos Winchester. It is inaccurate, improper, and inexact, and an *ill-whilly* thing to say."

Law stared at her silently.

"You forgot *inappropriate*," Ten said to Birdie without turning away from Law.

Law turned to look at Ten, who was staring at him with a threatening look in his eyes.

Ten continued with an arched brow and a warning grin at Law. "And that it was a mockit, manky, mingin, mauchit thing to say."

Birdie nodded as she pulled her gaze from Law. "You win."

Ten shook his head while he kept his eyes on Law. "No. I have not won, not yet, *Eun Beag.*" He added for Law's benefit, "She is the stepdaughter of the Duke of Leids, Alexander Hawke, and the beloved sister of War de Walton's bride, Lula. Her brother-in-law is Prince Darius Kir Khan."

Law flinched at that news. "Pity. I would have taken her for myself. However, I will not anger the Persian assassin, or dare to wreak havoc on Captain War with his fortress of men and his fists and cannons. Or, bloody hell, risk going against the legend that is *the Hawke.*"

Birdie glared at him. "Tare an' hounds! I do not need them to defend me. *I* would not let you *take me*, whatever that means!"

Law stared silently at her. He turned to Ten and tilted his head. "She does not know what that means, Number Ten? I am disappointed in you." He turned back to Birdie. "He has not seduced you into his arms with his charming grin and that dent in his chin? You must be special to him, indeed. If you are free for the taking, however, your acquiescence is typically not needed, but I would have made an exception for you."

"*Thunder an' turf!* You bampot, bowfin, boggin, blethering, glaikit idjut!" Birdie said loudly to Law. "Has it occurred to you that perhaps it is I that is seducing him? It is I who is keeping *him?*"

Law's eyes barely reflected his surprise. "She is Scottish. A *Highlander.* She is one of ours."

Ten nodded curtly. "Lady Egidia Ross is her great-aunt."

"Indeed? She is a Ross then," Law growled and turned his whisky eyes back on Birdie. "And Number Ten has not vowed to keep you?"

Birdie shook her head. "He dislikes me. *Terribly.*"

Ten winced and rubbed at his dimple.

She lifted a hand and counted off on her fingers. "I have rescued him one, two, three times! He refuses to tell me the truth of his role in this whole matter, yet expects me to trust him," she said, and waved her hand to the horses. "And still, he again and again says he dislikes me. And that is after I pulled his sister up from the ballroom floor and out from the icy water of the Thames. As well as after I defended him on his warhorse back in that street to the docks, after I slashed one of his enemies just as they were going to throw a knife at him and very likely would have hit him in the throat with that knife in the darkest of the night in an abandoned mews where he would have bled out his very life's blood into the pristine snow with no one there to hold his hand as he died," she scoffed, and stopped to take a much-needed breath.

Law threw his head back and laughed. He sobered and looked at Ten. "I want her."

"Leave off, Law," Ten snarled threateningly.

Law stared at Ten. "*Do* you dislike her?"

Ten hesitated. "*I dislike her terribly,*" he forced out with a quick scowl at Birdie, who was still staring at Law.

Birdie rolled her eyes. "Oh pish, you like me," she muttered. "Nevertheless, I dislike *you* terribly, too."

Law smiled. "I am glad to hear that you dislike one another." His smile turned ruthless as he stared at Birdie. "*I* like you."

Just then, Freddie finally made his way through the herd of horses with his arms full of saddles and several bridles over his shoulders. "Do not even speak to Miss Darley," he said curtly to Law.

Law sighed and turned to the blond man. "Very well," he said calmly as he looked back and forth at the two men glaring at each other. "You two can fight over her." His eyes went to Birdie again before his gaze came back to Ten and Freddie. "I do not like my seas crowded with smugglers trying to transport ships full of stolen horses to Napoleon." He smiled wickedly. "I sunk their ship, by the by. Before they could load the horses, of course."

Birdie leaned forward. "Are you a sea captain for the Royal Navy?" she asked with great interest.

Law turned his whisky-colored eyes back to her. His face remained impassive as he said, "If that is what you want to think, angel."

Birdie drew back. *"Tare an' hounds!"* she murmured under her breath.

With that, Law threw the end of the rope that he had tied the men with to Ten. Without a word, he turned and began walking down the street, leaving the four men in Ten's care.

"Law!" Ten called out.

Law turned to look back at him.

"Send the Runners."

Law nodded and turned back around. He waved his hand once in the air as he began walking again.

Ten watched him go. He turned to scowl at Freddie. "What are you doing here?" he asked in a low voice.

"What are *you* doing here?" Freddie demanded back caustically. "Be a gentleman. The Runners will be on their way shortly. *Miss Darley needs to leave.*"

Ten turned to Birdie and his eyes softened. "Indeed, he is correct. You should go, *Eun Beag*. You do not need your name in the *Morning Post* over this."

Birdie looked at the two men. "I must ask, êtes-vous fidèle à la Couronne? Do you know what I am asking?" She waited, wondering how they would answer her question: *are you loyal to the Crown?*

"Yes," Ten said as he scowled and arched an eyebrow at her.

"Of course," Freddie said sharply.

They stared stubbornly back in silence, saying nothing more. She sighed in exasperation. Had they answered her question about their loyalty to the crown? Or her question about knowing what she had just asked? She bit her lip, realizing they had not truly answered the first, most important question. Both men knew French, however. That did not help her know which one was the thief helping Schellburne.

Her heart was breaking. She did not want the thief to be Freddie, a man she had known since she was young and had counted as a friend. The man she always thought that she would marry. Yet, she also did not want it to be Ten Adair, the man she feared she was losing her heart to.

"What will happen to all these horses?" she asked wearily as she stared out over the herd in the street.

Ten grinned gently. "They will be returned to their rightful owners, *M'eun Beag*. The *Morning Post* will make an announcement. You should go. You are exhausted."

Birdie looked from Freddie to Ten. "I will go home, but I expect an explanation from both of you! And thunder an' turf, *I expect the truth*. Good *or bad*."

CHAPTER SIXTEEN

B IRDIE RODE MO into the Grosvenor Square stables and waved the grooms away. She wanted to see to Mo herself. She settled him into his warm stall, spread fresh straw on the floor, and gave him a bucket of clean water and a scoop of oats in his other bucket. She also gave him a flake of fragrant, dried grass hay. Then she spent a long time just brushing him and talking quietly to him.

She left him there with his head low and relaxed, napping after his ordeal.

Birdie walked into the house and straight to the parlor where she knew a warm fire would be lit.

She stopped in the doorway.

"*Oh Lud*. What are you all doing here?" she asked the room at large.

"Good God and bloody hell and the divil confound it! Here she is! What manner of havoc have you been involved in, little sister?" War de Walton said in his deep voice. He tightened his arm around his wife Lula's waist. "Lula has been terrified for you."

"War," Lula said with quiet reproach as she stared up at her big husband.

Birdie watched as War blushed and touched the brown curls falling over his wife's forehead with the gentlest of touches as he stared into her eyes, thoroughly captivated.

Birdie smiled at the two of them. Her sister Lula was dressed in a bright, parrot-green dress and had all her unruly curls bound up on the top of her head with a startling orange ribbon. She was also wearing her favorite jonquil yellow boots and a bright coquelicot-colored short pelisse with pompadour-pink pom poms. Lula was staring back up at War with a look of blissful captivation.

Birdie looked from Lula and War to her oldest sister, Julia. Julia's blonde hair was done up in intricate braids and curls with a sky-blue ribbon running through it. She wore a dress of cerulean blue that matched her eyes just so. The dress had a silver stomacher adorned with pearls, and around her shoulders was a shawl of softest blue and silver.

Birdie thought she looked like a princess.

She looked from her sister to Pasha, Prince Darius, who was dressed as usual in a blousy black tunic with wide sleeves caught at the wrists and full, silky, black breeches. An elaborately decorated silver curved Persian khanjar knife was strapped to a wide black belt around his waist. Birdie knew the black leather belt was full of the small and deadly kard knives that Pasha kept on him at all times to protect his beloved Julia.

"Interesting. She looks unscathed, *Azizam*," Prince Darius said softly as he kissed the blonde hair of Julia. He had turned from studying a painting to instead study Birdie.

"Pasha, darling, we cannot know for sure," Julia said as she stared up at her husband with a thoroughly besotted look. She caressed his cheek and brushed his glossy black hair off his forehead as she savored a moment to stare into his golden eyes. She then turned away from her husband to walk briskly forward to her sister. "Birdie, we were so worried about you," she scolded.

"Aunt Eggy sent a message, you see," Lula said as she too hurried away from where she had been standing next to War. "She told us about what you had gotten yourself into." Lula took

Birdie's hand and held it between hers. "Miss Octavia told us about the Frost Fair and going through the ice and then the horses being stolen. You have rescued your dear horse Mo, I take it? Do I need to make sure the poor horse is unhurt?" Lula said as she gently squeezed Birdie's wrist.

Birdie smiled and pulled her wrist from Lula. "You do not need to check my pulse. *I am fine*, thank you, Lu. I am alive. *Obviously*. As is Mo and all the other horses that were stolen."

Birdie looked over to see Octavia lounging on the settee pulled close to the fire. She was wrapped in blankets and had a steaming cup of tea held in both hands.

"You are well, Octavia?" Birdie asked quietly.

Octavia nodded fervently as she stared wide-eyed at Birdie and then looked around to all the people in the room. "Oh yes, I am most well, indeed! I find that your house is terribly exciting!"

Birdie's mother Amelia came forward with tears in her eyes and hugged her tightly. She was wearing a dark velvet gown. It was a darker blue than the one Birdie was wearing. "We came as soon as we heard, my dearling Birdie," she whispered with her black upswept hair against Birdie's. She had noted that Birdie's hair had come free of its pins and fallen down her back in curls and waves.

Amelia pulled back and studied Birdie's eyes. "You look...*annoyed?*" her mother whispered softly. "But...*happy?* If I did not know better, I would think you have fallen thoroughly in love," she said for Birdie's ears alone. She straightened her shoulders as she stared down lovingly at Birdie. "Tell me, dearling, what has happened?"

"Och, she has had an adventure! Leave her be, Amelia! 'Tis clear tae anyone with eyes that she is guid and fine!" Aunt Eggy said from where she sat on the other settee. She had a pipe stuck in the corner of her lips and blew a hazy white smoke ring that billowed above her head.

Empress Bibi was beside her, smoking her own pipe while holding an elaborately carved ivory cane embellished with gold.

She stomped it on the floor as she pulled the pipe from her mouth and pointed it at the three girls standing with their arms around one another. "She is a warrior, just like her sisters." She stomped the cane again. "Warriors, *all of them*."

Alexander Hawke smiled ruefully at the empress. He strode forward and put his arm around his wife. "Birdie, your mother and I sent a message to the queen as soon as we heard of your involvement in this smuggling scheme."

Birdie gasped. "Tare an' hounds, why? All is well, I assure you."

"Your Grace, as I said when I arrived, I will be happy to take her off your hands. Keep her out of trouble and all."

Bridie whirled around to meet the whisky-colored eyes of Law Winchester. He had been helping himself to the duke's brandy on a table just inside the parlor door. He saluted her with the glass and took a long drink.

"You will do no such thing," Birdie said firmly. "We are not having this discussion again, Lucas Amos Winchester!"

"What is this? Do you know Law Winchester?" Hawke asked Birdie.

Birdie pursed her lips and scowled at the man who looked more like a pirate than a sea captain. "No," she said curtly.

Law strode slowly forward with his glass of brandy, which he had refilled. "Indeed, she does. My friend Fairfax introduced us. Seems the two of them *dislike* each other, rather *passionately*, if I may say."

"Thunder an' turf, of course you may *not* say that! You *gallus, glaikit, rudeigin* man!"

Aunt Eggy snorted and laughed. "Dae ye ken that she just called ye a cocky, foolish, rude mon?"

Law turned his gaze to Aunt Eggy. "I know very well what she said, my *Lady Ross*," he said, and bowed his head slightly in her direction. "I am, after all, a Highlander myself." He spoke quietly. His voice was deep and rumbling like a storm threatening upon the sea, and his Highlander accent barely a hint, like a whisper in the brewing breezes of that storm.

Aunt Eggy stopped laughing abruptly and swallowed as she stared up at the big man.

War growled deep in his throat. "Do not frighten Aunt Egidia."

Law looked from Aunt Eggy to War. He bowed his head slightly in War's direction. "As you wish." He turned and went back to refill his glass of brandy.

Birdie's mother stared at Law, then at War, and then to Aunt Eggy. "Goodness me!" She leaned toward Hawke. "Did your friend Law just intimidate Aunt Eggy?" she whispered to her husband.

Hawke concealed his grin. "I believe Lucas Amos Winchester just did that very thing, Amelia, my love."

"Interesting," Pasha said softly. "Most interesting. In that one is the strength and the calm that tames the seas, even in the strongest winds."

War grunted.

Pasha added, "He is a friend of my friend Hawke, so now a friend of mine."

"Birdie? What of your Freddie?" her mother asked as she watched Birdie's face closely. "Was he involved in this?"

Birdie bit her bottom lip. "I still do not know." She sighed in frustration.

The empress grunted. "Idjut."

"What?" Amelia turned to the empress with surprise.

"He is named Idjut. Egg Lady said that is his name," the empress said, and jabbed her pipe toward Aunt Eggy.

Aunt Eggy scowled. "Bibi Hibi Ibi, ye dinnae understand. 'Tis an insult, nae his name!"

The empress grunted again and stomped her cane. "I say it is his name." She stomped her cane once more, as if the matter was settled, narrowly missing Aunt Eggy's foot.

"Where is Ten?" Aunt Eggy demanded as she took Empress Bibi's cane from her with a frown.

"Oh goodness, yes! Where is my brother?" Octavia asked in a rush.

Law looked over at the girl covered in blankets, lying on the settee. "Number Eight? Is that you?"

Octavia blushed and smiled bashfully. "Hallo, Law. Good of you to finally notice me," she said shyly. "I have been lying here the whole time."

Law stared at her. A large, white smile appeared on his sun-kissed face. "You were buried under all those blankets, Number Eight. I could not see you."

"I am used to that," she said softly as her eyes flitted away.

"Forgive me?" he asked in his soft, rumbling baritone.

Octavia smiled with pleasure as her eyes returned to his. "Always," she said.

Suddenly, Mr. Druckbert appeared at the parlor door. His chin was in the air as he stood at attention in his faded, out-of-date uniform. His hands were at his sides as he puffed out his chest. He cleared his throat loudly.

"Frederick Rockingham, the Duke of Trenton, is here, Your Grace."

Hawke and Amelia faced the doorway to receive Freddie.

Hawke's face was grim. "Rockingham," he said with no emotion.

"I have come to make sure that Miss Birdie arrived home safely and that Miss Octavia has suffered no ill effects after her fall through the ice."

Birdie made a soft, scoffing noise as she rolled her eyes and crossed her arms. "Now you come to visit me," she said under her breath. "I am quite well. Go see to Octavia, Freddie. You and I shall have a talk later."

Hawke and Amelia stepped aside to let him pass so that he could walk over to the settee.

Mr. Druckbert appeared in the doorway again. He stood at attention and cleared his throat once more and spoke even louder. "Ten Adair, the Earl of Fairfax." Mr. Druckbert glanced at

Aunt Eggy and gave her a tiny, hopeful smile.

Birdie bit her bottom lip. Mr. Druckbert, like Aunt Eggy, was full of surprises.

Aunt Eggy put two hands on the cane and hoisted herself up from the settee. The pipe was still stuck in the corner of her mouth. She scuttled over to Ten and placed a hand on his chest.

"I heard ye got intae a wee bit of a collie shangles. Ye look unharmed. Are you?"

Ten grinned down at her. "I am unscathed, Lady Ross. And may I say that the pipe and the cane are enchanting embellishments that only enhance your engaging and enticing countenance." He pointed at her hair, making a circle with his finger. "May I?" At her blushing nod, he gently pushed the crooked, thinning knot of her white hair back to the center of her scalp from where it had come to rest on her ear.

Birdie rolled her eyes. She held up five fingers for the five words he had come up with that began with 'e'.

Aunt Eggy blushed all the way to her pink scalp. "Och, ye charmer ye!" She patted his chest once again as she sighed while looking at the wide breadth of his shoulders.

Mr. Druckbert appeared at the door again, looking rather frazzled and harried. His face was bright red with excitement and he seemed out of breath.

He started to speak, but then corrected himself. He cleared his throat first and spoke very loud with great importance. "Robert Banks Jenkinson, Earl of Liverpool, *the Prime Minister!*" He bowed his head and backed out of the doorway as the prime minister entered the room.

Robert Banks Jenkinson came into the room and stopped as he took in all the people staring back at him. His austere but intelligent eyes surveyed them all. He scratched at the side of his long, full nose and then stroked a hand through his graying blond hair before placing his fingers onto his full lips. His eyes landed on Ten Adair.

Ten walked forward to the prime minister and the two quietly shook hands.

Hawke and Amelia, War, and Pasha also came forward and welcomed him.

Just then, Mr. Druckbert suddenly flew back into the doorway, clearing his throat several times as his hands flailed in the air. His face was even redder, and the thin shock of gray hair sticking straight up from his head was vibrating with his excitement. He tried several times to speak, but only a squeak came out. Finally, he managed in a high-pitched voice, "Good heavens! The queen!" He recovered somewhat, puffed out his chest, and shouted, *"Her Royal Highness, Queen Charlotte!"*

He hastily backed all the way out into the hallway as Queen Charlotte walked briskly through the door into the parlor. She was resplendent in a full-length pelisse of gold brocade. It had a full-length tuxedo trim of golden fox from the Americas. She carried a matching fur muff.

Amelia's hand went to her throat. She quickly recovered and curtsied, as did all the ladies in the room, save Empress Bibi, who took her time rising from the settee. She went to stand beside Aunt Eggy.

Aunt Eggy was glad to have the cane. She curtsied as well, though it was not low, and then let Ten and Empress Bibi help her back up.

Octavia struggled to her feet with Freddie's help. She managed to curtsy but then fell sideways. Freddy caught her quickly with an alarmed look on his face, but Octavia stared up at him with an apologetic look.

The men all bowed from their necks.

Hawke walked forward and bowed his head again. "Welcome to our home, Your Majesty."

Queen Charlotte nodded at him. She looked around at the people in the room and then leaned toward Hawke. "I received your message and thought it wiser that I come here instead of requesting that you all to come to me. This is far more…private. The palace has ears, you know."

Hawke bowed his head again. "I understand, ma'am."

Queen Charlotte stared around the room. "Robert! What are you doing here?" she asked the prime minister. She waved her hand at him. "Never mind. I am sure that you are here for the same reason as I." Her eyes had come to rest on Birdie. "Miss Birdie!" she commanded. "Come to me."

Birdie jumped, but hurried forward.

Amelia joined Birdie and walked with her to the queen.

Hawke moved to stand beside his wife and Birdie.

"Well, gel? What have you to say for yourself?" the queen demanded.

Hawke took a step forward. "Your Majesty, as you are aware, I do not like that my stepdaughter is involved in this."

Birdie placed a hand on his arm. "Thank you, but I asked to help. In fact, I insisted."

"She did indeed," Queen Charlotte said to Hawke. She looked back down at Birdie with sharp eyes. "Tell me."

Birdie looked up at the queen. "It is not who you suspected."

"That cannot be!" the queen responded with surprise.

Ten strode forward and stood beside Birdie. "I have proof that the perpetrator is General Schellburne, and very likely his son Davis is helping him," he said solemnly.

The queen's eyes turned to Ten. "Ah, the charming and dash-ingly handsome Earl of Fairfax." She tried to control her smile at seeing him, but could not.

Ten grinned back at her with his dimple-showing, gleaming-white-teeth smile.

Birdie made a scoffing sound.

The queen cleared her throat and raised her nose in the air to resume her serious royal countenance. "What proof do you have that one of our greatest *generals* is guilty, Fairfax?"

The prime minister walked away from where he had been speaking to War and Pasha to join Ten. "Did you say Schellburne, Fairfax?" He turned away in consternation. "No," he said in a low voice. "I cannot believe it of him!" He glanced briefly over at

Freddie Rockingham, who was standing behind the settee where Octavia was seated. "What of the other?" he said quietly as he motioned with his head toward Freddie.

"Yes, what of the other?" the queen demanded of Birdie and Ten.

Birdie shook her head and frowned. "Excuse me, Your Majesty, and Mr. Prime Minister, but I do not think he is involved, at least in that way."

The prime minister scratched the side of his long, full nose as he stared at Ten. "Fairfax? Explain."

Ten cleared his throat and arched a brow at Birdie before turning back to the prime minister. "He has been seen repeatedly with Schellburne, who the smugglers admitted was their leader. We cannot know for sure exactly what Rockingham's part in this is." He glanced back at Birdie. "Though he *is* involved."

Birdie glared at him. "You do not know that."

"I do," Ten said in a harsh whisper.

"You make an assumption based on an injury to his wrist that could have happened anytime, anywhere. He was not necessarily injured by me and the knife hidden in my crop. *''Tis better to change an assumption than to persist in a wrong one.'*"

Robert Jenkinson looked at Birdie with great interest. "The knife in your crop, eh? Fascinating! However, I do believe that quote is about changing your *opinion*, eh, Miss Darley?"

"Nevertheless," Birdie said without even glancing in the prime minister's direction. She was scowling at Ten.

Ten held her eyes as he shook his head once toward the prime minister. "Miss Darley changes quotes to suit her will, Robert."

"To suit the *situation*," Birdie corrected him sternly. She lowered her voice. "Your assumption about Freddie is wrong," she whispered emphatically.

Ten rubbed at his dimple as he scowled down at her. *"'Tis foolish to give merit to a man that does not place others first over himself.'"* He leaned down closer to her. "You give merit to a man that does not deserve it."

Birdie sucked in her breath. She knew that quote. It was a favorite of hers. She was just about to retort when the queen cleared her throat. *Loudly.*

"Enough," Queen Charlotte commanded. "Though 'tis amusing and interesting to watch you two spar. Am I correct that Miss Darley disobeyed my instructions, which were explicitly to *only observe*, certainly not wield a knife hidden in her *riding crop?*" She arched an eyebrow at Birdie and pursed her lips.

Hawke sighed while Amelia covered her mouth.

"She is a Darley," Aunt Eggy called out loudly from where she stood by the fire. "Of course she willnae be tae afraid tae fight alongside Ten Adair *and tae protect him!*"

Ten groaned and rubbed at the dimple in his chin as he stared down at the floor.

The queen nodded over at Aunt Eggy. "I see that you can hear quite well, Lady Ross."

"*Sards,*" Aunt Eggy mumbled.

Empress Bibi knocked her elbow into Aunt Eggy's arm and whispered, "Now you will be sent to the dungeons!"

"Hush, Bibi Babi Ibi!" Aunt Eggy whispered back as she peered at the queen.

The two old ladies jammed their pipes into the sides of their lips and puffed away as they watched the goings-on with avid fascination.

Queen Charlotte turned frosty eyes on Robert Jenkinson. "What do you know about this horse smuggling affair? Do not disseminate. You will tell me."

Robert Jenkinson pulled on his lapels and rocked up onto the balls of his feet before settling back on his heels. "I know the London connection is a military one. That is all the information we had."

"*We?*" the queen demanded.

Robert Jenkinson nodded to Ten. "Fairfax and I."

Birdie whirled to Ten. "Thunder an' turf! You *were* working with the prime minister! You could have told me!"

Robert Jenkinson straightened his shoulders as he stared indignantly at Birdie. "He could *not*! *I forbade him.* You see, as the queen knows, we have been making plans to exile Napoleon to the island of Elba and end this thing! Now, we shall do it as soon as possible!"

"When?" demanded the queen.

Robert looked down at the floor as he grasped his lapels, deep in thought. He rocked back on his heels and announced, "I should think we can accomplish his exile very likely by April. That is less than two months away."

Ten turned from the prime minister to grin contritely at Birdie. "You see? I had to know I could trust you."

Birdie rolled her eyes. "Do you typically kiss women that you do not trust?"

Hawke leaned forward to stare at Ten. "Excuse me?" he growled. *"Explain yourself,"* he said in a warning tone.

"Birdie!" her mother exclaimed in a shocked voice. "I thought you two disliked each other?"

"We do!" they said as one.

Hawke's jaw tightened. "It does not sound like you dislike each other. It sounds like you should marry, *immediately!*"

The queen raised her hand imperiously. "Not now, Hawke. Besides, three men have asked for Miss Birdie's hand in marriage."

Ten and Birdie both whirled back around to stare at the queen in astonishment.

Queen Charlotte was looking over their heads to Freddie Rockingham, however. She pointed at him. "Frederick Rockingham. If you value the title of Duke of Trenton, which I know you are waiting to be given, you will come here this minute and explain your part in smuggling horses for Napoleon."

Freddie walked forward and stood like a soldier in front of the queen. "I have always served the Crown's interest, Your Majesty."

Queen Charlotte narrowed her eyes on him. "You have." She studied him standing there so confidently. "Yet you have been seen working *with the smugglers.*"

Birdie started to object, but Freddie spoke first. "Who accuses me of this?" he demanded quietly with a furious glance at Ten Adair.

"I do," came a voice from behind them all.

CHAPTER SEVENTEEN

L AW STRODE FORWARD with his arms crossed over his immense chest. He stopped and stood with his feet planted apart like a man accustomed to balancing on a rolling ship. He stared unfazed at the queen.

"You?" Freddie said.

The queen gave Freddie a quelling look and then turned back to Law.

"Lucas." She nodded her head and gave him a smile as she fluttered her eyelashes. "I received your request."

Law nodded once and remained silent.

The queen cleared her throat and controlled her reaction to the big man with hair kissed by sun and sea salt. "You say Frederick Rockingham has been working *with* the smugglers?"

"I do, ma'am. As I am frequently at the docks, I saw him myself."

The queen stared at him a moment longer and then caught herself. "Yes, well! There you have it! Schellburne *and* Rockingham are our traitors."

Birdie, along with Amelia, Julia, and Lula, started speaking loudly, unable to believe Freddie could be a traitor.

Ten stared at Freddie who was standing there in furious silence. "Tut, tut, tut, Rockingham. Do explain yourself," Ten growled in a low voice.

Birdie and the other's voices rose even louder in denial as they offered their opinions.

"Hold, *hold*, I say!" Queen Charlotte commanded as she held up one hand.

Silence immediately ensued.

Ten kept his eyes on Freddie. He held his arms across his chest. One brow was arched and he had a sardonic grin on his face. "This ought to be interesting," Ten murmured.

"Do you have anything to say, Rockingham?" Queen Charlotte asked sharply.

Freddie took a step forward. "I do. I was acting on orders."

"Whose orders?" she demanded.

"I was working for the Crown," he said firmly.

The queen narrowed her eyes at him. "*Which* crown?"

"The king," Freddie bit out.

The queen paused as she studied him shrewdly. "My husband mentioned a military connection. He also mentioned there was a man we could trust who had served us well in the past. But then he said there was another we could not trust. Was he talking about you, or General Schellburne?" she demanded.

Freddie spoke through gritted teeth. "He was talking of General Schellburne, of course. *I* have served you well in the past, as the Darleys are well aware."

Amelia nodded adamantly. "He did help us with the matter at Tattersall's and those men who murdered Henry Darley and were trying to murder our horses at Aldbey Park."

The queen nodded and turned back to Freddie. "What else did the king tell you?"

"He asked me to see what I could find out. To do what needed to be done to find proof. Acting along with the smugglers was the best way. The king's valet can attest to this conversation." He glared over at Ten. "Fairfax is correct. The general was the mastermind in coordinating men to steal horses to send to France."

"You were a double spy," the queen whispered.

"I was," Freddie said proudly.

The queen looked over at Ten Adair.

"And you work for the prime minister, I must assume," she said.

Ten nodded.

"And you can provide the man that told you that Schellburne was indeed the head of this smuggling ring?"

Ten nodded again.

Next, the queen looked over at Law. "And you work for?"

Law stared at her and smiled very slowly. "Myself."

The queen looked away from his whisky eyes with a grin. "Arrogant man," she murmured to herself, and then sighed and shook the smile from her face.

Ten turned his whole body to Birdie, who was standing beside him.

"Pray tell, why were you really involved in this?" He grinned. "Who do *you* work for, *Little Bird*?"

"She works for me!" the queen said imperiously.

Birdie grinned and arched her eyebrow. "I was watching *all* of you," she said with a pleased look. "Save for Lucas Amos Winchester. I did not know who Law was until you introduced me to him, Ten," she said cheekily.

The queen grinned as well. "No young lady should be introduced to that one." She looked over at Law and sighed before pulling her eyes away. She smiled proudly at Birdie and motioned to Freddie. "And did you cut Rockingham's wrist with the secret knife in your crop?"

Birdie looked over at Freddie. "Did I? Was that you in the mews that night or not?"

Freddie sighed deeply. "It was, and yes, you did cut my wrist. Cost me several stitches, in fact."

Birdie bit her bottom lip and turned to Ten. "I saved you. Admit it. You are most grateful to me, else surely you would have perished, multiple times! And you like me," she added softly.

Ten laughed once. He grinned at her, showing his wolf's grin as his green eyes glittered down at her and crinkled at the edges, giving truth to his smile.

Amelia and Hawke and Birdie's sisters and their husbands began talking all at once. War, in particular, was grinning like a fool at his best friend, Ten Adair, and Birdie.

The queen cleared her throat. "There is another matter."

All eyes turned back to the queen.

"Three men have asked for Miss Birdie Darley's hand." She looked over at Hawke and Amelia. "I should like to show my appreciation for Miss Birdie's fine work in this smuggling debacle, and my gratefulness to her for saving my dear friend, the charming Earl of Fairfax. I would like her to choose her own husband."

Ten tried to speak. "I would not say that she actually saved me..." he grumbled, but Lady Amelia Darley spoke over him.

Amelia was beaming with joy as she interrupted Ten Adair. "Yes, *yes, of course.*"

Hawke's jaw tightened. "A moment please, my love." He looked over at the queen. "Who are the three men?"

The queen smiled and spread her arms wide. "Why, the three men in this room who do not have wives, of course." She smiled at Freddie, and then at Law, and finally at Ten Adair.

Ten growled low in his throat at Rockingham.

Freddie snarled at Ten.

Law gave a slow smile of anticipation.

Birdie's mouth fell open.

She looked over at Freddie. "You have not given a scant moment of time to me, yet now you want to marry me?"

She turned to Law without giving time for Freddie to respond if he had even wanted to. "And *you*, Lucas Amos Winchester! You do not even know me. I just met you today!"

Then she whirled to Ten and glared at him. "*Ten Adair! You* have been telling me that you *dislike me terribly* since I met you! Yet you give me perfect kisses. Tare an' hounds! Now you want to marry me?"

The three men remained silent.

Freddie was silent with embarrassment.

Law just continued to stand there with his arms across his chest and a smile of amusement on his face.

Ten was glaring at her as he rubbed at the dimple in his chin.

"Choose, Miss Darley," Queen Charlotte commanded.

"I have to choose *now?*" Birdie asked in a startled voice. She stared at her mother, who nodded and smiled at her and then she looked over at her stepfather, who looked sternly at her and crossed his arms over his chest. Her eyes found Aunt Eggy. She looked calm and pleased as she nodded at Birdie.

"The heart, or the lie, is in the kiss," Aunt Eggy said quietly as she stared at Birdie.

The queen nodded as she looked over at Aunt Eggy. "Lady Ross is correct. Evidently, only Fairfax has truly had the opportunity to kiss Miss Darley, multiple times if I understand correctly." She lifted her chin as her eyes sparkled in anticipation. "Let them *each* kiss her." Her smile grew with eagerness. "Then she will choose!"

Birdie whirled to stare at the queen.

Hawke and Ten growled deep in their throats.

"This is highly unusual, ma'am," Hawke said in annoyance.

"This is in contravention of all polite codes," growled Ten. "'Tis a casual, capricious conflict and contravention of polite society," he said loudly.

Birdie arched a brow at him.

"Rockingham!" the queen shouted. "You first." She pointed to Birdie. "Kiss her!"

Birdie frowned and whispered to herself, *"Thunder an' turf,* she means it." She watched Freddie walk toward her with his face emotionless. "Well, this is indeed discomfiting, disturbing, and discommodious," she murmured.

Freddie stopped and looked down at her with his perfect, golden, artfully coiffed hair and his blue eyes. She had thought him handsome once.

"One cannot say no to the queen," Birdie said quietly to him.

"I am all too aware of that," he murmured.

He leaned down and placed his lips chastely against hers and then pulled away.

That was it.

His lips had not lingered on hers.

Her heart did not speed up. Her breath did not catch. She was not melting like hot wax, nor did a bolt of lightning race through her.

She felt…nothing.

He smiled gently at her and nodded once. Then he turned and walked back to stand behind the settee.

Birdie watched him. He was a man accustomed to blending into the background when he wanted, and then being the focus of attention at other times. He could change at a moment's notice, it seemed. He was a man that had all too frequently played two parts. Spy and double spy.

Birdie glanced at Aunt Eggy. She was glaring at Freddie.

"Lucas!" the queen called out loudly. She waved him forward. "Kiss her!"

"I am happy to do as my queen commands," he said with a silky smile.

"Oh, Lud!" Birdie whispered. She watched Law stride confidently forward to stand in front of her. He stared down at her.

He spoke in a soft baritone. "You'll be wanting to hold on to me, angel."

Birdie frowned. *"What?* Why would I want to do that?"

He leaned closer. "Because my kiss will make your head spin."

Birdie's frown turned to a scowl. "Pish! I do not like my head spinning. If you make my head spin, you will also cause me to vomit on your boots, and then I—"

He kissed her before she could finish.

Somewhere in her brain, she heard Ten growling.

A tiny fissure of lightning shot through her. His kiss was

demanding, thorough. His lips moved over her mouth as he held her face in his large hands.

He is a very skilled kisser, she thought to herself.

"That is enough!" Ten said in a warning tone. "Let go of her. *Now!*"

Law pulled his head away and took a step back with a wicked smile on his face. He winked at her and sauntered away.

Ten glared at Law then he turned to Birdie and took a deep breath and let it out in a huff.

He looked at all the people in the room and then back to Birdie again.

Without any warning, he strode forward, scooped her up into his arms, and turned to her family.

Birdie put her arms around his neck and stared at him in surprise.

"I will not be kissing my future wife in front of all of you. 'Tis wrong. This is between Birdie and myself," he said in an annoyed, husky voice.

Birdie tilted her head at him. "You like me," she whispered.

He arched a brow at her and walked out of the parlor with her in his arms.

Hawke started to go after them, but Aunt Eggy stepped forward and put her cane out, thwacking him in the chest with it.

He stopped and frowned down at her. "Aunt Egidia, I do not approve of him taking her away."

Aunt Eggy shook her head. "He isnae. He is kissing her oot in the hall. *In private* as a *guid mon should dae.* He is also vera probably asking tae keep her. Just wait. He will bring her back."

⇛⇚

TEN SET BIRDIE down on her feet in the main hall. He stared down at her with annoyance and frustration.

"You want to kiss me. And you want to marry me," Birdie

said to him in a hushed voice.

Ten grinned painfully. "I asked the queen for a special license to marry because we had kissed. It is required of me. I took liberties with you."

Birdie bit her bottom lip. Tears threatened to cloud her eyes. "No." She shook her head adamantly as she stared up into his far-too-handsome face and his glittering green eyes. "I release you of any obligation to marry me. For it was I that seduced you."

Ten grinned. "You *thoroughly seduced* me, *M'eun Beag*." His voice lowered as he frowned in consternation. "But I willingly let you, for I had no willpower to resist you." He touched her cheek reverently with his fingers. "I—"

"Do not say that you dislike me terribly," she said before he could finish whatever it was he started to say. "I don't believe you dislike me. You are not a liar, Ten Adair," she said with tears in her eyes. "In fact, beneath that charming grin you endeavor to keep on your face, you are the most thoughtful, courteous, considerate, tender, respectful man I have ever met."

"*M'eun Beag*," he whispered as his finger traced her cheek-bone.

"Are you worried about your responsibility to your eight sisters and finding them husbands?"

Ten nodded quietly.

"I can help you, and them, you must know this."

His eyes found hers. "It took me a while to see that. You have already helped me tremendously with Octavia. You rescued her twice, after all."

Birdie grinned and arched her eyebrow. "And I rescued you three times."

Ten shook his head. He whispered in a husky voice, "You will have rescued me for the rest of my life if you agree to be my wife."

Birdie drew in a breath as hope filled her breasts. "You like me."

Ten shook his head once again. "No."

Birdie drew back in disappointment. "No?"

He shook his head slowly as he grinned at her. "I love you, *terribly*," he whispered. "From the moment I met you. I disliked that you had chosen Rockingham. *I disliked that terribly.*"

Birdie's smile lifted. "Can I tell you a secret?"

When he nodded, she said, "At first, I thought I wanted to marry Freddie because I had known him since I was a young girl and thought him so handsome. Then, it was about staying close to him to see if he was involved in"—she flitted her fingers in the air—"*all this*, for the queen, you see? I had to keep up the charade, even though I no longer knew who Freddie was, and knew that my family did not approve. It was very difficult." She stared up into his eyes. "More so when I met you."

Ten let out a long, relieved sigh as he closed his eyes and tilted his head up to the ceiling. Then he lowered it and stared into her eyes. He pulled her close and smiled down at her with his smile lighting up his eyes.

"I like you. *I love you.* I want to kiss you. I want to marry you. I want to keep you. I want to hold you close and safe in my heart, for always. I want to tell you daily that I love you and to hear you say that you love me, *M'eun Beag.*"

Birdie stared up at him as her breath caught and just as he had described a bolt of lightning blasted throughout her body. She felt like hot wax melting just hearing Ten's voice, just staring up at his beloved face.

And he had not even kissed her.

Yet.

A stomp of a cane came from the parlor door.

"Kiss him, dearling! Tell him ye love him and ye'll merrit him!"

Birdie looked over to the door to see Aunt Eggy and her whole family gathered there grinning at her. Even Law, who looked most pleased with himself.

The queen pushed her way through. "Well?" she demanded. "Do you love Fairfax and agree to marry him?"

Birdie smiled at them all. She nodded to the queen and turned back to Ten.

She smiled up at him. "*I love you*, terribly," she said quietly.

"I know," he said back with his Birdie-winning, dimple-showing, gleaming-white-teeth grin. "You love me. You want to kiss me. You want to marry me."

"*I do*," she whispered.

Ten threw his head back and laughed. He stared down at her with love shining in his glittering eyes. "I win."

He pulled her into his arms and kissed her. Blissfully and most thoroughly as the queen, Aunt Eggy, Empress Bibi, and Birdie's entire family watched and cheered.

EMPRESS BIBI LOOKED over at Aunt Eggy after the wedding of Birdie Darley to Ten Adair, Earl of Fairfax. "What will you do now, Egg Lady? Your great-nieces all have husbands."

Aunt Eggy thought a moment. She looked over to the group of Ten's sisters. They were all standing off to the side, huddled together like shy ducklings.

"There are eight Adair sisters all needing husbands," she said with a mischievous smile. She looked over at War and Lula. War's sister and nephews stood with them.

"And there is War's sister, Loveday de Walton. She asked me tae find her a guid mon over a year ago. She also has three sons that need a guid and loving father as much as she needs a guid and loving mon." She tilted her head and stared at the woman with her hair in a tight, severe bun at the back of her neck. She was wearing a layer of white powder or cream that totally covered the skin of her face. She was also wearing an elaborately ruffled, full-skirted, golden gown from long ago. "I dinnae know what she looks like under all that white face cream she hides behind," Aunt Eggy murmured past the pipe stem stuck in the corner of her lips. "She is tae busy crying and hiding in her room most days tae meet anyone, much less a mon. She will be a challenge, Bibi Ibi, aye, a vera great challenge." She pursed her lips as she studied Loveday, and then inhaled from her pipe. She blew a large smoke ring as she grinned at Bibi.

Bibi watched as the billowy cloud of white smoke hovered above Aunt Eggy's head.

"I will help you, Eggy Lady. We can find them all husbands!"

"We shall see, Bibi Babi Ibi," Aunt Eggy murmured. "We shall see."

EPILOGUE

"**Y**OU ARE AN insatiable little bird," Ten murmured with contentment. They had been married for several months and he was blissfully happy. He tightened his arms around his wife in their large bed in the fire-lit bed chamber. "You are most *ardent*," he whispered, and kissed her on the nose. "And *amorous*." He kissed her eyelids. "And terribly *arousing*," Ten said, and kissed her lips.

Birdie smiled and snuggled closer against him. "And you, my beloved husband, are potent and powerful and, and seductive, and *tare an' hounds*, I am lost in you and cannot think of the words I want."

Ten smiled. "I win."

Birdie lifted her head and kissed him. The kiss was teasing and playful at first, but it turned into a slow, deep kiss of passion and love and the most intimate joining.

Birdie loved to hear Ten groan and gasp and sigh when she kissed him and caressed him and matched her body to his. "I am happy to let you win anytime," she whispered later against his lips and then kissed him again.

Much later, as they were letting their racing hearts calm down, she was staring over his chest at their room. "Why did you never tell me that you lived in a castle, my husband? I can stare out and see the horizon over the green hills. I could ride for hours and hours toward that horizon. 'Tis wonderful."

Ten's laughter rumbled in his chest. "I wanted to win you for myself. My own, *very charming* self. After all, you came to my rescue on a big, dark horse. What could I do but at least surprise you and impress you by bringing you home to my castle, my beautiful *Eun Beag*?"

Birdie laughed and kissed his beautiful chest. "I am getting too big to do this much longer," she whispered as his hand moved to her increasing belly.

Ten kissed her forehead and then moved lower to cradle her belly and kiss that as well. He looked up at her with a grin. "With eight sisters, I hope this babe is a son."

Birdie grinned back at him. "I am wishing for a little girl. We shall just have to see who wins!"

FIVE MONTHS LATER, she was lying in bed, cradling their newborn son.

Ten knelt beside the bed, looking at her and their new son with love, pride, and gratefulness in his eyes.

Birdie was exhausted and damp with sweat from the exertion of the long labor. The sun was just starting to rise outside the windows of their room when she felt another sharp pain.

"Thunder an' turf!" Birdie whispered under her breath as another pain tightened across her abdomen.

Startled, Birdie looked over at the midwife, who hurried to exam her.

"'Tis another one coming, my lady!"

Birdie handed their son to Ten, gritted her teeth, and struggled to push once more.

Within moments, a little girl was born and Birdie collapsed back on the pillows once again, totally exhausted.

"I have a little girl," she whispered to Ten as the midwife

handed her the dark-haired baby. "I win," she said with a tired smile.

Ten sat down next to her with their son in his arms. *"We both win, M'eun Beag.* We have two perfect babies."

"'Tis miraculous, marvelous, so meaningful," she said sleepily as she nuzzled the dark hair of both of her babies with her lips.

Ten kissed her forehead. "I should like to call our son Weston, after my father, as we talked about. But what should we call our little girl?"

Birdie looked up at her husband with love in her eyes. "Well, we cannot use Egidia because Julia and Pasha have named their new little girl Egidia Bibi."

Ten grimaced. "Though I love Aunt Egidia, I cannot imagine a little girl being called Eggy, or Eggs."

"Perhaps she will be a Giddie, or a Dia? I don't believe Aunt Eggy was always called Eggy." Birdie smiled. "How about *Win*? Because indeed, of a certainty, we both did win, after all, *mo graidh.*"

Ten smiled. "If you are going to call me your beloved, you shall have to just call your horse Mo, not Mo Graidh. I want to be your only beloved."

Birdie smiled up into his eyes. "You *and* our children," she whispered.

Ten nodded. "Win Adair and Weston Adair. *Tare an' hounds*, I like that. So it shall be, *M'eun Beag.*" He leaned down and kissed his wife. "There are many people waiting out in the hall to see you and our babies. But let me take this moment to tell you that I love you *terribly, Eun Beag.* Thank you for *thoroughly seducing* me with your sultry eyes, your shining black hair, your mixed-up quotes, and your words that begin with the same letter. I must add, your remarkable riding, and your bravery for *always rescuing me*. You are my love, and I am keeping you for always."

I love reading through history to find ideas for my stories! Birdie's story was a treasure trove from historical facts:

The River Thames Frost Fairs were held on the tideway of the River Thames in London, England. They occurred in some winters, starting as early as the late 7th century until the early 19th century. Most were during the period of that time which was known as the Little Ice Age when the river froze over most frequently. The British winter was more severe than it is now, and the river was wider and slower, further impeded by the 19 piers of the medieval Old London Bridge, which were removed in 1831.

From 1400 until the removal of the medieval London Bridge in 1835, there were 24 winters in which the Thames was recorded to have frozen over at London. The Thames freezes over more often upstream, beyond the reach of the tide, especially above the weirs. The last great freeze of the higher Thames was in 1962–63.

Frost fairs were a rare event, even in the coldest parts of the Little Ice Age, and in times of thaw, many people fell through the ice, and lives were lost.

Some of the recorded frost fairs were in 695, 1608, 1683–84, 1716, 1739–40, 1789, *and the last, was in February of 1814 during which this story was set.*[1]

The smuggler's ship with the lower port ramp in this story was indeed used to load and unload livestock when a dock was not available. The lower port ramp was also the method used for smugglers that could not sail into port, but unloaded their contraband in the middle of the night, away from shore. It was then picked up by fishermen that worked with the smugglers.

The lower ramp became most useful in times of war when a warship could not just sail into their enemy's dock and unload an army of horses. This typically required a shallower inlet that enabled the horses to swim only a short distance. The tides of the

[1] https://www.historic-uk.com/HistoryUK/HistoryofEngland/The-Thames-Frost-Fairs/
https://en.wikipedia.org/wiki/River_Thames_frost_fairs

channel helped.

A secondary means of loading and unloading was to winch the horses aboard.

Any of you horsewomen or men out there can see the dangers of this method. And indeed, it did often go horribly wrong.[2]

During the Napoleonic war, horses were one of the greatest assets an army required for multiple purposes. Napoleon did start up what he called his 'remount program' to rebuild his Army. An army typically had to procure over half of the horses they required with the other half being purchased. There was then at least a year to two years to train these horses to be ridden. After his devastating losses in 1812 and 1813, he needed horses that were mature, trained, and ready to ride.

None of these horses were experienced in the terrors or hardships of war, however, making it difficult for their riders who were too often unskilled in riding themselves.

Most horses did not make it home. They were either killed or taken by the enemy.

The greatest amounts of horses, outside of France, came from Germany in the Hanover and Hamburg regions, as well as Warsaw. There were also horses from Denmark, Jutland, Holstein, and Mecklenburg.

It is a well-known part of history that many stud lines and breeds were entirely wiped out, not just from this war, but from the wars to follow.

There are records from Napoleon's remount program that show around twelve thousand horses were 'donated.' Forty-five thousand horses were purchased and fifty-thousand were 'volunteered,' with another twenty thousand 'obtained' in Germany. As this was too slow a process, the practice of conscription began in earnest to look for ready-to-ride horses and heavy draught horses or mules.

---

[2] http://annearundelhorses.blogspot.com/2010/12/transporting-horses.html

By December of 1813, Napoleon had increased his cavalry to over two hundred and twelve thousand horses.[3]

This gave rise to my story of the smuggling of horses for profit to France.

Only Birdie Darley could have been brave enough, daring enough, and caring enough to go on this adventure with Ten Adair, the charming Earl of Fairfax!

---

[3] https://www.napoleon-series.org › c_remounts1813

About the Author

Chantry Dawes lives on her horse farm in the south east where she raised her four sons and wrote historical romance in her spare time. She has two dogs, a cat and several horses. Once her four boys were grown up and gone, she turned to writing full time.

Chantry's stories always have strong women, oftentimes a horse or two, and men who very often think they are coming to their ladies' rescue, only to find out that it was themselves who were *blissfully* rescued by their lady. A self proclaimed history nerd, she is fascinated by the massive part that horses have played all throughout history. She believes that no tale is complete without that sigh worthy hero who comes riding up to his lady on an equally swoon worthy horse.

Step into her new Aldbey Park series and see for yourself... beginning with *Thoroughly in Love*.

Ingram Content Group UK Ltd.
Milton Keynes UK
UKHW021951130323
418485UK00014B/852